I0825406

TRUST
The Novel

TRUST
The Novel

Tawanna Marsh

Mitchell Marstin Media

Mitchell Marstin Media publications and entertainment may be purchased for educational, business, personal, or sales promotional use. For information, address formal inquiries to Mitchell Marstin Media, PO Box 382826, Duncanville, TX 75138, or contactus@mitchellmarstin.com.

First Edition 2018 Designed by Tawanna Marsh

Library of Congress Cataloging-in-Publication Data is available upon request.

ISBN 978-0-692-16027-5

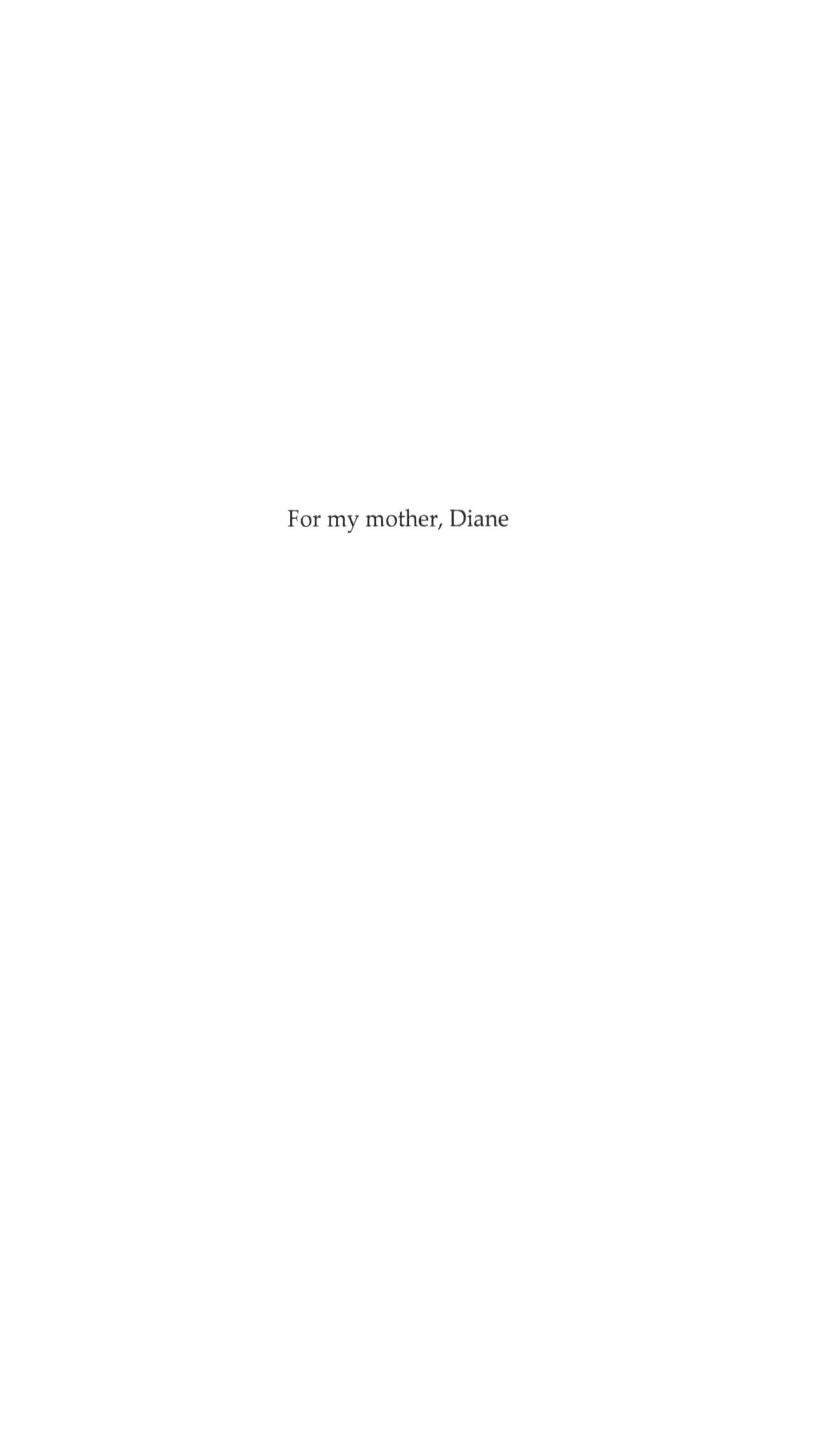

For my mother, Diane

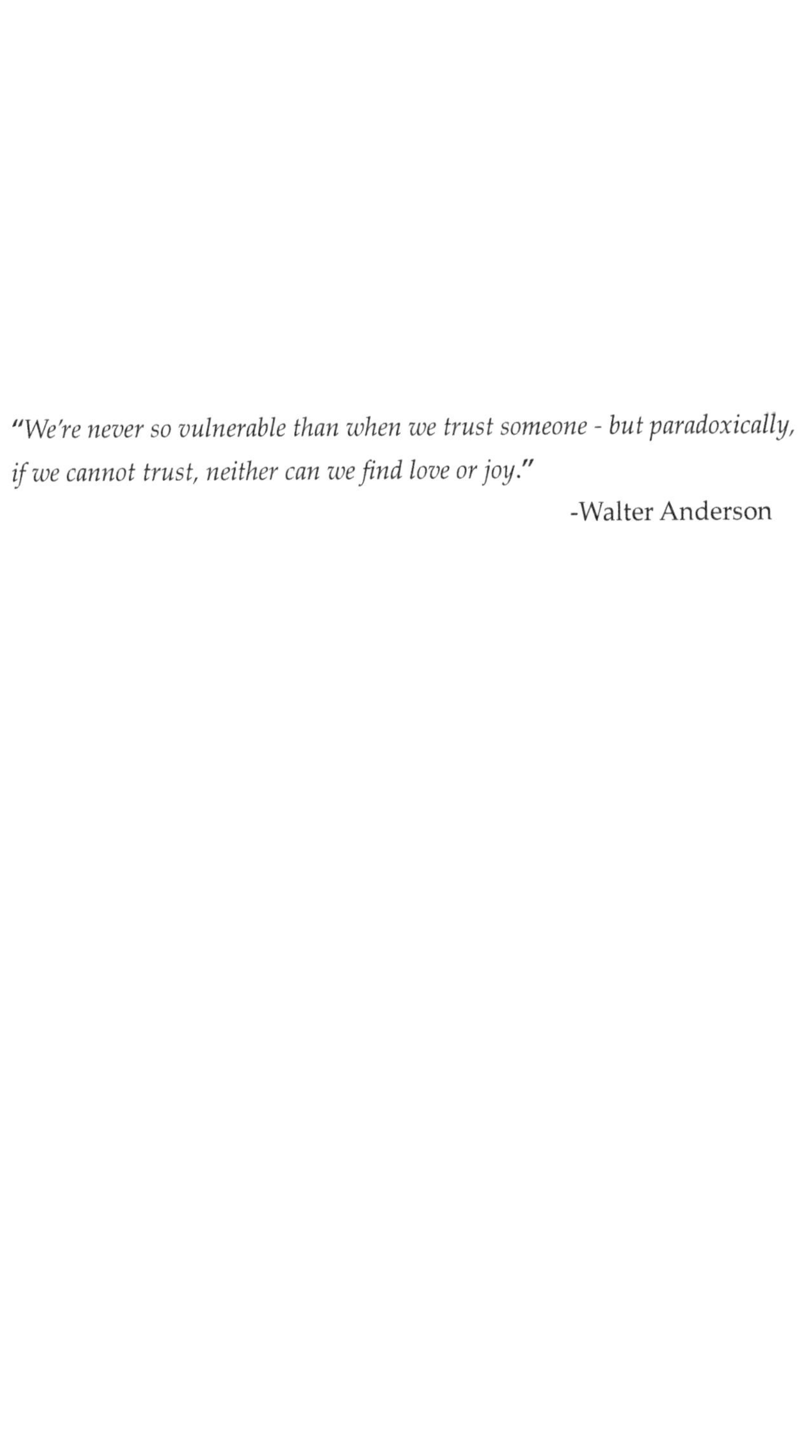

"We're never so vulnerable than when we trust someone - but paradoxically, if we cannot trust, neither can we find love or joy."

-Walter Anderson

TRUST

The Novel

PROLOGUE

"Tony, do we have everything?"

"Yes, babe. We've got the climbing gear, the ropes, the first aid kit, water bottles, cell phones, hooks…oh wait, I forgot the hooks," he said, while pushing the items around in the trunk.

"Ok. I'll finish loading the gear. You get the hooks from the garage, muscle man, and I'll meet you back here at the jeep."

It was early springtime. The sweet smell of new Oceania roses in my garden sashayed through the air. I pulled my shoulder length hair back into a ponytail. Tony glanced at me while walking to the garage. I smiled back. We were excited to spend our tenth wedding anniversary rock climbing in sunny Southern California. Tony chose Mount Whitney, which is the highest summit in the contiguous United States, with an elevation of 14, 505 ft. To us, this particular climb symbolized the challenges we'd faced together, and had conquered over the past ten years. Climbing the highest mountain meant conquering the highest heights as a couple, as an unbreakable unit, as ONE.

We finished loading the jeep and headed to Sequoia National Park where it was beautiful this time of year. We marveled at the sites along the scenic drive from Texas to California. The winding hills and statuette mountains of Arizona were almost wonderful enough to make us forget the smoldering 104 degree heat while driving through the desert at night. Almost…even with blasting air conditioning the heat was inescapable. 'This must be what it feels like a thousand miles away from hell,' I thought to myself. This was the nighttime heat. Daytime was much worse. The temperatures were sizzling through the desert at 1:00pm in the afternoon. Scenic, my ass. I was sure to fly to Cali on my next trip.

We arrived at Mount Whitney at 6:00am Friday morning, and immediately began unpacking the gear. Tony decided to begin the climb at Mountaineer's Route, a gully located on the north side of Mount Whitney's east face. The east face routes are the finest big-wall climbing in the high Sierra. This impressed Tony, who was quite the enthusiast. Mountaineer's Route was a semi technical-free scramble, considered a class 5.4 climb, and was perfect for me who was the least experienced climber. Although the route was technical-free, Tony required, that to ensure our safety during the climb, we affix the ropes and hooks correctly.

We walked a little over an hour from the parking area to Keeler Needle, a large rock with a sharp needlepoint peak that pointed due north. The Needle was safe to climb, as long as we stayed away from its pointy peak.

Tony went ahead of me climbing up the side of the needle at a three-minute pace. He was good at it. I followed trying to keep up, but fell slightly behind.

Twenty-five minutes into the climb we were beyond the point of return. The climb had become grueling on my arm, core, butt, thigh, and leg muscles. It was the kind of challenge that offered a first-class survival-of-the-fittest workout, one that had been laced with a tiny bit of fear, and that left your entire body tender and aching with pain the next day. The taxing activity on my body caused me to envision how nice a warm Jacuzzi bath would feel, especially one shared with my Tony. I thought of calling the hotel concierge to have housekeeping prepare a bath in our room, and to have it waiting for us by the time we finished the climb. I wondered about cell phone reception that high up on the rock, then proceeded to make the call.

While waiting for someone to pick up at the hotel, I suddenly came to a small cliff on the rock. I reached for the cliff with one hand, while the other held tightly to my cell phone. Big mistake. I missed the cliff, and it caused a quick stumble down two feet. During the stumble, I accidentally dropped my cell phone, and heard it crash into pieces about seventy-five feet below. I no longer felt secure. I used my upper body strength and grabbed a nearby piece of a large rock. I locked both hands tightly into it, and with all my might, I slowly began pulling myself up to a protruding foot rest of which to place my feet and gain stability. The rock piece was unstable. I slipped down even further, missing the foot rest altogether. While struggling to hold onto the rock with one hand, I used the other to try tightening the thick rope around my waist. I had discovered that for some reason my rope had too much slack, and any attempts at tightening it were useless. My body began dangling off the side of the rock.

"KoShari, you ok!?!"

Tony was at least 12 feet ahead of me. Consequently, I was too frightened to speak right away.

"Tony, Ahhh!" I screamed, while breathing heavily.

He saw me in danger and quickly rushed down to help.

"Hold on baby, hold on. I'm coming. Get a tight grip!"
"I'm trying, Tony. I can't."

Tony got within three feet of me when…

I felt the cool breeze on my face as I held on in utter fear for my life. I dared to look down, I was at least seventy-five feet from the bottom. Falling would likely end in death, given the sculptured rocks that were oddly jutted below. At least one of them would break my fall on the way down, forceably knocking my bones, like a car tumbling fast over a sloping cliff.

There was no time for past thoughts. The only thing that came to mind was, 'God help me.' I'm not ready to die.

My fingertips were bleeding from the pressure of the rocks. I began to fall.

"Tony, I can't hold on any longer. I love you," I whispered.

Chapter One

"Doctor, her vitals are normal. Her lungs are reacting well to the mild steroid treatments. I'd say she's a surefire for a steady recovery."

"Ok. You're excused, nurse Abby. I'm just gonna check one more thing here and I'm done."

"Alright, doctor. Page me if you need anything else."

About three minutes later, I heard what sounded like the shutting of window blinds, and the click of a door lock. Suddenly, I felt my hospital gown slowly roll up my body, exposing my lower torso, and breasts. The silence in the moment was resounding. Two fingertips began gently stroking my breasts, and then had traced a line down to my lower belly, stopping at the tip of my pelvis. It tickled, but I couldn't respond. He licked, and softly suckled my nipples, both of them. While his mouth was preoccupied with my breasts, he used his fingers to remove my panties. With the careful hands of a surgeon, he slowly slid them, one, and then the other, into my vagina. They felt lubricated. My guess is he had dipped them into petroleum jelly. He began pleasuring himself. I felt his heavy breathing, and heard his low moaning. I loathed the drops of what I imagined were sweat or drool falling on my neck.

Suddenly there was a loud knock at the door. The doctor abruptly stopped, and cleared his throat. I heard him zip his fly, and flap his doctor's coat over his pants. He quickly pulled down my gown, and covered me with the sheets. I heard the snap from his gloves as he hurriedly placed them back onto his hands. He opened the door.

"Doctor, you have a family member appointment for the coma patient in room 203 in five minutes. Would you like me to escort them to your office?"

"No, I'll be right there. Have them wait for me in the lobby."

"Ok."

The doctor closed the door behind her.

"You are one cute piece of ass. I hope your husband enjoys that pussy as much as I would." He exited the room four seconds later.

I lay here violated with nothing but retrospection. No one can hear me speak these thoughts. The doctors weren't aware that I hear them fussing over my care. The perverted doctor doesn't know that I feel his violations. I can't say I don't enjoy it. In some weird, and indescribable way, I do. Often he gets carried away, like the time I felt the twist of a dildo inside of me. I wonder if I can prove the assault when I come out of this coma. Doctors can get away with the violations claiming coma patients lose all sensory perception while in the comatose state. Science has yet to prove them wrong. I can feel every single touch. I'm not sure what's worse, the fall that got me into this coma, or the sick twisted doctor who has come to help.

His lustful acts reminded me how tender Tony made love to me, and how much I longed to feel his warmth again. While lying here in this coma, I think of Tony and how he changed my life. I think about who I was before I met him, and who I became after. He grew me, that man.

There were many troubles between us, troubles that could anger a person to extreme frustration. Troubles that…let me just put it this way... Those with weak hearts won't understand, and will be left feeling disoriented, confused, and furious after hearing about our troubles. I say this because my story is complicated. Although he is vastly different now, for seven years, my Tony, my precious, he cheated on me. He was what I called a habitual cheater. He cheated with all types of cyber-sluts, obese phone-sex whores, strippers, co-workers, my girlfriends…you name it, he cheated with it. He was like a junkie who gets high off some illegal narcotic. During the high, the junkie can care less about anyone or anything around. The high becomes the single most important focus of their universe. Nothing, not the safety of their children, not their employment, not personal hygiene, not anything, can keep them from getting the high they wanted. This is the type of fiending he would display just before having sex with other women, or men. Hell, it didn't matter, as long as he got off. He acted like he had to do it. Like it was calling out to him, and he'd lose his life if he didn't answer. Like a vampire in desperate need of a bloody fix. Oh God, but I loved him inexplicably.

The experts, my family and friends, even my OBGYN, they all advised me to leave him. All except for my mother. I didn't. I couldn't. He was my soul-fit, and my best friend. He was my match in every way, and my compliment, the guy who made me smile at the end of a hard day's work. He was filled with so much peace, that each time I'd lay comfortable on his chest, I'd fall asleep like a baby wrapped in warm blankets. That didn't happen with just anyone. It had only happened with him. The guy who genuinely belly laughed at my jokes, and never, ever, not once, made me feel that my strength threatened him. As far as I was concerned, that alone earned him my total devotion for life. It's rare to find a man, another person even, who's confident enough to allow a strong, independent, and opinionated woman to share in their shine. Sometimes he was my anti-, but always the anti- that brought out the best in me, like a freakishly difficult strength-training workout. He was the yin to my yang, and the other side of my reflection. He made me better, stronger, wiser, and smarter. He was what I needed, and by far the choice for what I wanted. How could I let all that go just because he cheated?

I can say with all certainty his cheating paled in comparison to the joy that only he could bring to my heart. I guess what I'm trying to say is if anyone out there knows what it feels like to have found the true love of your life; the one match to your soul, well then, Tony was it for me, the great love of my life.

I know what others who knew about us and our challenges would think. They'd think I'm some dysfunctional freak too blinded by love to recognize when I'm being bamboozled. They think what all the shrinks have told them about people like me. I'm blinded by my own insecurities and low self-esteem, and am searching for a father figure to fill the void left absent by my own father's emotional and/or physical abandonment in my life. And that explains why I allowed my husband to cheat on me. They might think I feared his leaving would take away my security, like he's some sort of security blanket I need to hold onto while walking around like a child with pouty eyes, sucking my thumb, and using my fingers to twirl my bangs. Or, they probably think I'm a typical control-freak chick, that because of my issues, I seek to run this man's life, which may explain him occasionally escaping into the arms of another, as opposed to running into mine.

They'd all be wrong. I'm not a typical case. I'm not in denial, and I don't have daddy issues. Well, maybe I had a few. I've always had a very healthy relationship with my father. In fact, I was the consummate daddy's girl growing up. There was nothing my father wouldn't do for me. I'm quite mentally strong, actually. Both my parents raised me to become a confident and well-adjusted woman. There's nothing lacking by way of self-assurance, here. I'm beginning to believe "they" might just be "me" thinking all these crazy things about myself, trying to rationalize my decision to remain with Tony after he cheated so carelessly. Certainly these thoughts are attempts at justifying my decision to stay in the marriage. There is a confusing dichotomy inside me. Anguish and agony are constantly bombarding my mind.

So, why? Why I allowed his cheating is a great mystery, or maybe not a mystery, but an act of deep interpersonal conflict, or blind faith. One theory of why I stayed is that I needed only to look around at friends who'd divorced their cheating husbands. From what I know, some were relieved. Others deeply regretted the decision to leave the love of their lives. I focused on the ones who'd left the love of their lives. Had I left, I would've fallen into that category. The effects of their decision were devastating, and severely interrupted their day-to-day lifestyles. Some of those with regrets blew up the size of a sumo wrestler from attempting to eat away at their painful emotions. They completely gave up on men and their hopes of participating in a fulfilling relationship. That was downright depressing to me, and not exactly what I envisioned for myself. Others either tried cheating themselves with other men, or decided to start dating women, seemingly to give the other side a try, since the main man in their lives had caused them such pain. As women we're so emotional, so protective of our hearts. We will over think a situation to death, justifying and analyzing. We can become as poisonous as snakes when our feelings are on the line, and as weak as doves when dealing with the pain.

Tony was the kindest, gentlest man I'd ever met. But when he would succumb to his addiction, he was the most heartless, vicious, ruthless, and selfish viper around. It's safe to say Tony had two different personalities back then; the real Tony, and the sex-addicted Tony. The real Tony was the man of my dreams. The sex-addicted Tony was every woman's nightmare. I, being the young lady that I am, NEVER would've married the sex-addicted Tony. That Tony wouldn't have gotten a second glance from me. I hadn't met the sex-addicted Tony by the time we got married. Friends told me that I knew all along, but had decided to ignore the warning signs due to my love for him. This very well could've been true. I don't fucking know. All I do know, is I was a sweet and sour siren who was extremely hard to get before meeting Tony. I never would've dated a cheater before meeting him. I was the one. I was the cheater when dating, back then.

I was on my way to the top when I was in law school. Since I was five years old I knew my professional destiny was to become a lawyer. All throughout my adolescent years I envisioned of one day becoming a successful attorney. The idea of parading in front of others, eloquently arguing a case before a judge, and giving the world the opportunity to witness how intelligent I was, thrilled me. I liked to be at the forefront, and was a born leader. I liked persuading others by being powerful and taking control. I took good care of my body with the work ethic and dedication of a German soldier. I always dated the best of the best. Of course I planned to marry money, and to have a beautiful house on a hill overlooking a drop-dead gorgeous skylight. I'd have 3 children who I'd raise to take over the world. My grown life would begin at age twenty-eight. I'd marry three years after graduating from law school, and two years after meeting my powerful husband. Course I'd be in love with him for the rest of my wonderful life. It was all planned out, and was gonna be picture perfect. Well, I pretty much got what I wanted, the beautiful home, the children, the career, but with a caveat. The caveat was a husband that cheats.

I had become well-known for my good looks, intelligence, and those slamming parties. People traveled from all over just to come to one of my get-togethers. It was primarily because guys both near and far knew they could come to a KoShari Alexander soirée, and find the hottest women who were all making it happen in some huge way. I and my friends were upper crust, beautiful to look at, ambitious, and educated. I prided myself on the "trophy" group I called my female friends and associates. Most of us were professionals, judges, politicians, doctors, architects, entertainment artists, pageant queens, lawyers, top saleswomen, corporate sharks, entrepreneurs, and high-end educators. We didn't need a guy for anything, accept of course for the occasional male-to-female sex that many of us needed only half the time. For some, an active vibrator would cure that good ole' dick craving just fine. I know because my good friend Miranda told me so. I myself couldn't go too long without an occasional booty call. Admittedly the penis is the best muscle on a man's body. I confess to the love of using my best muscle to stroke and massage theirs, often. Very often. I guess one could say I was hot like that. Being of the zodiac sign Scorpio, I believe the love of sex was somewhat just a part of my nature. Ha, it still is. Nevertheless, men were accessories, and not necessities, in my world. We certainly wouldn't take any bullshit off any man. Let a motherfucker think he would cheat on any one of us. Boy...He'd definitely have another thing coming. If he was slick enough for us not to have sniffed him out beforehand, the idiot would get dropped fast like the average Joe. We'd all worked hard to get to where we wanted in life. When you work really hard for something, you don't easily allow anything to threaten your dignity, and to swipe it away from you. We were elite. As far as we were concerned, we didn't care who'd judge by calling us snobs. We'd earned every ounce of respect born to wear the title. I'd say we were all something quite special. Tony caused me to lose my membership in the Trophy club, and to go back on everything I'd always bragged on, about myself. Ironically, I didn't drop him when he cheated on me. Not him. Regarding my dignity? Well, it went out the door, along with my self-respect, for a time.

One particular party stands out above the rest. It was the night of the "Full Moon Blast." My moon-shaped 3-D invitations had gone out two months in advance to everyone as far east as Puerto Rico, and as far west as Washington State, and California. I expected an exclusive crowd of over 175 confirmed guests to the party. That year we elected to host the party atop Hotel Derek in Midtown Houston. I'd invited one-third men, and two-thirds women. The ratio of men to women was a carefully orchestrated concoction of beauty, competition, jealousy, intelligence, scheming, and fun... All the right ingredients for the perfect party.

I sent two invitations to two different guys I was dating at the same time, both who lived on separate ends of the country. Piers lived in Washington DC, and Mason lived in Seattle. I didn't expect them both to show up, given Piers had previously stated he'd be traveling on business the day of the party. Apparently something had changed that allowed him to come. Shit, whatever. I wasn't in love with either of them, but had developed a heartfelt soul connection with both, and had been either too busy, or too lazy to choose between the two of them which I wanted to continue screwing. Both ran a cool fourth to studying for law school. There was rarely time to go out and party, let alone to nurture any real relationships. The times I partied were few and far between. However when I partied, I partied hard, and made sure to do as many different things as possible. The outlet always made the studying a bit more bearable.

I first met Piers, a musician, at a Prince concert I attended alone while on a trip to DC for a moot court competition at Georgetown Law. He was there with some chick that had gotten angry at him for something stupid. She stormed out of the concert, leaving him behind by himself. I can imagine he'd decided to stay to prevent wasting at least one of the tickets he'd purchased. I discovered later that he didn't care much for Prince, but respected his guitar skills. The guitar happened to be his favorite instrument, and mine as well.

My seat was on the next isle behind him and his date. Fortunately, or unfortunately, I'd witnessed the entire argument between the two of them. I thought it was cute the way he justified making his point in the argument, I didn't care whether he was right or not. He was tall, brown-skinned, had a banging body, and a bald head. He had the look that told me I could see us hooking up together. I walked up to him after the concert and introduced myself.

"Good going, Smoky," I said with a smile.

We started talking, went for sushi in Georgetown after the concert, and had been enjoying each other's company ever since.

Mason. I met him through my friend Alicia at a water-skiing party on Padre Island. He was visiting a college frat brother, and had been on vacation from his job as an IT Executive with Microsoft. When I saw him, the first thing I noticed was his sculpted shoulders. He had broad and muscular shoulders that slanted down enough to highlight the taper along his neckline. "Another sexy suit-brother," I said to myself under my breath. At around 205lbs, he looked the part of a fire fighter. He had ear-length dreads with sun-kissed blonde tips. The sun-kissed dreads matched his amber colored skin tone and hazel eyes. Oh, those eyes. They were spellbinding. I was attracted to the way he made eye contact with everyone around. The eye contact spoke confidence to me. I liked a strong man who wasn't afraid to look a person in the eye, or to make difficult business decisions on the spot. I wasn't sure of his business acumen, but somehow he looked the part.

We hit it off after a couple water ski rides together. I told myself he'd be a pen pal, a friend I could visit on occasion to Seattle. He'd been making time to visit me at least twice-a-month since we first met. He was adventurous, and we always had a good time together. I wasn't ready to end our friendship just yet. Oh, the decisions.

"So did anyone help you put this together, or did you do it all by yourself like the superwoman I know you are," asked Mason, as we slow-danced on the dance floor to a sexy R. Kelly song. I think it was the Caribbean one, about rolling the body, or working the hips, something like that. All I know is we were linked together like a braid. He held me very close that night, for some reason. "His" gently rubbed up against "mine," and it made me light-headed. The sensation sent a shaft of butterflies up my belly with each soft stroke against my pelvis. There was a rhythm to his movements, and I had completely surrendered to it. Slowly back, front, side-to-side he moved my hips, while his hands barely touched either side of them. Good thing I wore my 3 inch heels that night, or else his bulge would've stabbed me in the abdomen. I couldn't speak as he stared into my eyes, those hazel weapons had lassoed my mouth shut. All I could do was grin, silly, like a mischievous little girl.

"Excuse me, KoShari. Can I speak to you for a moment?"

I ignored the interruption, hoping it would go away. This was feeling too damned good. I could tell the sex with Mason was gonna be worthy that night. I was completely caught up.

"Uh, HELLO! You hear me talking to you. I SAID, do you have a moment?!"

I turned around with a raggedy frown ready to read someone their rights for being so rude, when to my surprise Piers was standing there with anger written all over his face.

"Oh, Hi Piers," I said, semi-hesitantly.

I wasn't afraid of what might happen next. Odd and uncomfortable situations never made me sweat. All my life my parents had put me through an intense training of recurrent high-pressured situations as a method of preparing me for the corporate world. I guess they wanted me to learn how best to maintain self-control in the midst of spontaneously unsettling circumstances. My training had been perfect for this little minor predicament.

Suddenly I awoke out of Mason's spell. I slipped his hands off my hips. He was resistant to my dismissal. He almost wouldn't let go at all.

"When did you get here?" I asked Piers, while Mason looked on in disappointment.

"I just walked in, KoShari. I asked someone about you, and they said I could find you making love on the dance floor. I see they were right."

"Ha ha, whatever, Piers. I was merely dancing with my friend Mason, here. Mase this is Piers. Piers, Mason."

"What's up man? I see you all up on my girl," said Piers.

"YOUR girl?! KoShari, who is this dude?" Mason replied.

"Look guys, I'm dating you both. You both knew I wasn't looking for a serious relationship when we met. I told you we'd be free to date other people, and you agreed that was ok. So don't go acting all brand new, and cause some ghetto scene or some shit, while we're out here on the dance floor."

"Yeah, but I didn't know I'd actually meet the other guy," said Piers.

"Ok, see Piers, don't go there. You and I both know you're seeing someone in DC. What's with the possession all of a sudden? And since when did I become YOUR girl?"

"That was a discussion I was gonna have with you during my visit this weekend. Things were going so well between us, I wanted to discuss taking our relationship to the next level. You know, seeing each other exclusively."

"Wow. I didn't know, Piers. We'll have to talk later. Let me finish up with Mason and I'll come find you. Now please, go mingle. There are lots of interesting people here."

"Go mingle??? Oh, alright. I'll do that while you dance with ole California dude, here. I ain't got time for this sh..." Piers said while walking away.

"Say, man! The insults aren't necessary. The woman has obviously made her choice. Some men need to mature and learn to concede rejection when it happens," said Mason.

"Brother You Don't Know Me!" Piers shouted as he stopped and turned to face Mason.

"Oh, Lord." I sighed.

I had worked hard earlier that night on my hair and makeup, and wasn't about to get in the middle of a brawl. I quietly stepped back and got out of the way. Piers charged at Mason and grabbed his throat. He clocked Mason dead in the nose. Oddly, it took people a good two minutes before they noticed the fight on the dance floor. Guess they didn't want to bring too much attention to something that could end the party right then.

Both Piers and Mason had to know my true feelings for them. I believe a guy knows when a woman is truly into him, just as a girl knows when a guy is truly into her. Seems like a sixth-sense sort of thing. When the deep chemistry is apparently absent, sometimes, out of desperation or boredom, one tries to disguise what they know to be true, and that is the lie that something real exists between them and the one they want. They even force themselves, and the other party, to believe that fate or destiny was involved in the union. If the one being pursued is passive enough, they can be convinced to go along with the lie. Nevertheless, the truth is always apparent, whether or not it is acknowledged. The truth, in these instances, is that neither one is really into the other. I for one cannot settle for some pseudo-situationship that might look good to the public, but is actually empty behind closed doors.

I hadn't given off the vibe of being in love with either Piers or Mason, so not sure what was happening there. I believe at some point it turned into a bravado contest among the two of them. Men can be territorial by nature. I think at the point of the brawl Piers might have felt Mason was infringing upon his territory, regardless of his feelings for me. Or, maybe not. Maybe he was falling for me. I wasn't falling for him, so that didn't matter.

"What the hell! Now why don't y'all take this shit elsewhere? This is a good party and I'm not ready for it to end. Somebody please bust up these savages! Damned fools. KoShari, what's with you? Don't you know how to control your men?" Alicia was harsh.

She had gotten frustrated at the fight, or rather at the typicality of a fight at a party between two black men.

"Hee, hee," I snickered, overlooking Alicia's seriousness. "Girl I didn't tell them to start fighting and acting like buffoons. You're right. This is just plain ugly. Not to mention, I don't want either one of em,' like that. Damn. What a way to spoil a good time in the sack."

"Yo hot ass... Is that all you think about? KoShari, I swear," said Alicia. I sneered at her words.

I had gestured one of the bouncers to come break up the fight. Big Luke pulled the two of them apart, and forcefully pushed them in opposite directions. Piers left the party right away. Mason stood there looking at me in disgust. He shook his head without a word, and then left.

"(Clap, clap) Alright, alright. The craziness is over, people. DJ kick that music up, and let's get this party back on track," Alicia said, while walking thru the dance floor, attempting to convince the others to keep enjoying themselves after the fight had occurred.

Both Piers and Mason were incredible men with great pedigrees, but there was something missing between me and each one of them. Although I had developed good friendships with them both, there was no burning desire. I hadn't felt what it was like to fall in love up to that point, but I knew it hadn't happened with either Piers, or Mason. They were both good sex partners, but love was something altogether different.

After the fight incident at the party, I began to take a good long look at myself in the mirror. I wasn't raised to be such a heartless bitch, and wondered why I'd let things get so far out-of-hand. I didn't feel good about myself after that. Nevertheless, I came to the conclusion that I didn't tell them to react the way that they had. Who knew they'd actually fight like school kids over me? I was mature enough to take full responsibility for my own actions, and had thought of ways I could've prevented the fight that night.

Sure, I could've chosen to invite only one guy. It would've been the right thing to do. However, that would've presumed I cared enough about Piers and Mason to think things through before deciding to invite them both. That's just it; I hadn't cared enough about the men to prevent the blow-up. I admit to the carelessness and rude behavior of inviting them both, knowing potentially something bad could happen as a result. Honestly, we were all seeing other people at the time, and although I liked the guys, I found myself more infatuated with the idea of having alternate travel destinations, and someone to escort me during the visits. A good time. That's all that both Piers and Mason had amounted, for me. I was so engulfed in law school at the time, I couldn't allow myself to waste precious moments with men I didn't terribly long to be with.

The reckless behavior changed when I met Tony. He became the one man that caused me to care more for him than I did my own self. It was dangerous and risky, but true.

Chapter Two

I remember when Tony and I first met...

I was out shoe shopping at the Galleria while on the phone with my friend Courtney, who was telling me about an exclusive party that would take place that night in River Oaks. I'd spotted a nice pair of shimmering silver heels at my favorite shoe boutique when Courtney began telling me all about it. She said it promised to be one of the best parties that year, and was trying desperately to get me to drive my jeep, since she knew I was the only one of our clique that didn't drink hard liquor. Courtney began her clever petitions for me to drive to the party that night.

"Ok Shari, so you comin' over, or you want me to come over there?" Asked Courtney.

"Sweetheart, you know you're driving tonight. Last time I drove, y'all heifers earled all over my backseat. It cost me $1500 for the leather treatment alone. And you divas hadn't offered to pay one dime."

"KoShari, you're the only one who doesn't drink. We'll pitch in for gas or something, but you know it's safer if you're the designated driver."

"Ok, since you gotta break it down like that. If you throw up in my jeep again, I'm sending you a bill you'll pay, or else. What time will you be ready?" I asked.

"You can get here around 9:30pm. I'll be ready by then. Oh, yeah. Alicia said she's off tonight and wants to hang."

"Ralph must be out-of-town."

"You know it. He's in Cali for the weekend on business."

"Ok, girl. Tell her to come to your house. I'm no taxi driver, you know."

"OK. Toodles!" Courtney was halfway in the tub before she hung up the call.

I arrived at Courtney's at 9:30pm sharp. As usual, Courtney was still getting dressed. Alicia was, of course, on the phone with Ralph, telling him who she wanted him to say hello to in LA. She and her boyfriend Ralph had plans of moving to LA to start an intellectual property practice after law school. They planned to represent their friends in the entertainment industry and publishing. They were already engaged, and set to recite the nuptials during the summer before our third year. While on the phone, Alicia looked up at me and smiled. She briefly interrupted her conversation with Ralph to acknowledge my entrance.

"Hold on, baby," Alicia said to Ralph. "Hey Shari, sweetie, how are you? She's not done yet," referring to Courtney. "She's probably meditating, searching the stars for favor so she can meet her soul mate at the party tonight, ha ha." Alicia let out a smug laugh. It was like her to be lightly sarcastic.

I smiled and walked to the back to find Courtney putting on her mascara. Courtney was the prettiest of us all. She was a medium build at 5' 7" around 130lbs, perfectly hourglass slim-thick shaped, and well-framed. Her hair was brown, long to her waist, and lusciously thick. She had a honey complexion, and often wore natural make-up to accentuate her simple elegance.

"You here, already?" Asked Courtney, while looking at me through the mirror. "I should've known."

"Aren't I always on time?"

"I was hoping you got held up at a street light or something. Give me ten minutes and I'll be ready."

My patience ran thin because Courtney should've been ready ten minutes ago. She knew how I hated, I mean HATED, to wait. I could tell by the way the night started out that I was in for some unpredictability that night.

"Shari, Ralph asked if you're ready for moot court." Alicia yelled from the other room, while still on the phone with Ralph.

"Tell him of course I'll deliver. As always I aim to please, never to disappoint. Tell him his briefs better be ready, and fully researched. He knows professor Jamison is looking to get him, ever since he dissed her at the last lecture."

"Ok baby, I love you. I got a surprise for you when you get back. I'll see you tomorrow. Goodbye, I love you!" Alicia told Ralph.

"Y'all are wayyy too in love for me," I told her.

"That's my man, baby."

"Let's go," said Courtney as she breezed through, scanning the living room for her keys. She grabbed them from an end table in the foyer. "I want us to get a good parking spot."

Houston never looked so alive that night. It seemed everywhere you looked people were out in groups, walking the busy streets, laughing, and enjoying Houston's wild nightlife. It was particularly busy down Westheimer Street near the Galleria, along the way to Uptown. People were out everywhere, at Starbucks having coffee, hanging out at The Cheesecake Factory with friends, riding in horse driven carriages, walking along the Galleria waterfall, all appearing to be free and loving the night out.

Hip Hop was playing on the radio when Courtney blurted out, "Did you hear Freda and Jake broke up? It's really over this time."

"No!" I replied.

"Yep. He said he's glad its over. He got tired of dating a baby. Said he needed a woman who could hold her own with him. Somebody who wouldn't let him get away with whatever he wanted. Somebody with respect for herself."

"Somebody like you?" I interrupted.

"What!? Girl, please."

"Courtney you've had the biggest crush on Jake since 1L orientation," I said.

"Yeah, he does look good. Not to mention he's a shoe-in at Fulton & Jabronsky for next summer. The guy has a bright future ahead of him. But I don't take seconds. He should've noticed me before wasting time with Freda."

"Hey, seconds aren't all that bad. Ralph was still with Priscilla when we started con law together." Alicia noticed Courtney and I look at each other and roll our eyes. She played us off like she didn't care we were thinking she was a man-thief. "Anyway-ya! I think he's totally different with me. He never smiled this much when he was with her. I don't think she knew how to bring out the best in him. You gotta know how to do that, you know."

"We'll see. I can't develop anything with anyone till after this semester. Professor Tate is kicking my ass in Torts. I need all my brain cells working with no interference just to get a B+ in her class. I need at least a B+ to get the clerkship at Time Warner-New York this summer. Anything less than a B will drop my chances," said Courtney.

Courtney had big dreams of becoming a member of the legal team at a major entertainment company after graduation. She lives for the challenge of the high-life, and loves to party both personally and professionally. She was sure to secure an associate spot during her clerkship that summer.

We arrived at the party at approximately 10:20pm that evening, and parked across the street from the place. It was packed. There weren't many familiar faces right away. One of the lovely things about the big city of Houston was the clique diversity. Rarely did you run into the same faces while you were out. I liked this about Houston. In most places, there are only a select number of people going in a young black professional direction. You always run into the same faces at parties and events. Houston offered an alternative to the norm. The city is so big, with so many young black professionals, and so much to do, you literally can hang out each weekend of the year and do something different with a different crowd each time.

"Let's go, ladies," I said while walking to the venue from the parking lot.

We headed into the party like a herd of cattle. "Mingle well, not too much huddling tonight," I said. Courtney and Alicia laughed.

"Robert! Hi baby!" Said Courtney. She drifted into the crowd. Alicia and I continued waving at people we knew.

"Alicia is that Octavia? I better go say hi. She hooked me up at the dentist the other day. Octavia, how nice to see you," I said while walking up to her. Octavia was a dentist who was married to one of our law school buddies, Zach. She frequently accompanied him to our law school socials and was sure to pass out tons of business cards while there. "How'd you hear about the party?" I asked her. It's always good to know who knows who. In case you want to expand your circle of influence, you have an up by having pre-judged a person based on their affiliations.

"Jimmy told me about it last Sunday at the Houston Rockets Golf Tournament Fundraiser in Sugar Creek. He said I should come, so I did. I'm not regretting it. This is a nice crowd," said Octavia.

"Right…right," I said while looking around for other familiar faces. I was growing disinterested in talking further with Octavia.

"Let's dance," said this handsome man with a distinctive low beard, who had walked up from behind. He was sexy, but he seemed a bit out of place at the party. He looked to be in his mid-fifties. Fortunately I am attracted to handsome older men.

"Ok," I said without hesitating.

As we danced, I could tell he was taken by me. I played the card by flirtatiously dancing around him, and making him feel nice and relaxed on the dance floor. He was blushing, so I had a sense of the pleasurable upper hand.

Suddenly, I noticed this guy staring at me from the patio outside. The room was separated from the outdoor patio by a wall of French glass doors. I could easily spot him checking me out. I looked away and turned to my dance partner as though I was enjoying myself. The song ended. He asked, "What's your signature drink?"

"I don't do alcohol."

"Good. It's rare I meet a woman who doesn't drink. What's your name?"

"KoShari, (pronounced Ko Shah ree). KoShari Alexander."

"Nice name," said the guy.

"I'll take a water with lime."

"Sure. I'll get it. I'm Jim by the way. I'll be right back."

'I guess if I wanted your name I would've asked,' I thought to myself.

I had said my name, KoShari Alexander, like I expected him to know of the Alexander name. The Alexanders were well established in Houston, Texas. My family had built a name for themselves in the high-end Chandelier business. My maternal grandfather started the business thirty-six years ago in Houston. He began his career as a young glass blower for a small glass company in Kansas City, Missouri. There, he had designed exquisite and unique chandeliers and glass sculptures. The glass company closed its doors after seventeen years. Somehow my grandfather continued in the industry on his own, by acquiring several contracts with five-star hotel chains and entertainment venues in Kansas City. Soon the word of his unique design and disciplined business tactics spread across the country. He acquired business in Houston after a contact connected him to a wealthy oilman with ties to the local colleges, universities, and the museum district. He installed new chandeliers at the University of Houston, University of St. Thomas, Texas Southern University, and three Houston Community College campuses. The Museum of Fine Arts-Houston, as well as the Johnson Space Center, also became clients. One year later, he opened his first gallery in Houston, "Dubaki Chandeliers." In the absence of any sons to take over the family business, my grandfather passed control of the company along to my mother, who in turn granted conservatorship to my father, once they had been married for 14 years. When Dad took over, he renamed the company, "Dubaki-Alexander Chandeliers." Dad took the business to new levels, acquiring several more contracts with many worldwide hotel chains, and other places located in the Houston Uptown and surrounding areas. Soon we owned three galleries in the Houston metropolitan, and twenty-four worldwide. I was certain that mentioning my last name to my dance partner would remind the guy of seeing one of our billboards in bright lights off the 59 or 610 freeways.

While Jim was getting my drink, I noticed the stalker again eying me from the patio. This time he walked toward the front of the place, never taking his eyes off me, and oddly enough, not bumping into anyone along the way. My eyes followed him. We scoped each other for a moment, and then someone else caught my attention.

"Be careful there, you don't want to brush-up on any of your Dad's buddies, ha ha!" Laughed Courtney. She'd walked up behind me.

"He's pretty nice, but I'm not interested in that way."

"John David asked about you. I told him he should talk to you in person, and that you didn't like shy guys. Besides, I don't have time to play match-up," said Courtney, as she continued looking around the room.

"Yeah, well little did he know, he ruined his chances when he asked you about approaching me. Courage is a mandatory characteristic of all potentials."

"You said it good sister," said Courtney, while waving at the DJ. "You taking any requests tonight? I want to hear some old school LL."

"What's your pleasure good-lookin?" Asked the DJ.

"Rock the Bellzzzz!" Courtney replied.

The DJ put it on while she was still singing the word bells. The crowd went berserk. Almost instantly the dance floor was packed. I noticed Alicia with two different guys who were burying her on the dance floor. Alicia was short, about 5'4" very petite and quite cute. She was a light-skinned shawty with shoulder-length straight, and black hair. The guys were swallowing her whole. I gave Alicia some relief by dancing with one of them. Courtney soon joined us. We bourgeoisie people know how to party. You never knew whether cool or wild was appropriate, of course it depended on the crowd. We didn't dance like animals, but certainly had a good time, as much as we could, while still keeping it cute. Always. After the hype died down we all ended up back at the bar together.

It was as if I could feel those eyes staring at me again. Sure enough, there he was.

"Alicia, Courtney, do you know that guy?"

"Who?" Asked Courtney.

"Over there, near the corner," I pointed in his direction. "He's looking right at me."

"Can't say that I know him, sweetie," said Alicia.

"He keeps looking over here like a stalker or something. I hope he's safe. I'm going to the ladies room. I'll be right back."

While in the ladies room I ran into soror Danielle Piedmont.

"Hey Danielle! How's it going?" We hugged.

"How've you been, KoShari?"

"I've been good, trying to enjoy a study break at the moment."

Danielle was a 3L at UH Law. She'd pledged Delta a year before me at TSU undergrad, and had no love for me when I was on line. She was cool, though. We had nothing against each other as far as I knew.

"I was hoping to get some signatures for the petition to renovate the law library at school," she said.

"You sure you want to talk school business, here? Seems people tried to get away from the routine by coming here tonight."

"You mean YOU tried to get away from the routine, K. I see you're still wet behind the ears, lil sis. Always be networking. Especially in places where people are laid back and feeling relaxed. Some of the most critical business transactions have occurred in this type atmosphere."

"I guess," I told her, as I took the petition from her hands and added my signature to the list. "Well, I'm out. Enjoy yourself!" I said with a smile, handing the petition back to her.

"Oh don't worry, I will. Thanks for your signature, lil sis."

Just outside the bathroom door stood the stalker. He had followed me, and had been strategically waiting near the exit door of the bathroom. I was shocked. I slowly walked over to him while never losing eye contact.

"Hi," I said with an eye-smile.

"Hi."

"You think you know me?"

"No. I just really wish I did."

"I noticed you looking at me earlier."

"I like the way you noticed me. So what's your name?" He asked, while walking a step closer to me, making the moment even more intimate.

"KoShari."

"Hi KoShari, I'm Tony."

"Hi Tony."

I was purposely trying to appear uninterested, but couldn't help shining a deceptive smile. He started small talk about how nice the party was. I really wasn't feeling him. I began looking around for someone else I knew. I wanted to walk off.

"So KoShari, what's your story?"

"I'm a 1L at UH Law."

"Oh, really?" I graduated from Harvard Law a year ago."

"OH REALLY!" I excitedly replied. Suddenly he had my undivided attention.

"So do you practice here in Texas?"

"As a matter of fact I do. I'm on the legal team at Total Entertainment Group. I handle the contract negotiations."

"You like it?"

"I love it."

"So what do you plan to do with your JD?" He asked, as if to quickly switch the focus back to me.

"International Business Law. I want to oversee mergers and acquisitions, as well as strategic alliances between domestic and international companies."

"Sounds about like what I do," he said with a smile.

For a moment we look into each other's eyes, capturing the others' graces.

"Tony, hey! I see you came," said Danielle Piedmont. She had walked up during our conversation.

"Hey woman, I hadn't seen you all night. What's up?" Tony asked Danielle.

"Do you want to dance?" He looked at her, and then looked at me strangely, as if to silently express, 'I know she saw us talking.'

"Maybe later. I'll come find you."

He turned his back to her while facing me. Danielle slowly walked away. She looked back at us with a crimped expression of disappointment on her face. I'm thinking this guy must really be special if Danielle made a point to come over and interrupt us. It seemed she had something to prove, like she was trying to stake her claim. Clearly he was interested in me, not her.

I was turned on by Danielle's interest in the guy. Her actions showed me there was much more to him than what I saw. Oh, but I was feeling what I saw. He was very tall, 6' 5" maybe, and had an athletic physique. He wasn't dressed too fancy, sort of plain even, in a simple but elegant sort of way. He had a confident calmness about him, a charm that made him very attractive to me. He seemed self-assured and satisfied with himself. I liked that. Not to mention, learning that he was a Harvard alum was the cherry-on-top.

"Hey why don't we call each other sometime?" He asked.

"I don't know, I'm kinda busy with school and all." I was fronting. At this point I was interested in getting this man in between the sheets to see what he was made of.

"Yeah, yeah I know the routine. Been there done that. Tell you what, give me your number, and if there's no chemistry after our first conversation, I'll do us both a favor and won't ever call back. Can we make it a deal?"

I grabbed a napkin and wrote down my number. I handed it to him.

"You got it. Hey, I'm going to find my girls. I'll see you around," I told him. I began to walk away.

"Ok. It was nice meeting you, KoShari. Bye. Beautiful."

"Goodbye, Tony."

I looked back at him. Our eyes were glued as I walked away. We didn't break eye contact till I reached Alicia, who was several paces away.

After taking Courtney and Alicia home, my thoughts wandered about Tony. I remembered thinking how comfortably real our conversation was. He seemed like a sweet man, like he could be fun to hang out with. Sometimes I could be a tight wad. He seemed the type that could loosen me up and make me laugh. I was intrigued. Well, what'd ya know. A man finally had achieved what I was beginning to think was the impossible. Someone finally made me sincerely consider him after a chance encounter. It was refreshing to have these thoughts about a fellow. I was impressed, or was it that Harvard Law degree that impressed me??

Chapter Three

"Ma, you here? Hel-lo! Shari's home!" I yelled while going through the back door of my parent's home.

"You better be glad I know your voice. You almost got hit with a bat, girl. Hey baby." She said, as we embraced.

I loved coming home to my parents' from time-to-time. It kept me grounded and refreshed. Visiting home was another great way to break the rigorous studying routine.

"The lovely Janis Alexander," I told her. I was excited to see my Mom.

"It's always wonderful to see you, dear. You been taking care of yourself? Are you eating properly? You look pale in the face and a little too slim in the waist," she told me.

"I'm fine mother. Where's Dad?"

"Oh he's out playing golf with the contractors for the new chandelier gallery in Chicago. He'll be home for dinner. You staying? I'm cooking smothered Norwegian salmon with steamed asparagus & red pepper, one of your favorites."

"No, I'm just here to pick up the case briefs I left on Monday. I gotta get going. I have a diving lesson at 5:30pm."

"Shari you better be careful going that deep under water. You might get down there and can't come back up someday."

"Never that, mother. That kinda stuff doesn't happen to me," I said, being cocky.

"You heard from Nana, how's she doing?" I asked.

"She's fine young lady. How are your grades?" I noticed she had quickly cut off my questions about Nana.

"They're fine, Mom. I should get all A's this semester. Don't worry. I'll make the Dean's List."

My mother was constantly on my tail about spending quality time in the books. She was a Stanford alumnus, with an MBA from Pepperdine. She helped run my grandfather's chandelier company after graduating. I attribute my good study habits to her. She taught me to earnestly work for everything I wanted, and to never expect favor from anyone, but to work hard at creating it for myself. I love my mother very much. She's full of wisdom and was always happy to pass it down.

"Let me know if I can help you, dear. Sometimes a fresh perspective on something is best."

"Ok. Can I ask about Nana, now?" I asked, sarcastically.

"Girl, you know that woman is fine. As long as she can go fishing every Sunday morning at the crack of dawn. Why don't you go by and see her sometime?"

"Yeah, I was thinking of asking her a few questions about men."

"Men! What men?! You got time to think about men?! Now Shari, I've told you the first year of law school is reserved for establishment." Of course she had stopped cleaning her plant pots, all her activities were halted at this point. She pointed her finger at me. She was preoccupied with letting me have it, the Janis Alexander way.

"You shouldn't worry about some knucklehead young man who half the time doesn't even know how to keep his ears clean..." she's going on and on.

"Ma, who doesn't clean his ears?" I laughed at her uncensored words.

"Who are you talking about? There's nobody, Ma. I don't have a boyfriend."

"Good, cause I was about to go off on you for not talking to me before my mother. What do you want to ask her anyway?" She asked while looking puzzled.

"I want her to tell me when you know you've met the one, if there is such a thing."

"Ah Shari, I can answer that one for you."

"But Ma, I want to ask Nana. She gives me an objective opinion. She tells me what the guy is thinking, mostly. I'd prefer that perspective, you know, how a man thinks he knows he's found, "the one."

"Honey whatever," she said in a brush-off sort of way. "Now hush-up and help me do this. Take that pot and put the soil in. Now saturate the seeds into the soil." I began helping her with the seeds. She went on and on, giving me instructions for potting the plants.

"I'm going to have to leave in a few...you, gotta, finish, this yourself..."

She ignored me and kept giving instructions while I was talking. I cut her a side-eye on the sly.

"Down!" Yelled the diving instructor. Everyone suited in diving gear took the plunge all at once. Looking down I couldn't see the bottom of the pool. There was a big black pit of darkness. I dropped down further. Five feet, then seven, then ten, then thirteen. At thirteen feet I flicked the headlight on my helmet. Tap! I hit the bottom at fifteen feet. I looked around to see the others who had made it along with me. The other students in the class, Natalie, Joe, Malorie, and Edgar, were all there, looking around as well. The assignment was to stay down for seven minutes practicing the proper breathing techniques with the oxygen tank, and then come back up. I began walking slowly around the pool noticing its dimensions and familiarizing myself with the surroundings. Malorie tapped me on the shoulder. Just as I looked around, she turned her back to me, placed her hands on her knees, and started twerking under water. I laughed. Joe got our attention. He tapped his watch to let us know the time was up. Immediately, we carefully pushed up to prevent a "bing" reaction, a stinging sensation often felt in the ears when trying to ascend too quickly in deep water. We slowly popped up to the top like floating devices. We applauded when seeing each person.

"Ok everybody!" The instructor shouted as we were cheering. "That was good. Remember to confirm the position of your equipment before coming to the surface. Take it nice and slow when floating up. Fantastic everyone. Let's break. I'll see you next week at 5:30pm. Oh yeah, don't forget the final certification dive at Galveston's Stewart Beach in three weeks. Stop by the front desk to pay your fees if you haven't already, check-in your equipment, and sign the clearances. See you next week!" Said the instructor.

"So what, you thought you were on soul train down there?" I asked Malorie, being funny.

"Girl you know how we do it. You wait till we get to Galveston. I'm gonna pop, pop, pop it!" She told me while twerking. We both laughed.

"Alright, now! Stay outta trouble, girl. I'll see you next week," I told her.

I gathered my things and headed to the jeep. I'd allotted six hours to studying criminal law concepts that night, and was pretty focused to start on time. Just as I placed my things in the passenger side of the jeep, who do I see? If it wasn't Mr. Confidence himself. I saw Tony coming out of the gym located next to the diving class, with some friends. He didn't notice me right away. I watched him for a moment. He and his friends were laughing about some football player's stupid fumble on the field. He looked kinda cute in those just-above-the-knee-length, wrangle-fitted Polo blue jean shorts, and top with the arms cut-off. Their conversation was ending. He looked up and noticed me getting into my jeep. Tony walked over to me while cutting the warmest smile I'd ever seen. He looked really happy at the surprise of seeing me that day. Of course I blushed. I did that a lot around him.

"Hello, Tony," I muttered.

"Well hello there, ma'am. What a pleasant surprise," he said, while leaning up against the car that was parked next to my jeep. With his forearms and legs folded, he was slowly looking me up and down.

"You work out?" He asked.

"No. I'm taking diving lessons next to the gym," I replied. I leaned against my jeep. I'm checking him out, looking into his eyes, searching for his character.

"So you like to go down deep, you say?" He said.

"Doesn't everyone?" I asked trying to match his humor.

"That's interesting. I love to dive. I've dived down in Belize before. They have some of the most beautiful coral just off the Ambergris Caye. Actually, it's one of the top 10 largest barrier reefs in the world. They also have a famous dive spot called, The Blue Hole. Its so big and deep, you can see it from space. Have you heard of it?"

"No I haven't," I replied.

"You'd love to dive there, the place is perfection. Tell you what, why don't I take you there someday?" He asked, as if he was certain I'd say yes.

"That's a bit forward don't you think? We should do coffee or dinner first, I mean, that's normally how first dates happen, right?"

"Ah-ha, so you're asking me out on a first date, I see... Well, I'm flattered. So be it," he said, while writing down his email address. "I'd love to have dinner with you Saturday night around 7:00ish. Email me directions to your place so I can pick you up. Say… you like venison?" He asked, while handing me his information. I noticed his subtle attempt at grammatical manipulation, also known as, trying to put words into my mouth. He had put a spin on my comment about how first dates happen, to his advantage, of course. I didn't know what to think of it right away. Was he being cute, or could this be cause for future concern?

"Whoa, whoa, wait. Sorry, Tony. I have plans this Saturday night," I was lying through my teeth, but I couldn't let him think he had the upper hand, especially after that little clever bit.

"You sure do have plans... To have dinner with me. Too late to back out now, I already accepted your offer to go on a first date. I'll look forward to getting your email," he said with a seductive smile.

I'll say… This dude basically just told me to cancel my plans because

I was going out with him on Saturday night. He seemed skilled enough to take the control that, he somehow knew, belonged to him. I was being swooned and I liked it. Hell, if I had plans, I probably would've canceled them anyways, the way this dude was making me feel.

"I gotta go," he said as he walked away. He waved back at me. He was about twenty feet out when he yelled, "Don't forget to send me your email address!"

I stood there stunned, looking at him as he walked into the parking garage. He must not have known who he was dealing with. I was not easy by any means. As enticing as he seemed I couldn't call him. I always play hard to get, always. Naw, I wasn't playing. I AM hard to get. If a guy doesn't have to work to get you, he won't appreciate you, right? I mean, who truly appreciates an A they didn't earn? Anyways, it was beneath me to give in right away. He needed to see how preoccupied I was. I was a busy person with a very active lifestyle who didn't rely on others for happiness. It was important he knew that. Yeah, that's it. Besides who asks for email addresses anyways? Why didn't he just ask me to text it to him? But…he was rather handsome. He had a good combination of intelligence and confidence that attracted me. I mean, really attracted me. Dang he was fine!! 'Ok. Maybe this one time I'll do the unusual and send the email tonight, just to let him think he got the upper hand,' I thought. I really liked this guy, and found myself liking him more and more each time I saw him.

From: KoShariA@yahoo.com, To: Tony@TBhome.net Sent November 3, 2005 19:30pm. "My address: 4545 Chevy Chase Blvd. #12, Houston, TX. 77062. See you Saturday night. - KoShari."

I decided to send a straight-to-the-point message with no fluff. I was determined to give him exactly what he'd asked for in the email. Nothing more. I'll show him who's the master of the game.

From: Tony@TBhome.net, To: KoShariA@yahoo.com Sent November 3, 2005 19:35pm. "Got it. Can't wait. – T."

Huh. To the point as well. I guess…

He arrived at my place at 7:00pm sharp Saturday night. He looked great in a khaki tan long-sleeved silk flannel, with a white T-shirt underneath, and jeans. The cuffs of the sleeves were folded to his forearms. The fact that he was clean cut was a plus. He had a nice casual and groomed appearance.

"Ding-Dong!" The doorbell rang. Before opening the door I gave myself one last glance-over in the mirror. I'd worked hard to create a modest but sexy look, that said I'm off to the neighborhood Wine & Beer to listen to some hot jazz. Yet my outfit suggested I looked well in anything, even if it were a nicely designed short jacket, and a pair of fitted jeans tucked into thigh-high boots, but flats no heels. The things that mattered most were well-together. The hair, nails, and makeup were flawless, always a must with me. I wanted to woo him with my body's scent. I found that most Dior scents drew men unto me. A bit of light layering with the crème and perfume gave me that naturally clean & somewhat floral, but not-too-sweet, scent. I made sure the smell wasn't loud enough to cause an allergic reaction, I kept it soft and subtle. Smelling nice was important to me on a date, with anyone. I opened the door to find another warm smile, and a single Oceania rose being handed to me.

"Hi KoShari. I hope you like Oceania roses. I thought this one was full of deep and rich color, like your eyes."

"It's lovely Tony, thank you," I said as I took the rose. "Why don't you come inside? Let me put it in water."

How did he know Oceania roses were my favorite? There was no way he could've known. He coincidentally selected a rose that happened to be my favorite rose of all time. How's that for a sign? I noticed him checking out my place as he walked through the foyer. I had put on some dinner-party music, and decided to leave it playing at a low volume. It set a proper mood for my return. The lights were low, and the miniature living room waterfall was refreshing. Needless to say he was flattered.

"Wow, KoShari. What an ambiance. Forget the Caribbean. I'd plan a vacation to come here. This is heavenly, very fitting for you."

"I call it home. I like to keep my space quiet, clean, and peaceful. It's great for breaking the frenzy of law school. I guess I prefer clarity over chaos, you know?"

"Yes, I do."

As I finished placing the rose in the flute glass vase, (pronounced vaas), I noticed him admiring the art piece on my living room wall.

"This is nice, who's the artist?"

"Oh that's an elegant piece from Italy. My Dad brought it back while on a business trip in Sicily. It didn't match any of my Mom's furniture so she gave it to me. I never learned who the artist was. There are nice colors in this piece. I like to think of it as, The Serendipity of Italy."

He looked down at his watch. "We better get going, we've got reservations at the Rainbow Lodge for 7:45pm."

After placing the rose in a water and ¼ cup Sprite mixture, we headed out the door. We arrived at the Rainbow Lodge at 7:40pm. He parked near a tree in the parking lot. He insisted that I remain in his Range Rover so he can be a gentleman and open my door. We walked up to the greeter, announced our names, and waited to be seated. The place was very nice. It looked like a hunting lodge with deer head on the walls. There were fireplaces and low lighting in many of the rooms.

"Right this way Mr. Bryant," said the maître d.

We followed him to our seats. Tony had requested a quiet corner table with a grand view of the garden outside.

"This way, madam," said the maître d, as he pulled out my chair. I was seated across from Tony.

"Are you ok with this, I mean, did you want to pull out my chair instead?" I asked with a laugh.

"It's ok. He can do it this time," he replied. We both smile.

"Your waiter will be with you shortly," said the maître d.

"Wow, what a selection." I said, while looking through the menu.

"Have you ever been here before?" He asked.

"Yes, a couple times. Once with my parents, and again with my college debate team. I've had the sautéed duck with vegetables. What do you suggest?"

"Let's hear the specials when the waiter returns."

"Ok. Um, chargrilled venison sounds good." Just as I was commenting on the menu item, our waiter walked up.

"Hello. I'm Jason and I'll be serving you this evening. May I get your drinks to start the dinner tonight?"

"Yes, I'll have a tea, and she'll have a water with lime," Tony told the waiter. Apparently he had payed attention to what I was drinking at the party the night we met.

"You're good..." I told Tony.

"Ok, I'll bring them right out," said the waiter as he walked away.

"You picked a great place for dinner tonight, Tony. I'm impressed."

"This is just the beginning, KoShari. I've got lots more in store for impressing you."

"Oh, yeah?" I asked, flattered.

"Yes, KoShari. I really like the woman I see in you. I think you would complement me well. Very well. You smell really nice. I could just eat you up." He drew closer to me. A moment later we laughed out loud together to break the electric allure that had become obvious between us.

"Here we are," said the waiter as he gently placed our drinks on the table. "Would you like to hear about our specials this evening?"

"Yes, please," said Tony while grabbing his glass to add sweetener in his tea.

"You'll be delighted to hear about our pan-seared venison over corn, tomato, and avocado relish, with buttered spinach. We also have a slow roasted goat stew with new potatoes, and a broccoli & cheddar soufflé.

"Tony, the goat stew sounds delicious, I want it."

"Ok, make it two, I'll have it as well," Tony told the waiter.

Previously, I was never comfortable allowing a man to order for me on a date. Tony was turning me on. I was receiving his energy as he sat across from me. His charm was working. Really working.

"Ha, ha!" I laughed out loud at his jokes. The more he spoke the more intrigued I became. After dinner we walked to his Range Rover, still chatting away. I was smiling so hard my cheeks were hurting. It was embarrassing to smile so much and to have him witness it. After driving for about ten minutes, we arrived at an undisclosed location in River Oaks. The only thing to distinguish the place was a white building with an unmarked blue door.

"Where are we?"

"I'm surprising you. It's called, "Marfreless." I think you'll like it. Come with me."

Of course I followed him. I would've followed him anywhere on that more beautiful than usual, evening. The door opened and it was like walking into one of the romantic greats on film. The lounge inside was nicely-sized with clear and lofty views to the second level. Downstairs was a dimly lit bar. Next to the bar sat a Baldwin, angled in the corner. A jazz pianist was playing a George Benson tune. In the loft area upstairs were couches on a large open floor plan surrounded by several private rooms. Each couch or oversized chair was accompanied by its own candlelight situated on a nearby side or center table. The furniture was of various random styles. Some contemporary, some traditional, but all with different design schemes. Around us were couples and small groups of friends socializing, fraternizing, and flirting. Many were holding drinks and having soft conversations. I admired the décor and laissez faire ambiance of the place.

"Follow me," Tony whispered, taking my hand as we walked upstairs. I was feeling high as a kite, and light as a feather. Again, I would've followed him anywhere.

There was a couple talking on the stairwell. We whisked by them. I almost knocked the poor girl over with my clumsiness. He led me to an empty love seat next to some stacked black boxes with books on top, and a closet.

"Have a seat young lady." He sat down an elbows length from me. I sat with my legs crossed.

"Let's see… I must be the fifth girl you've brought to this place," I said.

"No, you're actually the first. When a friend told me about this place a year ago, I decided I would save my visit for someone special."

"Aw, how sweet. So I'm special to you, huh?" For some reason I couldn't look away.

"Why yes, KoShari, you seem to be. Don't know yet. The verdict is still out. I feel really comfortable around you. You feel like home. You're likable." He quietly took a breath, inhaling deeply. "You smell great. I like looking at cha' cause you so damned fine." He moved closer to me as we began to cozy-up more intimately.

I could sense he was holding back a bit, the same way that I was. He felt good. I wanted to grab him to me so we could engage in a passionate kiss. The sparks were there. We were like two heated wooden sticks. A couple touches and we'd ignite into instant combustion. However, with all the electrical energy between us, we forced ourselves to cool, and to maintain a safe distance from each other. We didn't want to rush it. The attraction was obvious. There was no need to spoil it with premature interactions. Whatever was happening between us was special, and we both knew it. Conversing with him was more meaningful than any discussion I'd ever had. I could've talked with him all night long. Actually, that is what happened. Before I knew it we were in the parking lot, where we remained for two hours after the place closed. We talked about our life stories and individual short comings. That night I realized Tony could've been a missing puzzle piece in my life. God, was I digging him. A sudden urge came over me to have him as a constant, at all costs. He seemed like a glass slipper fit. After that night, something told me he was the one. Isn't it funny how "the one" always takes you by surprise? You never know when it's going to happen. What a sense of humor, God has. Humor about my life with Tony… There was absolutely nothing, in no way humorous, about what was to come.

Chapter Four

"Oh No! I'm gonna be late! Dang it!" I yelled.

I had hit my big toe on the bed rail while rushing to get dressed for a date with Tony. I'm a clumsy klutz. I don't remember ever being as suave and cool as I wanted to be. At each and every opportunity to show just how much Shari had it going on, I'd stumble and fall for no reason at all, lose a button off my shirt to pop somebody in the eye, sneeze my reading glasses off, or some insect would fly into my hair and I'd go berserk looking like a mental patient trying to swat the thing away, all the while making a bird's nest out of my hair. I guess I'm just clumsy. I can't be perfect, you know. If it weren't for my clumsiness, God would've made one perfect depiction of a woman in me, because I see myself as the epitome of the species. Although clumsy, I have other traits that nullify the klutz in me. I take a certain amount of pride in not being easily broken, like most women I know. Not much can ruffle my feathers. I'm not a very insecure woman. I attribute that to my notoriously happy childhood, and great relationship with my father. No daughter was ever the quintessential apple of a father's eye. What a princess he had raised me to become. Growing up, I knew I was loved. I remember at twelve my Dad called on his way home from work and asked me out on a date.

"Shari, how would you like to go out on a date with me?"

"Yeah, sure Dad," I replied, trying to play it cool, when inside I was bubbling over with excitement. That night he took me to dinner at my favorite Mexican restaurant, Chuy's in River Oaks. Afterwards, we went to a movie. When we got home he presented a half dozen bouquet of Oceania roses. Oceania roses became my favorite roses that night. I'll never forget what he said afterwards:

"Shari, always remember to never compromise and allow another human being to take advantage of you. Never settle for anyone who won't make you feel as special as your Mom and I think you are, and as special as you feel right now."

I looked away and cried. I had felt such love that night. He told me he loved me, and I deserved the world on a platinum platter.

"Be sure you marry someone who treats you like you are his prized possession, like a precious jewel, that he'll do anything to protect."

Those words penetrated in my brain. I vowed never to forget them, and to do just as he said. Dad had shown me in a great way how I was supposed to be treated as a wife. But, Tony... I forgot about the special night with my Dad when I fell in love with that man. Not that I thought Tony would mistreat me. Its just that once I realized how deeply I was falling in love with him, absolutely nothing else mattered, no talk from Dad, no amount of hearsay, not anything was going to stand in the way of me having that man. Even with all the love and nurturing my parents had given me, I literally had never felt this way before. When I fell for him, I fell hard. I loved him deep. I thanked God for allowing me the high amount of human pleasure that only seemed fitting for heaven while here on earth. I was a first year law student when we met, was making my debut into the legal profession, something I'd wanted since childhood. I'd fallen so in love with Tony, that if he'd asked me to drop it all and move away with him, I would have, without question. Tony had an effect on people. He never met a stranger, and you were immediately drawn to his consuming energy and confidence. He had a way of making you feel good about yourself while around him. Not to mention his insatiable sexual appetite. This man had me tingling in places I didn't know could tingle. As chance would have it, he was my first... my first love that is. My inquisitive nature wouldn't allow me to wait for sex until marriage, although my Mom and Dad taught me to wait. Yeah, like that was going to happen. My philosophy was to try each one on till I found one that fit. By one, I mean one penis, that fit. I didn't sleep around carelessly or unsafely, but I had been around the block more than most. I had already garnered quite a few really good lovers by the time I met Tony. I thought it fortunate to have such an experienced lover my first time in the falling-in-love game. He gave attention to every little detail about my body. At times he'd be tender. Others, he'd be dominant. He always sensed what the mood called for, and his timing was always on queue. His passion would slowly overcome me like hot candle wax over a smooth, steel surface. He brought something unusual out in me that I never knew was there. He equally excited my flesh, and my soul. He arrested my senses and consumed my mind. Maybe I wasn't so fortunate. After we'd make love I was like a dog in heat, wanting more and more. Never getting enough. He became a drug habit I couldn't kick. Tony had my nose wide open, as some would say. I stopped hanging with my friends. Stopped studying as much. I only wanted to be with Tony, nothing else mattered. What a fool I'd become. I didn't care. I would do anything to be with him, again and again. My Mom wrote me off as hopelessly in love and borderline obsessive. She got tired of me talking about him all the time. She'd tell me not to lose myself in him. She gave me all the good advice a mother is supposed to give, but I didn't follow that one. I did exactly what she said NOT to do, and completely lost myself in him. All I could think about was how much brighter my days were with him around, how much more meaningful my life was with him in it, how comfortable and beautiful I felt around him.

This was so good it had to be from God. And it was. It was the gift from God that drew me closer to God. I think back and realize this experience really did bring me closer to my creator, my heavenly father. What else can describe this deep and intense moment of goodness and heat? It was powerful and it had to be spiritual. I was getting high, but not with drugs known to man. I was high off his love. Boy…did I ever come to know Jehovah through my marriage to this lovely man whom I could not live without. No regrets, though. I love Tony with everything that I am.

I remember watching the Cosby show and noticing the transformation the actress, Lisa Bonet, had made. She played Denise Huxtable, the second oldest child of five children on the show. One day while watching the show, I noticed she started wearing her hair in dreads, and had changed the character, Denise's, personality. Shortly thereafter, I learned she'd recently married Lenny Kravitz while playing Denise on the show. She'd completely changed, so much so, that they had to change the script for her character. She was eventually written off of future episodes. I remember thinking she must've fallen hard for Lenny because she's altered her entire life, both personally and professionally, for him. I don't think they stayed together, but there's no denying how the relationship began. What kind of love is that? I asked that question while smirking as though it would never happen to me. Now I know you can actually fall in love in a way that nothing else matters. If you're blessed enough for it to happen the right way, you alter the plans for your life to be with them. You risk the shame and scrutiny from others. That kind of love is rare, and is the kind you fight for. It is unselfish. When you fall in love this way, you are no longer the most important person in your life anymore, your significant other is. If that means foregoing your dreams to help make theirs come to pass, so be it. You'll do whatever it takes to keep it. I remember Tony was a beer drinker when we first met. I swore I would never date a guy who drank beer, ever. Of course Tony had changed all that. I would rub that little pooch of a beer belly. I'd rub it, kiss it, lick it…whew, talk about change. I never would have done that for anyone else. How unhealthy, this love.

"KoShari, hello, are you ready sweetheart? The event begins in an hour. You know it takes thirty-five minutes to get there from here, and that's without traffic." Said Tony, while speaking through the outdoor intercom at my town home gate.

"Yes babe, I'll be right out."

Tony had invited me to an Entertainment Sports Lawyers Association (ESLA) convention where he was the acting chair of events. The convention was held in Houston that year. He was scheduled to give the welcoming speech. If you ask me, he was a bit calmer than I would've been under the circumstances. He was running late and I wasn't making it any better by taking so long to get dressed. I teased his frustrations. I liked the way I could make him change his tune with one of my "looks," and a sweet smile. Tony was crazy about me, and I knew it. I loved to watch how he melted in my presence.

"Hi, Tony."
"Let's go woman, before I miss my queue."

We zoomed off in his Range Rover headed to the venue.

Later that night…

"That was fun, Tony," I said in the car on the ride home. "You spoke well, babe. I was proud of you."

"Oh, yeah? Well, young lady, I'll have you know you were the perfect complement. I love being the envy of all my friends. Enough already, you're gonna make me believe I can walk on water."

He was driving along the 610 freeway when suddenly I gestured to him, "Hey, exit right here, on Sage. I want to show you something."

We quickly exited the 610 Loop in the Galleria area near Uptown Memorial and San Felipe. I guided him to the nearest Dubaki-Alexander Gallery. We parked, and made our way inside. It was late and after-hours, of course. I had kept a set of master keys to the galleries on my person, in case Dad ever needed anything. We walked inside the beautiful tall one story warehouse building. It was surrounded by razor sharp manicured lawns. I hit the main switch breaker inside and, viola, the showroom came to life. The crystals from the hundreds of chandeliers emanated a beautiful disco ball effect in the warehouse. There were soft hues of blue, red, pink, green, yellow, and magenta, all over the place. I felt nostalgic knowing my family was responsible for carefully hand-designing each one to the brilliance they so beautifully radiated. I flipped on the classical music Mom had programmed into the intercom system. It was just right for a lovers stroll through the gallery.

"KoShari, this place is beautiful. They all look handcrafted, and of the highest quality. Business must be wonderful for your family," said an awestruck Tony, while looking around as far as he could see.

"Yes, we're very proud of the business' success. We've put a lot into it over the years, worked very hard to establish the family name. Success has been even greater now that we've expanded into non-congested markets in other parts of the world. Last November, Dad took a trip to Geneva, Switzerland. He met with a prominent billionaire art collector who ordered one hundred and fifteen specially designed chandeliers for the ballrooms of each of his ski resorts. He gave special orders to design each one like a unique snowflake, each chandelier different in its own way. Dad let me do the research, and it was phenomenal. I never knew so many snowflakes had been recorded. I was fascinated by the different designs, all created by the hands of Almighty God himself."

"I see you were busy helping the family business along."

"Yes. My parents don't believe in giving away free money. Each dime was earned in my house. They made it fun, and exciting. I was able to select all one hundred and fifteen snowflake designs for the Switzerland project. The client really liked them. He raved at the meticulous detail in each crystal. It was a successful project. His referrals gave us a healthy presence in Switzerland. We acquired five more clients from his contacts alone."

"It must've been fun, working hard and engaging that way for the family business."

"Yes, it was pretty gratifying to participate on that level. During the project, Dad taught me about the pricing structure, and revenue breakdown of each chandelier. I sat in the design factory and watched the craftsmen chisel the crystal to design specifications. I'm very fortunate to have parents as focused as mine."

"Yes KoShari, your parents sound wonderful. I'd love to meet them someday."

"Tony, you are so going to meet them. And soon, I might add," I said, seductively.

I grabbed his hands and pulled them up to my lips. I bit each one of his Tiffany & Co. cuff links off the cuffs of his shirt. He smiled, showing off those charming dimples and strong facial features. His hands were the strongest and softest male hands I'd ever felt. Not a scratch or blemish anywhere. They were smooth, and sexy. After I bit off his cuff links, I lifted his hands to my mouth and gently kissed each one, as I thought to myself, 'is there anything I wouldn't do for this man?' My reply was no. I would do anything for him. At that point I decided I had to have him in my life. Forever.

Yes, I believe it was unhealthy to let go and allow myself to indulge so deeply. Unhealthy. There's a perfect idiom for what I was feeling. Unhealthy as it might have been I wasn't afraid to jump in, head first. It may be said that I shouldn't have allowed myself to become such a fool, but what's the use in falling in love if you don't get the most out of the experience? I never do anything halfway. It's all or nothing for this Scorpio. No matter the risk. Anything less wouldn't be worth the ride, right? So many of us women put the brakes on falling in love for fear of this, or that. We've been brainwashed into thinking we must be in control. We cheat ourselves of the deep, deep penetrating intimacy we can have by becoming control freaks. I say be brave and take the risk. If God sends it to you, become like Lisa Bonet and go all the way, no matter what happens. Yes, it's risky. There's a fifty/fifty chance things will, or won't work out. Jump in anyway. Take a chance on experiencing the bliss that comes from uninhibited love. Simply let it flow. Accept the good along with the bad. Feel the seemingly unattainable feeling of freedom that is in true love.

However, there is a price for the precious. It doesn't come for free. An unseen enemy doesn't want us to achieve such love with one another. It would bring us too close to blissful happiness. Therefore the enemy does its best to stand in the way and block the bliss. It uses people to accomplish its goals of trying to ruin marriages. It uses other women, other men, and most often our closest family members to interfere and tear us away from true love. It even uses the past, if it can. It will use past betrayals and past pain to push true love away. It reminds that we must protect our hearts from what can happen, again. We're fooled into becoming over-protective of ourselves and our significant others. No one should be forced to live in that kind of bondage. Actually, protecting our hearts is not our job. It's God's job. I asked God for His help with our marriage. For a very long time it seemed He didn't hear me. I later realized He heard me the very first time I prayed, and immediately went to work on my behalf. However, when I first realized a major problem existed in our marriage, I had to make a decision. Was I gonna fight for my enchanted love, or become a statistic and give it all up, like so many others?

Chapter Five

The Annual 'San Pedro Island Jr. Miss Beauty Contest' was well under way. While peeking thru a curtain to watch, I could see many locals assembled together, laughing, talking. They were awaiting the next contestant to grace the stage. A lovely young girl walked on stage who appeared to be around twelve or thirteen years old. It was as if the beauty of the entire island shone brightly thru her, from the inside out. Her smile immediately captivated the audience. With her beautiful curly black hair flowing around her, she floated across the stage while performing an interpretive dance routine. There was maturity about her beauty. An innocence, that could only have come from the honest energy on the island. My heart warmed as I studied her. I was pleased and at peace with my surroundings, when suddenly everything went pitch black dark. I could no longer see...

"Hey woman, no peeping toms ere'! Pay or you miss da show, madam."

It was Tony faking an island accent. He had placed his hands over my eyes and pretended to be the local law enforcement. It startled me. I turned around and we laughed together.

"Thought I was a cop, eh?" He grabbed me close. We hugged, tightly.

We were laughing when he scooped me up, placed me on his back, and carried me away from the festivities. I wrapped my arms around his neck and my legs around his waist.

"Oh, Tony. You should've seen her. She was so beautiful. I think they're having a junior pageant. The pageant stage was decorated with streamers and flowers all around. They were simple decorations, not the fancy productions they show on TV back home. Everything here is simple, almost primitive. I love this place, baby. It is unspoiled, a well-kept secret."

I sighed as a sign of total happiness and relief, and laid my head on his shoulder. My arms were still wrapped around his neck as he continued carrying me on his back across the white sandy beach.

"Yes, hunny. This place is perfect. I'm glad I got you, the perfect woman, here with me. God has blessed me to be able to call you my wife."

I kissed the back of his neck while giving in to an uncontrollable urge to do so. While enjoying my piggy back ride, I knew without a doubt that I was where I was supposed to be, and with whom I was supposed to be with. He felt so right. We fit together like two pieces of the same heart. He held me under the moonlight. I could feel the stars aligning as if everything, including our union, was in sync with the universe. Surely the heavens were celebrating that I was a part of him, and he was a part of me. Undoubtedly, our marriage had been written in the constellations since the beginning of time. What a honeymoon. I could've stayed trapped there in Belize, forever. Love was lovely that night.

We had sat on a bench ten feet from our bungalow. The bench was situated at the edge of a pier overlooking the deep dark blue waters that were glistening with silver streaks from the moonlight. There was a calm breeze blowing on my face coming fresh off the water. The moment was unforgettable.

Tony kissed me once… then kissed me again… and then exaggerated a kiss on my forehead.

"You hungry, baby?" Asked Tony.

"Not really, but I suppose I can eat something," I finally muttered with my eyes closed. My head was lying on his chest. My legs were crossed in his lap as I sat snuggled right beside him. We were locked tightly into one another. A crowbar couldn't pry us apart.

"I'm sure you're hungry, though. If you want to get something I'll go along with you to the restaurant," I told him.

"Shari…I'm hungry for you," he said, in a deep voice.

I looked up into his eyes. I knew he was serious. We fell into a kissing embrace. He pulled away after about seven seconds, but he kept his lips dangerously close to mine. I could feel his warm breath on my neck. He slowly but firmly rubbed my arms, then my back, and then my hips. With fingertips as light as a feather he cupped my breasts and nipples, which were as hard as stones. He suddenly, but gently, widened the cross of my legs, carefully placed his warm soft hands up my thighs, and into the V of my crotch. For a moment I lost my breath. He caressed that part of my body till the soles of my feet tingled. What felt like hundreds of little excitable nerves rushed from that intimate area of my body, up thru my stomach, and settled into my nipples. I felt lightheaded. I closed my eyes while my breathing steadily deepened. It was an intense moment. It took strong will power not to rip each other's clothes off right then and there on the pier. He wanted me. I wanted him. I was wet. He was hard. Before I knew it, he'd picked me up and took me back to our bungalow. We were French kissing the whole way there. At the bungalow, he slowly placed my body on a bed while still kissing. He crept on top, grabbed both my hands, and stretched our arms wide over our heads. His hips spiraled into mine. We made a combination of hot, slow, fierce, smooth, swift, and deliberate love by candlelight. It was ecstasy. It was heavenly.

Even later that night…

"Right this way, please," said the waiter.

He sat us on the stationary boat for a midnight dinner by moonlight. The boat was old and unrepaired, but seemingly sturdy and reliable. There weren't many people out having dinner that late into the night. The chill factor was trending on the high side, probably too cool for most. In fact, the wind blowing off the water made it seem somewhat icy. After making love, we had the munchies and were anxious to feed our ferocious appetites. We were happy to find something, anything, open that late.

"Damn I'm hungry," he said. He had a delighted look on his face, like he was very sexually satisfied.

"Me, too. What's on the menu?" I picked up the menu and searched for a good fish with veggies combination. It was late and I wasn't about to load up on carbs just before falling asleep.

"Hear that? Someone's having a party over there." He was referring to some loud Caribbean music off shore on the other side of the basin.

The party was at a big beautiful two story contemporary house with lots of large and long windows. From the boat, we could see the people dancing, partying, and having a great time.

"Let's crash the party."

"Tony, we don't know those people. They could have us arrested."

"So. Let's risk it."

"Ok. But if we go to jail I'll cook you burnt toast each morning for breakfast when we get home. I'll make you eat every bite, at water gunpoint."

Tony and I took a canoe across the water to the house where the party was located. We walked up to the front door, knocked, and the door flung open. No one greeted us, we walked inside. The music was blasting and there were people talking and dancing up and downstairs. Many had drinks, some didn't. The scene was picturesque, like something out of a reggae music video.

"Let's dance, babe."

He led me outside to the patio. It was the only non-crowded dance spot, people were dancing pelvis-to-pelvis. Tony and I grooved to the Caribbean music, swaying side-to-side, and locked into each other. It was as if we were moving in slow motion. We danced all night long at that party.

We caught a beautiful visual of the eastern sunrise on the canoe ride back to our side of the Island. While Tony was using the ore to advance our canoe across the basin, I cherished the uniquity of the sunrise, realizing that there will never be another like it to grace the skies, again. Its debut was hosted by a few colorful clouds. It was cold and quiet that early in the morning. The waters were pretty still, save for the waves caused by a few fishermen in their boats, whose lines were jerking from the catch.

We arrived back at the bungalow and crashed for about four hours; then woke up, and got out again. That day, we jet-skied and manned our own sailboat. Then took a helicopter to Belize City, climbed the Mayan ruins, hiked through the rainforest, and trekked around the city. We did everything imaginable that Belize City had to offer. The remainder of that evening was spent poolside at the bungalow while sipping rum runners.

The next morning, I awoke feeling rather spritely. "Tony, lets go diving. You're certified, right?" I had become certified soon after we met, and was anxious to see the blue hole and the coral reef he had raved about, before.

"Uh, duh, yes, I am."

"Ok, babe. Let's find a best place to dive."

It was around 11:30am and the temperature was very hot. Tony stopped a local passerby to get his recommendation. I saw him pointing north of us.

"The guy said the place up the beach about a mile from here is very popular, "Dive Sharks." He said they have good prices on oxygen tank rentals, and that we should dive earlier in the day, like high-noon, for the best views of the coral."

"Well, let's go," I said.

Back at the bungalow, I had changed into my swimsuit and grabbed a small wrap-around towel. Once dressed, I suddenly remembered to get my underwater camera, and heavily tinted athletic shades. We left the bungalow looking forward to diving and snorkeling.

The dive was great. I took numerous pictures of the coral and unusual fish that swam closest to it. I'd never seen many of the fish, before. I took pictures of Tony swimming with the nurse sharks and stingrays. Me,

I wasn't so brave. While in the water, the instructor had gathered my apprehension with the sea animals and had decided to tease me. He placed a stingray on my back.

"Hey!!! Whoa!! Tony!! Get it. Make him stop!!"

Clearly I was frantic. I was a scared fool, herkin and jerkin around. The instructor and the other divers, including Tony, all rolled with laughter while watching my reactions. Tony took pictures of the incident. I thought he was going to have a fit cackling at me while taking the pictures, he was laughing so hard. I guess they say it doesn't pay to be a scaredy-cat. Fear gets us nowhere. This is true. I remember a girl who'd gone on the diving excursion along with us. She was a pushy little thing. While I was jumping around in the water making a fool of myself, she was asking Tony to help secure her tank, like there was no one else around to help. I'd noticed her watching before, as Tony and I were talking and laughing on the boat ride to the diving destination, Shark Alley. She seemed captivated by us as a couple. I noticed her eying us, and decided to give her that "back off bitch" five second stare, but then, on second thought, I decided to give her something good to look at, since she was staring so damned hard. I began rubbing the back of Tony's head till his eyes rolled, and his head relaxed in my hand. I knew what he liked. She must've admired what she saw. As soon as Tony and I were separated, she moved in to vie for her own attention from him.

Sheena was cute with long and curly strawberry blonde hair. She was a fit and trim, well-tanned, sexy, woman of age; maybe in her mid-forties. Her eyes were glossy and hungry looking. Tony is a super nice guy who can never say no to a damsel in distress. Sheena had sniffed his kind a mile away. However, she wasn't the only guilty party. I think Tony gets some kinda kick out of the extra attention from other women. Of course he helped her. I looked up after swatting away the sea animals, and saw this woman smiling at my new husband. I'm not jealous, but I don't know what came over me. Suddenly I was like a mother bird watching a vulture fly around her young. The fear left, and then the animals left. I swam over to Tony and "Miss Needy," who was making the moves on my man.

"Hey baby, what's up."

"Oh, Hi. This is Sheena. She needed help with her equipment. You should be good to go now, Sheena."

"Thanks, Tony. I was afraid I wouldn't find enough muscle to help me, here. You came to my rescue. Thanks-a-million." She looked over at me.

"You got a real good one here, girlfriend. Don't take your grabs off him, not even for one second," said a desperate Sheena.

I smiled and told her, "Indeed God has blessed me with my very own gentleman. Don't be so desperate and maybe yours will come along someday." Oops. I knew I was being curt. I meant for the message to come off, catty.

Most men don't concern themselves with such feminine emotional sarcasm, like we women tend to do. Sometimes we tend to go overboard with the nastiness. I didn't seem to care that day. I had to stake my claim. I was having way too much fun on my honeymoon, and was not about to let some fleusy ruin it. I can imagine had the shoe been on the other foot, Tony would've done the same for me, or maybe not. Tony smiled and shook his head, like he thought I was acting just plain pitiful. He swam away from Sheena. Sheena looked me up and down, and smiled like she didn't care what I was saying. Like she was still going to find a way to get into his pants before we left the island. Anyhow, I swam on with my man as if I didn't notice her secret plotting. 'Tony would be too preoccupied with me, the newfound love-of-his-life, to give her a second glance,' I thought to myself. However, sure enough, he had made eye contact with her before swimming away, briefly, but it told me he noticed her enough to alert he got the message she was sending. 'Ah girl. He's a man. All men have roaming eyes regardless of how fine the china is at home. It's a man thing. Don't think anything of it. Get over it, and move on,' I thought to myself.

I remember the day we left the island. That morning, I had gone running along the beach and had spotted a 'For Sale' sign in front of a beach house. I swore that day that we would come back to the island and buy property. We'd bring our kids back in the summers. Kids? What a nice thought. I had reflected over the past year. I remembered when Tony and I decided to marry after I graduated law school and passed the bar. We did a rock, paper, scissors during a discussion about the number of kids we wanted. It was a coincidence that we both said three, two boys and one girl. I was excited to begin our new life together.

We arrived back to Houston on a Saturday morning. "Click Click," went the door to our new home. I dropped the bags in the foyer and sat down on the chaise lounge in the reading nook, that is nestled inside of our living room.

Our home was a gift from my parents. It is a lovely custom two-story Mediterranean style stucco, with a Spanish tile rooftop. The home was about eight thousand square feet, and slightly smaller than my parent's. He was flattered that my parents wanted to give us our home as a wedding gift. Especially since he knew it wasn't because he couldn't afford it. He had put away an attractive nest egg, plus some healthy investments that could make for a comfortable family lifestyle for a very long time. Tony was a great planner. He'd prepared for a financially secured family life early in his career, even before meeting me.

"Home sweet home," said Tony.

Both Tony and I were tired and jet-lagged after the trip. Tony didn't say, but I knew he could use at least three hours of personal time away from me, to collect himself, by himself, after so much time together on our honeymoon. Maybe that was my own secret wish for myself... Anyhow, we arrived home at 11:45am that morning. We planned it that way to have at least a full 24 hours to regroup before heading back to our Monday morning routines.

"Hello Mother, dear. We made it back ok. Just wanted to hear your voice since I haven't spoken to you in a while. We had a wonderful time. I swam with sharks and stingrays, can you believe it?"

I had called Mom to let her know we made it back safely. I mentioned nothing about my crazy incident with the stingrays and sharks. She didn't need to know everything. I hung up the phone and put on a Dave Matthews Band CD, before stepping into the shower. Afterwards, I was tired and had plopped down on the bed. Our bedroom window overlooked the backyard, the guest house, and the outdoor kitchen. I noticed Tony out on the veranda sifting through mail. Before I knew what had hit me, I'd fallen fast asleep.

Chapter Six

I was looking forward to practicing international business law for Dubaki-Alexander Chandeliers as its main international corporate liaison. Dad had made me an offer I couldn't refuse. The salary was fifteen percent more than the offer from Alliko & Shyman, and much more convenient than the ninety minute drive (one way, in traffic) to Bush Intercontinental Airport. The airport had offered an associate's position on their International Affairs Legal Team. Dad's offer gave me the opportunity to work close to the family, and to learn more about my inheritance. Dad was careful to train me for total control of our business in case anything had ever happened to him. He'd lost hope for a son after giving up years of begging Mom for another child. $273,000 as an annual base, my own huge corner office, and flexibility, was too sweet a deal to pass up, especially for a newbie attorney like myself. It seemed appropriate for me to take the role. After some slight negotiations, I was happy with the arrangement. Tony was set at his firm as well. He'd made junior partner a year after we met, and was well on his way up the ladder. He'd done well for himself. I was proud of him. He had raked in $380,000 for the year. We were as powerful a couple as any, and had equally ambitious business personalities. Our professional profiles would no doubt result in major contributions to our city's economy.

"Mr. Posh, we've already acquired a huge client base in Switzerland, thanks to you. We agree it is best to explore some other European markets. We're interested in opening a Paris gallery, that's been the plan all along. However, we thought it advantageous to gain a good reputation in Italy, first. The research on current Italian architecture yielded some interesting findings about some venues that can become potential clients. Ed in acquisitions suggested we follow a steady and slow path through Italian high society, and then strategize our infiltration into Paris from the line of personal contacts developed, there. I agree with his strategy. I'm not anxious. I believe timing mixed with opportunity is the best approach for generating contacts in a new market. Our time and opportunity have come, but for generating business in Italy. Not Paris, just yet. What's your take on it?" I asked, in a serious but calm demeanor.

"Yes, I can agree with you. I consider your assessments to be similar to what I had in mind. However, I believe Paris is ready for us. I understand you and the others believe the Parisian market is over-saturated right now, but my contacts have told me otherwise. It's going to be a simple task to work Italy, and I'm perfect for those. Tell your father to call me. I'd like to discuss our international projections going into next fiscal year." He let out a slight grin.

"Sure. Have a wonderful trip, in case we don't speak again before you leave." I escorted him to the door of my office. "Have Linda arrange your departure. Always lovely to see you, Mr. Posh. Enjoy the remainder of your stay here in Houston. Call me if you need anything. Goodbye."

"Farewell, my dear." He said, but was rather nonchalant. It was obvious he was already thinking of the next meeting while saying his goodbyes to me. I gathered he didn't like my decision about working Italy before Paris, but there was a communication of mutual respect between us that made the exchange more than comfortable.

Mr. Posh was the regional director of our Switzerland galleries. He was very interested in expanding his circle of friends in the Parisian chandelier business. He'd contacted me to discuss the possibility of corporate allowing him to facilitate the Paris connections. He figured along with his personal contacts, Paris would be a good move for the Switzerland galleries' public relations and marketing. Since many of his Parisian friends who were regulars at the ski resorts in Switzerland, were connected to the art, fashion, and entertainment industries there in Paris, he figured he had a direct entrance into Paris' high society. I for one saw no problem in allowing him to facilitate the venture. It certainly wouldn't hurt the company. He had been a very good curator for twenty-one years in the Swedish museums before joining the Alexander-Swede Team. He's had his feet wet in understanding how to maneuver through high society for a very long time. He would be one of the best representatives to send to both Paris, and Italy. Plus, he's loyal. I was confident he'd represent our full interests in Paris and Italy as savvy as my Dad, or I myself, would. I loved to watch Mr. Posh in action. He was stylish, and a most patient gentleman, yet ever the professional.

There were several briefings scheduled that afternoon. I decided to take lunch at The Japanese Tea Room in the Asian mall, on the southwest side of Houston. I'd had a big breakfast that day, and decided to have a light lunch to balance digestion. The atmosphere at the Tea Room suited well for my midday tasks. I'd wanted a change of scenery from the Midtown area. Southwest Houston offered no great scenery. However, I'm an avid tea drinker, and believe in having authentic foods with international roots. The Japanese Tea Room served delicious tea, and I loved the Asian atmosphere, there. The people and the environment gave the feel of actually being in Japan. I had a short meeting scheduled with Dad via teleconference in a couple hours, and needed to focus to provide him a thorough report. My Dad required excellence. He taught me the importance of being sharp and prepared. There was no slack because I was his daughter. He treated me like he did any other legal associate, stern and demanding.

After finishing up, I had a little time and decided to walk through the mall. I wanted to price the wild caught salmon at the Farmer's Market. The Asian markets were the best places to purchase Pacific ocean-seafood at reasonable prices. The Asian-American business owners traded directly with their Asian counterparts, straight out of Asia. The direct connections made it possible for Houstonians to get rare and fresh FDA approved Asian seafood directly from the Pacific and Indian Oceans. I purchased salmon, oysters, scallops, and fresh lobster, to add to my deep freezer at home. I'd placed the seafood in an empty water cooler container I kept in the back of my jeep.

"Tony???"

While getting into the jeep, I had noticed what looked like Tony's silver Range Rover at the stoplight on the corner of Synott and Bellaire. The intersection was located directly in front of the Asian mall. There was a woman I'd never seen before seated in the passenger side. They appeared to be laughing vehemently, and making energetic hand expressions during their conversation.

"Who is that?" I asked myself out loud. I squinted my eyes trying hard to get a better view. The car was too far away for me to notice the license plate numbers for additional confirmation. The light changed, and away they went. 'Oh well,' I thought to myself. 'I'll tell him I saw him later. Maybe he was headed back to work from a business lunch, or something.'

During the meeting with Dad, I received a call from Tony.

"Hey sweetheart, you busy?"

"Yes, in a meeting. I'll call you back, after."

"Wait a minute. You hungry for Indian food tonight? I got a taste for Bombay Palace. Meet me at 7:00pm at the Bombay Palace on Westheimer, behind P.F. Chang's."

"Ok. I'll call you if something comes up and I can't make it. Love you. Bye."

"Oh yeah, Shari wait… John and Cindy are coming. Do you mind?"

"Nope, not at all. Gotta go, sweetie." I hung up and got back to my meeting with Dad.

Bombay Palace was moderately crowded that night. I arrived at 6:55pm and requested seating for four. Tony and guests hadn't arrived yet. I ordered myself a water with lime, and began looking around at the people in the restaurant, eager to find a familiar face. Five minutes later Tony walks in while telling a joke, no doubt. He was laughing; both dimples were in clear view. John and Cindy were chatting along with him. They were fully engaged in a threesome conversation when they walked up to the attendant. She pointed at me, and all three headed my way. They continued laughing and talking as they walked to our table. It was like Tony to be the wittiest guy. He was never at a loss for words. His intelligent humor and fun loving spirit suckered me every time. John and Cindy were a cool couple. Tony met John at a golf tournament for the firm. They had clicked right away.

"Hello, hunny. You look lovely, as usual." He reached over and kissed me behind my left ear. He whispered, "I'm going to eat you up later, so get ready."

After his whisper, I abruptly spoke to John and Cindy in an attempt at escaping a blushing embarrassment in public. "Hi guys! It's wonderful to see you. I'm glad you could make it. How are things?" Everyone took their seats.

"Pretty great, KoShari. We're having an incredible time raising the twins. There's never a dull moment with them. John and I are juggling the work-and-play schedule. Been missing each other lately, though. I'm grateful for this time tonight. We can really use the get-a-way."

"I can imagine. Your alone time has gotta be few and far between."

"Ha, that's a great way to put it. John's literally been getting hard when I feel his penis in a passerby, and then he's forced to cool off when the kids suddenly demand our attention. Ha, ha! It's like a see saw. What an experience. I'm sure I'll have blue children should we try again. It's amazing," laughed Cindy.

"Speaking of penis, hunny, I got something special planned for us tonight. I got lil hairy Shari on my mind, hee hee," said Tony, out loud, and in front of John and Cindy.

It made me uncomfortable that he would joke like this in front of others. I felt cheapened, like I meant little to him. I couldn't understand why he was so comfortable making those types of jokes while others listened. That night I saw an unfamiliar side of Tony. He acted like a fourteen year old boy who had seen his first porno. Almost like a lustful imp, rubbing his hands together and licking his lips, while salivating at the anticipation of having sex. I mean, I'd never heard him speak that way before, in public. However, as uncomfortable as I was, I didn't respond to my discomfort. I guess it was the professional in me. My dad had taught me to never, under any circumstances, allow myself to come unglued in public. When I do, I demonstrate to others just how little character I have. Well, I didn't want that, so I went along with the conversation. I kind-of participated without adding my own jokes. I laughed it off like normal. After all, I'm the one who brought sex into the conversation with my probing questions about John and Cindy's alone time.

"So Cindy, have you guys been on any interesting vacations lately? Tony and I are always looking for the next big wonder of the world, or geographical discovery." I attempted to change the subject to something less sexual.

"Nevermind, that. I want to hear about the orgies in Germany," Tony said, and without shame.

I'd never heard him mention the word "orgies" before! Again, I played off my shock and hurriedly looked at John and Cindy like I was anticipating their response.

"Man, let me tell you," replied John. John had leaned in closer to us from across the table. "You and me got nothing on those big Nazi type Germans! From what I saw, I need some puff-up surgery. You know, the procedure that makes you more…ENDOWED," he said. He rolled into laughter.

I shook my head while smiling and looking down at the table. I was playing along with it all, when underneath, I couldn't believe my ears.

"Hey KoShari," motioned John. "Speaking of new geographical discoveries, you and Tony should come with us to this little place I know of, just outside of Amsterdam. Lots of swingers show up. It's a good time. You won't regret it. The S & M will blow your mind."

"Tony, what do you think?" I calmly asked.

"Could be fun," said Tony.

"We can talk about it later, Tony, I guess. So what are the requirements to get in?" I wanted to know as much as I could about this, even though I had no, absolutely NO, intentions of going. But I'm nosy, so I asked anyways.

"Well, let me tell you. People you and I know, I'm talking folks in our inner circles, do this. You'd be totally surprised. For one, you must be married, and open-minded. There, you'll see men with men. Women with women. It's quite an educational experience, its wild," explained John.

By now our food had arrived and we started eating. I noticed Cindy was quiet. She wasn't saying much after John and I's conversation. Probably the woman radar. She might have seen through my facade, and knew I wasn't interested in doing any of what we were discussing. Smart women can figure each other out, right away. I attempted to engage her anyhow.

"So Cindy, have you ever had a cause for concern about this place?" I was attempting to convince them that my questions were genuine.

"Not really, it's all clean. Most of the people are checked out for some time before they are granted participation. They've got a great system in place about STD's and stuff. In order to get in, you have to watch for one month before you can participate. For me, it's a great relief from my day-to-day lifestyle, particularly the parenting. Doing this helps remind me that I'm still a fun person, still hip. I like it. I was a major skeptic when John first told me about it, like you, KoShari. But it later grew on me. I decided to give it a try. I've been doing it ever since. Swinging is a stress reliever, for me."

Of course I'm listening to her while wondering, what the hell is wrong with this woman? More importantly, what was wrong with my husband? I had no idea he was into orgies, swinging, and S & M. I never thought for once my husband would invite me to dine with swingers. I guess I underestimated his life before getting married. Maybe I had seen the tendencies, but didn't care, because the love between us felt so good.

I maintained a poker face until Tony and I arrived home that night. I ended up asking him how long he'd been involved with swingers, how he got started, and who were his first participants. Course, he didn't say. I asked if he was bisexual. He replied, "no, not anymore." The more I questioned him, the more disappointed I became. I had to give him credit for being honest with me. And that, John and Cindy? Who gave them the right to stain their children by being so off kilter with each other? They were defiling their bed in a huge way.

"Shari, it's no big deal. We don't have to do it if you don't want to. I thought it was something that would prevent us from becoming stale and out-of-practice."

"So, is that what I am to you, stale and out-of-practice?"

"No baby, you're my wife, and I love you. I place your needs above everything else. It's ok. Calm down, and relax. Don't allow this to ruin such a productive day. We've got forever to be together. Forever is a long time. I was just thinking, you know, for the long term. Like I said, we don't have to do it. Here, lie down and let me rub your feet. You've worked really hard today at the office." He grabbed me from behind.

I took him at his word and lay down while kicking off my shoes to receive my massage. Tony had a knack for easing my frustrations, even when he had caused them in the first place.

"Ok Tony, I'm tired. It would be foolish not to accept this. But dear, didn't it strike you as strange how comfortable Cindy and John are with it?"

"Shari you'd be surprised what people are into these days. No, I don't think it's strange at all. Lots of people swing and do orgies. There's no surprise in that."

"I guess, baby. I for one know that you're all I want. I got too many other things going on in my life to be complicating it with that. I need clarity, so I can make sound business decisions. How can I focus on work if my mind is filled with porno images all day long? It's unreal."

I noticed the look on Tony's face. He smiled while listening as he massaged my feet. However, he didn't reply to anything I had just said. After about two minutes of sitting in silence, he hops up to get dressed for bed. I thought it odd that he didn't respond. I didn't want to argue with him, so I said nothing further about it. Besides, he's my man, and we discuss everything. If there was something I needed to know he'd tell me, or so I thought. I turned over in the bed and began snoozing less than five minutes later.

"Ms. Bryant I did the research you needed. Would you like to discuss it today?" Asked Rainey, my lead paralegal, over the loud speaker.

"Tell me this... Can I, or can I not sue for the right to sell chiseled glass in the open market place, along the streets of a Nigerian city?"

"Yes you can," But you probably won't win. There are African laws in place to protect the Nigerian enterprise from unknown and under-established American companies. The laws prevent American corporate coercion, by giving first difference to their own. Thereby, placing us on a waiting list that never moves. It's basically, strategic omission."

"Ok. Come to my office with the documents tomorrow morning at 10:30am. We will continue the discussion then. Good job."

"Yes Ms. Bryant. Have a good evening."

I turned off the speaker phone and flipped my hair back. I reclined in the easy chair, and placed my right index finger, and thumb, on my chin. I began thinking about Tony, and wondered how his meeting went. I decided to give him a call.

"Hi Peran, is Mr. Bryant back from his meeting yet?" I asked Tony's secretary.

"No ma'am. Not yet. Can I forward you to his voice mail?"

"No. I'll try his cell. Thank you."

Peran was Tony's middle-eastern secretary. She was a decent assistant, always punctual. Her accent was thick, and her work ethic was stellar. I had called his cell phone and got his voice mail.

"Leave me a message on the voice mail, Beep!"

"Honey just checking with ya, nothing special. Call me later. I was thinking about your merger meeting earlier, and wondered the outcome. Love you. Bye."

That was strange. He always took my calls, no matter what. I briefly wondered where he was. I began packing my things to head home for the evening.

"(Beep!) Shari, it's me. Sorry honey, I'll be home late tonight. We decided to celebrate the partnership with Alkstein. We did it honey, can you believe it! I'm excited. Listen, I'll call, or see you later. I love you baby! Did you ever marry a winner, Ha-Haa! See ya. (Beep!)" Tony had left a message on our home phone.

I played Tony's message twice that night. I was so proud of him. I only wished he'd called me on my cell so I could congratulate him, personally. It was ok, I knew he was out celebrating with the firm. Besides, I had lots of contracts to review for Dubaki-Alexander Chandeliers, Italiano. Yep, the team had finally done it. We broke into the Italian market. I was very happy about it. Mr. Posh had been pushing that deal for a while.

I fell asleep with a pen in my mouth, glasses falling off my face, and a stockpile of contracts on my chest. And then, I felt him. In the middle of a deep REM sleep, I felt him. I felt those soft lips gently kiss my nose, then my lips, then my forehead, then each eye, and then my chin. I slowly opened my eyes to a warm smile and gentle strokes on my arms. I moved all the papers to the nightstand, removed the pen and glasses, and grabbed Tony by the neck. He had triggered my erotic alarm.

"Whoa, whoa woman. Slow down, there. I'm dead tired. The firm rented space at the top of the Renaissance Glass Room. We danced and partied all night." He slowly pulled away from me.

"Yes, dear," I replied. I looked over at the clock, it was 4:00am.

"Dang, I guess you did have a great time. It's late. That still doesn't affect me wanting you." I proceeded to kiss him on the cheeks and temple.

"Babe, I need rest. We'll have to continue this some other time."

"Well…ok."

I had a pouty look of rejection on my face. I admit I allowed myself to feel rejected. Usually it didn't matter when he had walked in, he was all over me. Instead of forcing it, I crossed my fingers together behind my head and lay back on the headboard. Tony had walked into the bathroom. He began a conversation while in the shower.

"Hey Shari, I saw your friend Rosie tonight."

"Who?"

"Rosie, you know, who meets with you and your friends at Zha Zha's."

Zha Zha's was our favorite coffee house in law school. Several of us girls would meet there from time to time, to discuss books we've read, or whatever else outside of school and studying.

"Yeah, ok. So what was she doing there?"

"She'd just made partner at Alkstein."

"Oh, really? Good for her. I'll have to congratulate her next time I see her at Zha Zha's."

The thought had crossed my mind as to why he would be thinking of her after coming home to me. I let it pass. I wasn't always right in those instances, and was admittingly a bit possessive when it came to Tony. Then again, I remember thinking there was something preventing him from wanting to be intimate with me. Could it have been his thoughts of her? I dismissed those notions, convincing myself that they were bad leaps in logic. I rolled over and eventually fell back, lifeless.

Chapter Seven

"...Call the International Trade Association and check with them. I need up-to-the-second accurate information about Italy. Listen, do what you can, just provide the info. by this afternoon. Got it?" Said Dad, while on his office line.

"Mr. Alexander, Mr. Bryant is here to see you," said Debbie, my Dad's secretary. "Debbie show him right in," he told her over the loud speaker.

Unbeknownst to me, Dad had asked Tony to stop by his office one afternoon. Tony opted not to tell me about it right away.

"Henry, it's nice to see you. I came right over when I got your message. Is everything ok?"

"Sure Tony, have a seat."

Dad began reclining in his chair, and rolling a pair of stress balls in the shape of golf balls that Mom had purchased for him. He must've been stressing.

"Tony I'm hearing some strange things going around about you, son. I heard you've been having sex with other couples, going to orgies and such. Is this true? I mean, I didn't raise KoShari to participate in mess like that.

Don't get me wrong if that's what you're into, it's fine. You're free to do as you please. However, I happen to know my daughter wouldn't approve. Kinky sex...Who doesn't like to experience it every once in a while. I believe once you're married you've decided to give up the experimenting, you know?"

Tony rudely interrupted him. "Hold up. Let me understand why you took time out of your schedule, and mine, I might add, to ask me about my sex life. I don't think that's any of your business, Henry." Tony shrugs his shoulders and sits back in his seat sulking in frustration.

"Tony, you're wrong. It's every bit of my business where my daughter is concerned. Not to mention my family name. Brother you're taking my name to places it's never been before, and that's to snake parties. Sure I care about my daughter's well-being, but I'm also very concerned about protecting both the Alexander and Dubaki names in this town. My wife and I have worked hard for our family, too hard for some insecure Casanova to ruin it all. Son, there aren't many places you can go around here, and someone not know about you and Shari. Your wedding was announced in a full page Chronicle ad, for God's sake. At the least, you should've taken your fancy elsewhere. It's your carelessness that disappoints me. It would also crush my daughter to no end."

"Henry, I'm not ashamed of anything. KoShari knows about everything I do. Would it surprise you to know we had dinner with a potential couple the other night? I guess you really don't know your sweet Shari. Furthermore, Shari is a grown woman, now. She can fight her own battles. She doesn't need her parents butting in, and neither do I, so back off. KoShari is your daughter, but she's my wife. I'll protect her now. As affluent as your family is, I would've thought you knew that. I don't deny what I've done. I'm simply saying it ain't none of your business." Tony attempted to walk out of dad's office while hopefully getting the last word on the discussion.

"Son, don't be coy with me. KoShari believes we don't choose who we fall for. I think we can choose that person. You were not my first choice, you were hers…"

"Well that's all that matters now, isn't it. You know Henry, I'd hate to create a problem and cause KoShari to distance herself from you. I really want her to remain close with her family. Please keep this little unnecessary conversation to yourself, or I'll be forced to drive a wedge."

Dad let out a tiny laugh as he watched Tony leave his office. He was let down. He'd thought one thing about Tony and had discovered another.

You see, I'd known all along Tony had some bad boy in him. To be honest, it's one of the things that attracted me to him. Yes, I'd had an idea that he was more promiscuous than me. I overlooked it in hopes he would show me some of what he'd learned. Don't get me wrong, cheating is cheating. I don't condone it in anyway. All I'm saying is this whole predicament wasn't nearly as upsetting to me as it was to my Dad. I understand Dad doesn't want our family name tainted. But Dad had no idea that people, a lot of people, were into some freaky shit. A lot a people Dad knew were doing it. Had he known who they were, maybe he might not have come down so hard on Tony.

In a way, Tony was right. My parents were probably a bit old-fashioned when it came to sexual perversions. At the same time, my family was also right. I knew in my heart that sex with multiple partners while married wasn't moral. However, I was beginning to feel it was typical, or common behavior in our circles. After talking with my husband, how can I not believe my thinking was behind the times? He made me feel that I'd missed out on something by not trying it. I'm no dummy. I knew my friends weren't into this sort of thing, or, were they? Realistically, I would have no way of knowing what they all did behind closed doors unless we discussed it. We hadn't discussed this with each other. Tony seemed open. I couldn't hang. Tois' aren't my thing, never have been. And since I wasn't into it, I thought for sure my husband wouldn't be, either. I know my Dad was looking out for me, but the truth of the matter is… I'm a big girl. I am capable of making my own decisions. I don't need Mommy and Daddy fighting for me. I can handle this, or so I thought.

"KoShari, I spoke with your Dad, today," said Tony, that night at the kitchen island, during our naked dinner by candlelight. We liked doing this from time-to-time. It was a sneaky aphrodisiac. He'd tell me it was fun to eat dinner in the nude, and I would be dessert afterwards.

"Apparently people are talking, saying I'm hanging out too much in the orgy crowds."

"What?" I asked, puzzled.

"Your Dad was chastising me. Me… A grown ass man."

"Tony, my Dad is a serious businessman. I wouldn't have taken any discussion with him like that, lightly. Well... Do you? Do you participate in orgies?"

"No. I'd never do that without you. What do you think, I'm some insecure Casanova, (something my Dad would say), that can't keep his pants up?"

"I don't know Tony, are you?"

"Shari, I can't believe you asked me that." He stroked my right leg as he spoke.

"Are you trying to butter me up by rubbing my leg?"

"No, dear. I was showing the support that I need from you. It seems our marriage is not what they wanted it to be. They, being your parents."

"Maybe not, Tony, but it doesn't matter. The only thing that matters is that I know you. I love you. I'm on your side, unless you quit us. Have you been misleading me all this time?"

"No, Shari. I haven't. I just didn't think it was necessary to drudge up my sexual history as a prerequisite to marrying you. When we met, I knew you were the one, instantly, and unconditionally. Regardless of what you or I had done in the past. Regardless. I knew you had fallen in love with me the same way I fell for you."

"So you mean to tell me, if you learned that I was a lesbian before we met, without me having told you so, you'd be ok with it?"

"Absolutely, KoShari."

"Tony, you lie."

"No, really, I'd be fine with it. See maybe you didn't give any forethought to those nuptials before you met me. I did. I knew that when I met my wife I would accept her no matter what. If she was good enough to make me fall in love with her, she deserved my total devotion. My everything. My all.

My wife would be someone special. She had to be, to nab me. I'm a piece of work and I know this. She would have to be a strong and soft woman, who was completely comfortable in her own skin. Being comfortable in your own skin sometimes means that you've experimented with some unconventional things, good or bad, wrong or right, that life has to offer. I for one am not intimidated by an experienced woman. So you see, accepting "my wife," if in fact she's able to wear that title, is no big deal to me. She's my one and only true love. I'd do anything for her. As I'd do anything for you, baby." He relaxed back on the bar stool after his words, and stared dead into my eyes while awaiting a response.

"Tony, are you giving me this speech because you want me to be as understanding with you, as you would be with me?" I displayed a look of disappointment as I continued. "I bet you are… Honey, I believe in acceptance and unconditional love. But too much experience can be costly. What if you experimented and got AIDS, or an incurable STD? Had you experimented badly I'd deserve to know of your 'past experiences.' Sometimes there's just no good excuse for sexual promiscuity. Sometimes a slut is just a slut," I said, matter-of-factly.

"Ooh, ouch, that stung." Said, Tony.

"Anyways, why don't you show me some of that experience right now?" I said, as I walked, in my 4 inch crystal slippers, over to him and sat in his lap. He had oiled my naked body down just before dinner. I slid atop his lap with ease.

I sat spread eagle wrapping my arms around his neck while licking the edges of his left earlobe. I felt unusually close to him after all that effective communication. Realizing how deeply meaningful my husband and I's conversations were, was a major turn-on. To me, it meant there was no one on earth he connected with more than I. The thought was refreshing. It was security. It was confirmation that I'd met my soul mate. I learned I'd fallen in love with a born leader, a free spirit, a wild stallion that was not easily tamed. When I'm away from him, I crave his company. When I'm with him, I wish time would stand still. Dangerous is a word that described Tony Bryant. You just never knew when he'd suddenly become bored with you, and would dance off to the next thrill, and then come back when he wanted, like he knew you'd accept him in a heartbeat. He is irresistible; a guilty pleasure that pulled you to itself. Maybe that's just how I felt. Maybe it was just me being in love. NOT! I soon realized other women had caught on to my pot of gold and wanted a piece of my sunshine. How do you contain the uncontainable? I knew he'd break free from any restraints. I'm ashamed to say I greatly longed for him, anyways. This was my first mistake. I could see myself tripping. I came to depend on him for sex and reassurance, among other things. My first "snowfall out of the haze" wake-up experience was soon to come...

The next day I decided to stop by the local floral shop.

"Well, if it isn't my favorite daisy! How are you, young lady? I've missed you around here," said Iris, as I walked into her shop.

Iris was the owner of the neighborhood floral shop near our home. She herself wasn't a florist, but had acquired the shop at a business auction. She didn't know much about flowers and plants, but was a winner at customer service. She had hired a great staff. They pride themselves on being called the best floral arrangers in Houston. Iris was a good listener. Everyone who came to her shop loved talking with her. She was either a great listener, or the biggest gossip in town. I hadn't figured it out yet.

"Hi, Iris. Those tulips are lovely." I had approached some bright and deep yellow tulips in the corner while gazing at their beauty.

"Mom would love these."

"How is your mother, dear?"

"Mom is great. You know her, always into something."

"Yes, and that handsome husband of yours? Oh that's right… He was here last week. JoAnn sold him some beautiful wildflowers. Did you get them, were they for you?"

"Yes I did, Iris. They were gorgeous. Were they imported?"

"Naw, dear. We grew them in the greenhouse out back. They were some of our finest."

I had no idea Tony had bought wildflowers the week before. Who had he bought them for? Rosie had crossed my mind, but only because of Tony and I's discussion the other night. I quickly dismissed the thought. I try to make a habit of giving Tony the benefit of the doubt. I was beginning to think on something I didn't want to believe, so, I perished it. Maybe it was a secretary's birthday, or something. And if so, why hadn't he mentioned it to me? Anyhow, I purchased a dozen yellow tulips and headed to my jeep. Just then with tulips in hand, my phone rang. It was Mom.

"Hey, Ma."

"Hello, Lady. Did you get my message about Martha's Vineyard?"

"Yes, ma'am. You know you can count me in, I'd love to go. It's been a while since I was on The Vineyard. What you got planned?" I asked her, while placing the flowers in the back of the jeep.

"Well honey, Paula and Walter are hosting a fantastic wine tasting at their home, and then the art exhibit is immediately following at the new Folk Art Museum."

"Mom, it's going to take a minute to get back and forth from the wine tasting to the exhibit, right?" During the conversation I was driving to Amagio's for a Caesar salad and Italian bread for lunch. I'd begun slowing down to make a right turn into the restaurant parking lot.

"Shari, you got some nerve. You know I always set a strict itinerary for each and every trip. I've planned the flight arrangements so we can be where we need to be, on time. I've even planned to make a spa appointment so we can freshen up in-between. Shari, you remember Stella's? I love that spa."

"How can I forget? I hear about it at least once a month when you're reminiscing about your East Coast escapades." I was trying to be funny.

"Don't be funny, dear. You haven't quite mastered that part of your personality yet," she says with a chuckle. I let her laugh a little while smiling on my end.

"You know Courtney lives in New York. I'd love to stop and visit her. Last I spoke with her she was calling me while standing on a street corner in front of a hot dog stand, claiming she was a real New Yorker now, because she had bought a hot dog while strolling through Central Park. I miss that crazy girl."

"Shari, call me when you get home. I'm in favor of that law; you know the one about not using cell phones while driving. I want you to be safe. Bye, sweetheart."

After her sarcasm about my humorless personality I thought twice about giving her the tulips, and had decided to keep them for myself. Still love her, though. When I got home I placed them on my kitchen island in the crystal Waterford she had bought us as a wedding gift. The yellow tulips were a perfect complement to the cherry wood cabinets and black and silver appliances in the kitchen.

It had pleased me to think of going to New York with Mom and seeing old friends while there. Mom, Dad, and I had good times in the summers hanging with Daddy's friends on Martha's Vineyard. 'It will be like old times,' I thought to myself. 'Who the hell had he bought those wildflowers, for?' I wondered.

Chapter Eight

"KoShari I'm taking your jeep this morning. Yours are the first keys I see and I'm running late. Catch you later, babe!" Yelled Tony, while I was still in the shower.

"Damn." I muttered.

Tony knew I didn't like for anyone else to drive my jeep. It was a law school gift from Dad. I'd grown attached to it, and was very selfish about it. I didn't understand it, or care to explain it to anyone. I just out-right didn't want anyone else driving it. Tony and I had countless discussions about it. So many times he'd wanted to drive down to Galveston Island with the top down. I'd tell him, "you'll hop on a hawk's back and fly to Galveston before I let you take my jeep and get it full of sand." Eventually, he backed off and quit asking.

I took his Range Rover to the office that morning but had secretly sworn to pick up my jeep by midday. I decided to be real slick about it. First, I'd call his office to ensure my jeep would be in the parking garage at his building. I'd swap the vehicles, then send Tony a note to tell him what I had done. I wouldn't even do him the courtesy of leaving his Range Rover keys with building security. I figured it would teach him not to make the mistake of taking my jeep again.

"Pixie, I'm off. I'll be back within the hour," I told one of the receptionists on the way out of the office that afternoon.

I set out on a mission to recover my jeep around 1:00pm. I'd already called ahead and checked if Tony was there. His secretary said he was in a meeting until 2:30pm. I had it made. He'll never guess I came to get the jeep at this time. I hopped into the Range Rover and headed Uptown to his office. I figured with traffic and all, I'd arrive at his building around 1:15pm. I arrived pretty close to that time, 1:12pm, and pulled into the parking garage. I knew the code to gain entrance through the contract side of the gate, and proceeded thru, once the lever lifted.

Tony would often park on the ground floor. I drove there first. I looked up and down the aisles, while driving five miles per hour, ensuring I didn't pass up anything familiar to my jeep. I circled the entire ground floor and still hadn't seen it. I thought maybe Tony had taken off just before I got there. Along the way to the garage exit, I thought to try the basement floor, just in case. The strange attachment to my jeep had become daunting by now. I was about to get frustrated, when I spotted a tan ragtop in the corner about forty feet away.

"Is that my jeep??" It was very dark in the corner. If it were not for the tan ragtop I wouldn't have seen anything. The jeep itself was black and had blended in with the darkness around it. I decided to drive a little closer for a better view. As I got closer to the jeep, I realized two things: (1), that it was in-fact my jeep, and (2), there were people inside. I got even closer and began to feel a sickening pain in the pit of my stomach. It was as if the pain layered itself in my belly one degree more terrifying than the other. The windows were fogged. I could barely make out what I thought was a woman rapidly rocking back and forth while sitting on top of my man's lap, rubbing the back of his head, and digging it into her breasts. She looked like the same woman that was with him when I spotted his car at the stoplight near the Japanese Tea Room in Southwest Houston. The woman was moaning up a storm. I could see that it was good to her. It was passionate. I was envious! That's right, my first reaction wasn't anger, it was jealousy. I was jealous some other woman was all up in my space feeling how my man makes me feel, and enjoying his passion, feeling him go deep, while forcing himself inside of her. I slowly pulled up beside the jeep. That idiot. He didn't even come up for air enough to notice I was parked right beside him.

I got out of the Range Rover and walked up to the jeep. I noticed his hands were firmly gripping her ass, and pulling it with each forward movement. The sucker was still wearing his wedding ring. I didn't knock on the window. I used my spare key to open the door wide open. As soon as the door flung open I was hit in the face, "WHOOF," with the smell of their steamy sex.

"Hello, Tony. Looks like you're having a great time. Don't let me interrupt, I just, NEED MY JEEP RIGHT NOW!!" I yelled.

She and Tony finally stopped and looked at me like a deer caught in headlights. They were disappointed I'd interrupted the flow. Tony, of course, was speechless. She looked at me, then back at Tony. She chuckled while struggling to catch her breath.

"This must be the wife," she said.

"Bitch, get your ass outta my jeep!!"

I grabbed her by the hair and yanked her slutty ass to the ground. She was still buttoning her shirt. I didn't give her a chance to finish.

"Tony who is this slut?! What the hell are you doing, Tony?! What are you thinking! Is this what you borrowed my jeep for! You jerk!!"

I tried really hard to stay cool, like I had played it well, for so long. However, I was largely unsuccessful at it. While I was yelling at Tony, the woman had run off.

She was almost to the elevators when I yelled, "Heifer, I may not know you, but I will!! I'm gonna look you up, sorry ass, Bitch!!"

"Yeah, yeah. It was great honey, I don't regret it. You should try these episodes with him, yourself. Maybe then he wouldn't call me. No, I don't care that he's married. He's a really good fuck. You can't keep a man like that all to yourself. He's too good to be with one woman, hun." She said.

I took off running toward the elevator trying to catch it before it closed so I could finish pulling out the rest of her hair. Just as I arrived, the elevator doors shut on me.

"Damnit!" I shouted.

I turned to head back towards Tony, and didn't see him anywhere. He'd disappeared. Gone, just that fast. I was left standing there looking frantic, like a damned fool. The Range Rover was still running, and the jeep car door was still open. The beeping from the door ajar was getting on my nerves, big-time. I paced back and forth between the two cars while running fingers, from both hands, thru my hair.

"Ok KoShari, calm down. You'll get thru this," I told myself.

I kept trying to encourage myself, but it wasn't working. Suddenly, I fell to my knees and screamed at the top of my lungs, "AHHG!!!"

I held my face, and cried like a baby. "Why, why!!" I asked.

I'd only been married for a year. Why had this happened, and so soon? I was numb with pain. I remember wondering how I could go on after that. What could I do? What should I do? What will I do? As I sat on top of my legs there in between the two vehicles, I tried as best I could to collect myself. Tears flooded my swollen eyes. My hair and make-up, the all-white three-piece Donna Karen pant suit, were all shot. I had even ripped a huge hole in my pantyhose after yanking old girl out of my jeep. After about seven minutes of entertaining the pain I was feeling, I very quickly decided, there definitely are other men out there.

'I don't need Tony…' I thought to myself. But actually, there was no one else like him in the world, as far as I was concerned.

I couldn't believe it. Even after that fiasco, I still wanted him. I tried really hard to remind myself of the high self-esteem I had, of how much I had going for myself. It would appear that I could quickly recover after this, and just move on. There were men waiting in line to be with me.

Shoot, Malcolm told me at the wedding, "I'll give it three years. After that, look me up, KoShari. Tony is not the settling type. No woman can hook him. When he fails you, come find me. I'd give anything to be with a woman like you. Anything." Malcolm was serious.

When he spoke, I smiled and walked away not realizing I'd actually be entertaining the thought a year later. But it was too late. I'd already given so much of myself to Tony. Surely no man could enjoy me after him. I'd given mind, body, and soul to Tony Bryant. What's shocking is I wasn't ready to take it back. Even through the pain, I could still feel my heart burning for him. It was as if God himself had intervened, and had locked Tony into my core. I couldn't shake the connection, no matter how hard I tried.

That day, in the midst of it all, I made a decision. To fight the burn in my heart would be foolish. I absolutely must have what, or who I had longed for. Therefore, I had to find a way to make it work. That's right. I was strong enough (or stupid enough) to still want to be with the love of my life, after catching him red-handed, smack-dab, in the middle, of cheating on me. I wasn't ready to give him up, not yet.

I was wise enough to know there was something else, something dysfunctional happening, or was it? I was also wise enough to know that I will hurt and suffer for a time, but it wouldn't last forever. I decided to resolve in my mind that it will be hard, but Tony and I would get through this. I still wanted my husband, and I didn't care what anyone had to say about it. I had weighed the benefits versus the risks, like I had been trained to do professionally. I determined the benefit of having him in my life far outweighed the risk of losing him. This one, would become the most important benefits/risks analysis of my life.

In that moment, I thought about what Dad had taught me when I was fifteen:

"KoShari, it is never acceptable to lose your head personally, or professionally. You must always maintain a cool head, especially during tough times when things go wrong. Rest assured something will happen that will catch you off guard, and will make you feel unprepared, and afraid. Don't give in to the fear, and watch the situation work itself out. Fear will remind you that you have everything to lose. Faith will remind you the situation is temporary, and will soon pass. It will be hard, but force yourself to be in faith, and you will see the best possible solution will gravitate towards you. Force yourself not to lose your cool, and you will find things will calibrate, naturally. They always do. KoShari, dear, this takes practice. Start now, and when you're grown, having a faith mindset will come easily. No matter what happens, keep your cool."

Dad was right, but he might've underestimated certain levels of difficulty. Maybe he was only referring to sour business situations and bad corporate deals, surely his advice was not referring to interpersonal life relationships. Maybe he hadn't, underestimated. All I know, is I've come to face my difficult moment, and it is time for me to keep my cool. I had an idea… I decided the next time I saw Tony, I would do the opposite of what I wanted to do. I would grab him to me, and hug him as tightly as I could. I wanted to show him that our love is deeper than an act of adultery. I wanted him to know that I supported him no matter what, that my love for him was unconditional. Besides, I don't know who that woman was in the white Donna Karen, who showed up at Tony's office parking garage. She must've been an impostor, or some'n. Carrying on, grabbing folks by their hair, and stuff… That woman couldn't have been me. Oh, but it was me. It was the me who had been pushed to a breaking point, and had lost all control. So much for keeping my cool in that moment... That evening, I heard him walk into the house. I was out on the veranda having hot tea and watching the sunset in the west. He rushed in like a crazed hyena.

"KoShari, where are you? Shari baby, are you ok?"
'Am I ok…? What a joke,' I thought.

I slowly placed my teacup on a small, circular, end table, turned to him, and smiled warmly. Poor guy. He didn't know what to think. I gestured for him to come over and give me a hug. He looked puzzled, at first. He probably thought I was gonna strangle him to death. I didn't. He came to me, and I embraced him tenderly. He broke down.

"Shari, baby, I'm so sorry." He was sobbing his eyes out. He grabbed me tighter than he ever has. "Baby, she meant nothing to me. I don't know what I'd do if I ever lost you. I'd die. Oh God, Shari, please forgive me. PLEASE!"

"Tony. You are my husband, and I am your wife. When I said for better or for worse, I meant it. I'm not going anywhere. Ever. I love you Tony. I. Love. You," I said, while holding his face and looking into his eyes.

He held me close to him. We said nothing. Instead we sat there holding each other for minutes, that seemed like hours. He continued sobbing through the embrace. Later that evening we had dinner without a word. We went to bed holding each other the whole night long. The next morning, he mentioned how we should plan a vacation in a couple months. He said we needed to get away from it all, to sort things out. The scene of that woman on top of Tony and their heavy breathing in my jeep, went racing through my mind as he spoke…

"Hi Mom. Call me back. I need to talk to you. I'm…"

Mom picked up the phone while I was in mid-sentence. I'd called her on my way into work that next morning.

"KoShari, I'm here. How are you? Is everything ok?"

"Mom, yesterday I caught Tony in my jeep with another woman."

"What!?"

"Yes, Ma. Tony was having sex in my jeep with someone else. Yesterday he took my jeep into work. During lunch, I went to his building's parking garage to swap cars, and found him in the jeep with another woman, screwing her brains out. He and I talked about it. I decided to forgive him. Ma, I'm confused. I'm hurting. What should I do?"

"Huh. I see it's time for a family jewel with me and your grandma. KoShari clear your schedule the next couple of days. We're going fishing."

"Fishing? Ma, you know I don't fish."

"KoShari, just do it. Call me later after you've settled in at the office. Everything is gonna be fine. I love you, dear. Bye."

We hung up. I sensed in her voice that she had a peace about it. Knowing that she was ok, helped me to believe, that somehow, I would get through it. Some fucking how.

Chapter Nine

"HAPPY NEW YEAR!!" The crowd shouted in an enormous roar, at the Sugar Creek Country Club in Sugar Land. The party that year was sponsored by the Fort Bend Rotary Club.

"Happy New Year, baby!" I said, as I lovingly leaned into Tony's chest.

I was slipping in my four inch diamond stilettos, and had used his chest as a crutch. I fell awkwardly, and gracefully into his body. He smiled, and gently caught me, as though catching his very own delicate dove. Tony's chest had always been my soft place to fall. That man has an authoritative gentleness about him that cradles me to a harmonious equilibrium. His touch is poetic. 'Let's see,' I thought to myself in that moment. 'I love him more this year than I did last year. I absolutely cannot see my life without him.'

"Shari, lets go talk to Ahmed and his wife. I haven't seen much of him this year."

"Ok, babe. I'll freshen up and meet you there afterwards."

The whole night was vibrant and exciting. People were dancing, laughing, joking, gambling at casino tables, magicians doing magic tricks, karaoke… all at the same time. I stood outside the ladies room, and had spotted Tony across the dimly lit room, making his way through the crowd to Ahmed and his wife. I looked away, and then looked back before taking off to walk near them. Just then, I saw Tony slowly walk past a gorgeous Asian woman, and give her a card, placing it in the palm of her hand. I thought my mind might've been deceiving me. Maybe I was mistaken. Even then, I tried not to think the worst, first. Who wants a weak and insecure woman? I'm positive Tony (or any man for that matter) didn't. So I played it cool, and decided to meet with Tony, Ahmed, and his wife anyhow. I walked up behind Tony, touching his back and moving my hand up and down his right shoulder blade, standing alongside him, while facing Ahmed and his wife. Like John, Ahmed was an attorney at Tony's firm. They started at the firm as first year associates together. I smiled at them all, first looking at Tony, and then at Ahmed and Leena.

"Hello, guys. This is fun isn't it? Hi, Leena. It's nice to see you."

"Thank you, KoShari. Yes it is, and its always nice to see you, too."

Tony kissed me on the cheek, and whispered in my ear, "I've hired a private horse and carriage to meet us tonight at 1:45am, in front of the Williams Towers near the Galleria."

I looked up at him and rubbed my nose against his, like two Eskimos. Leena and Ahmed, chuckled.

"We'll leave you two alone. We've got more mingling to do." Said, Leena.

"Ok. Leena, please call me. We must do a 3:00 o'clock tea one afternoon." Tony nibbled my ear as I spoke.

"You got it, KoShari. Take care."

She and Ahmed walked away. I was basking in his kisses. He had me shying away like a school girl. Suddenly I noticed from far across the room the Asian woman in white, whom Tony had sneakily handed a business card. She was studying our behavior, and our happiness. She looked for a moment, looked down, and then looked away, as if to hide her stalking. She walked out the front door while making a formal exit.

I wondered to myself if she was trying to signal Tony by gracefully walking outside. Could Tony have been entertaining yet another woman for an affair? Thoughts of last year's pain crept into my belly. What a terrible feeling. It felt like a bad acid reflux. The thought of him being with another woman made me want to vomit. But I chose to let go of the thoughts. I decided not to ruin the night with probing questions and non-trusting notions. Besides, we were enjoying ourselves, and having a wonderful time.

One thing I think is important to mention, Tony and I had not had a big argument since getting married. I remember Mom telling me as a young girl how to properly carry-on with a husband. She would say to never, ever, sweat the small stuff. No man likes a nagging wife.

I remember watching her and Dad closely at public functions. I wanted to learn how she carried herself in the presence of other flirtatious women around my Dad. I also wanted to watch her show and prove what she had been teaching me all along. You see, Henry Alexander is an attractive and distinguished man, with stature. He turned quite a few heads, and still does. Mom would amaze me each time. She has a healthy build, and was often the thickest woman around her friends, and Daddy's female associates. Others were slim, and thin. She was the plump sister of the bunch. It didn't matter. She had an unwavering confidence about herself, that made her the draw of the party. She was witty, and full of smiles, always the funniest woman in the place. Everyone always adored her, including my Dad. His eyes sparkled when he watched her work a room. He would be checking her out. She'd make quite an impression on him. She did something magical. After coming home from those functions, they'd lock the door to their bedroom and place a, "DO NOT DISTURB, MAN AND WOMAN AT WORK," sign on the door. Each time, like clockwork. I loved watching the way they loved each other.

Anyhow, I listened carefully to her advice, and was now putting the wisdom into practice in my own marriage. I weighed the thoughts of Tony reverting back to old form against all the reasons that I loved him. The good outweighed the bad. I used the idea to propel my decision not to ask about the Asian woman. Suddenly, I drew confidence from the mature decision. I thought I was being the bigger person, by not causing a problem when I could have. I squared my shoulders and got cocky, started walking around like I know my man wouldn't cheat with this one, like he cheated with the last one. Listen at that, 'like he cheated with the last one,' some cocky bitch, am I…

And then I noticed something funny about Tony at the party that night. He had caught my boost in confidence and acted like he could care less. Although he was fully aware that I'd noticed him and the Asian woman make contact, he paid no attention to my tactics. It was as if he expected me to be the confident woman on his arm, and it mattered not, what he'd done. Even though he showed no reaction to my charade of acting as though I didn't mind that he was flirting right in front of me, I knew that he was proud of the woman on his arm. He often appeared to be a happy husband. I knew I had something to do with that. Any man married to a woman that doesn't nag him is a happy, happy man. Never really had time to nag him, I guess. I'm too busy. Not to mention all my needs are met. Regardless of what he does. His problems are his own, and not mine. Yet, our marriage would survive our individual hang-ups. Or, so I thought.

I wasn't expecting a big reaction out of him after he noticed that I'd caught him flirting. But maybe I expected him to respond to me how my Dad responded to Mom, when Dad caught on that she knew another woman had captured his attention. Dad would immediately address the situation. I guess Dad didn't want any confusion back home. It didn't happen that way with Tony. Tony acted as though he did absolutely nothing wrong by handing the woman his business card. He treated the incident as innocent as he wanted me to believe that it was. He continued being the life of the party. But I didn't leave his side anymore that evening, just in case...

I had grown tired and asked Tony to cancel the carriage ride. He did, and we drove home early that morning around 1:15am.

"Oh yeah, Shari. I forgot to get a fax off yesterday to the Adams Group regarding an answer to a legal question they had," said Tony, on the ride home.

"Sure, baby. Just pull it up on the network and fax it from home," I suggested, attempting to get him to stay home that night.

"Yeah, but there are some documents I need that aren't on my home PC, or laptop. I left them at the office. Tell you, what... I'll drop you off, then shoot by the office. It'll only take a minute." We had made it home, and were just pulling into the drive.

"Tony it's 1:00 o'clock in the morning. Come on, now. You should come inside."

I couldn't help but wonder why he wanted to go. Maybe he's going to meet the Asian woman he gave his card to at the party. 'Is he going to hook up with her?' I thought to myself.

"Tony I think you're being a bit anal about this. It's New Year's Day, for God's sake. Can't it wait till Monday?"

It took all my strength not to ask him about the Asian woman, although I had every right to. I did everything possible to keep the peace and to not cause a problem, even though he was the problem. I wasn't prepared to deal with the stress that night. I was exhausted from the party. It was easier to just, trust him, and to let him go to the office.

'Let him throw me away. I'll have another man in a month,' I thought to myself. I further justified his leaving by thinking I could always reach him on his cell if I needed to contact him.

He dropped me off. I kissed him, smiled, said goodbye, and walked into the house. On the way to the house I stopped and waved him down to say one last thing.

"Hey. Your Caribbean slave girl will be waiting for you when you return."

It was my last ditch effort at keeping his mind on me, when he was with the other woman. He smiled, briefly, then drove away. His smile waned not two seconds after leaving the drive. I knew in my bones he was going to meet with another woman, but I couldn't bring myself to fight about it. Somehow, I felt my complaining would tear away at my image of having it all-together emotionally, the image that I had portrayed for so long. All during this marriage I'd presented this strong persona to him, like nothing ever shook me; excluding my immediate reaction to the jeep incident. I was too proud to give him an advantage by thinking he'd ruffled my feathers. He wasn't going to witness me losing my cool over anymore of his actions. After all, he wasn't in control, I was. I was determined to show him that if he wanted another woman after all that we had between the two of us, it was ok with me. I'm not some frail weakling that cannot get another man. Had I reacted negatively, like so many women do, by yelling and screaming, he would've known that he had the upper hand. I wasn't going out like that. If in fact I was going out, he was gonna realize that leaving me was his loss. I was sure of it. How dare he challenge me by going to see another woman in my face, inherently knowing I knew full well what was going on. Sorry. He wasn't getting a reaction out of me on this one.

My feet were killing me that night. I dropped my purse on the kitchen island and went into the master bath of our bedroom suite. I ran some bathwater, and took a hot bath in fresh lavender and green tea leaves with glycerin oil; got out, dried off, and hit the bed. I had scheduled an early morning workout for 6:00am the next day. I wanted to start the New Year off right by continuing to work at staying in shape. My trainer, Markus, liked to meet early. I wasn't looking forward to it but I didn't mind. I had planned to stretch, nap, and rest for the remainder of the day after the workout.

"Buzz!" My alarm clock sounded off like a loud fog horn. I popped up, hopped into my workout gear, and headed to Rice Stadium to meet with Markus. I tried as hard as I could to block out the idea that I had noticed Tony wasn't home before leaving.

I arrived at Rice Stadium at 6:00am sharp worn out from the night before. I'd learned the fortitude of functioning on minimal sleep while in law school. The lack of rest didn't bother me. After a quick cup of coffee, I was raring and ready to go.

"Hey, girl. On time as usual, I see. I like that. A dedicated person who likes pain," joked Markus.

Markus was a terribly handsome personal trainer. Terribly. GOD, he was fine! He was an olive-skin colored, Louisiana Creole brother with wavy and curly black hair. He had big voluptuous eyes that beckoned you, and a perfect naturally tanned complexion. His body was a chiseled work of art, extremely sexy. I'd always said if I wasn't married I'd jump right on that. However, he wore a cross on his neck that acted as a crucifix to my wicked thoughts, like something vampire slayers would hold up to keep vampires at bay. He was a Godly man. Not interested in anything lustful with anyone, but his wife. By the way, he was still single, and waiting to find "the wife" as he often put it. The fact that he was willing to wait patiently until he had found THE ONE, made him all the more delectable to me, just scrumptious. Anyhow, I knew he was hands off. We did a good job of keeping our relationship professional, even though an attraction existed between us. He was serious about his training. I found out, the humiliating way, that he was not interested in mixing business with pleasure, especially with a married woman, and at least not with me.

"Let's get started. I got another session in a couple hours across town."

I ran up and down the bleachers of the stadium for ten minutes. Afterwards, I ran a timed ten minute mile around the track. And then I sprinted in two-minute increments, off and on, for fifteen minutes. It seemed more like forty-five. By the end of the workout I was exhausted, listless, and immovable.

"Markus," I called, while completely out of breath.

"You work the hell outta me, you know that, don't you?"

"Yeah, baby. That's my job. I realize you're a runner, but you need to do these types of hard physical challenges more often than you do, at least four to six times a month. I'll see you next time. Keep it real," he said, as he walked away, headed to his car.

As soon as he was out-of-sight, I collapsed in the middle of the football field. I didn't think about Tony until the ride home after the workout. I wondered what time he made it in. I decided to call him from the car.

"Hi. You've reached Tony Bryant. Leave a message, please." I had called Tony and got his voice mail after the first ring.

"Honey-y. You can't be gone already. Call me. I don't like going so long without talking to you. Call me right back," I said on his voice mail.

'No he didn't, just, not answer his phone,' I thought. My mind went racing with thoughts of him being with someone else.

"R-ring," went my cell phone.

"KoShari Bryant."

"Shari, where are you?" Asked, Tony.

"I'm headed home. Good Morning, you. I didn't see you when I awoke this morning. You got out early, I assume."

"Hey, baby. What's up?" He said. He had ignored my comment.

"Oh, I just wanted to hear your voice. You know, to start the day off right."

"Yeah. I guess I'm pretty focused right now. I got a big day ahead. Don't be disappointed if I don't see you until tonight."

I had thought of asking him what time he returned home that morning. He sounded as though he was about to get busy with the day. I decided it could wait til later.

"Ok, Mr. I'll check you later. I love you."

Dang. I didn't even ask him where he was headed. 'Anyhow, let me prepare for my day,' I thought to myself. Thoughts of where he might have been, and who he was with the night before, flooded my mind. It was very hard to fight off the thoughts. I chose to remain in a state of denial. The obvious was too difficult to digest. I wasn't ready to go there, this year. It was early in the New Year, and I wanted to start the year off right, even if I was living a lie. There was something comforting about turning a blind eye to Tony's indiscretions. I had already surveyed the outcome of a big argument on what I knew in my heart to be true about him. I'd resolved that I didn't want to be without him. I just didn't. I loved him too much. That day, I chose not to delve further.

Mom and I had gone shopping together later that day. She was always my favorite shopping partner.

"Mom, how does this look?" I asked, as I tried on the diamond laced necklace at Tiffany's, in the Galleria.

"Shari, that's beautiful. What about this brooch? Look at the combination of gold and platinum. I think it's a lovely butterfly. I can see this with a nice contouring two-piece suit, or even a scarf."

"Mom, we have different taste. I would never wear that brooch with a scarf." I gave her a mildly disgusted reaction.

"Shari, speaking of different taste, I see we also have different taste in men. I hear your Tony has been exploring with Asian women."

"Mom, don't do that. Don't go accusing and assuming based on what you've heard. I find it hard to believe anything from your circle of friends. Most of those women live for drama."

"Shari, your Dad saw him with his own eyes the other night at this private little Japanese place. He was sitting with his legs crossed on the floor next to this woman. They were very intimate, while drinking sake."

"Mom, Tony has lots of business meetings. He may have been treating a client."

"No, dear. Your parents aren't dummies. We know a flirt when we see it. According to your father, she and Tony were star gazing into each other's eyes. Shari, you should discuss this with Tony. We didn't raise you to be humiliated by a husband. Not to mention the Alexander name...Our business was primarily built on reputation, and word-of-mouth, about our products and services. Our good name is not to be tainted with the incompetence of a philandering spouse in our family. I need you and Tony to get it together."

"Ok Ma, since you put it that way, I'll be sure and ask him about his dealings," I said, sarcastically.

"Shari, let's discuss this. You're a beautiful woman both inside and out. I'm very proud of who you've become. I trust your judgment. I won't say that you've picked a loser."

"Mom, really. A loser?"

"I didn't say he was one, even though you've already caught his ass in YOUR vehicle having sex with another woman in a public place. I know we've discussed this already, but, well you know, it looks bad for business.

It's just that he's so damned careless with it. Just work it out, ok?"

"Sure, Mom. I understand you're concerned. I'll pull him aside, today."

"Yeah, well, you better. The nerve of that fool! I'll jack him up! Who the hell does he think he is, anyways? He ain't that handsome, funny looking asshole…" she shrieked.

Mom went on and on about Tony. I could tell she was upset at the thought of someone cheating on her daughter, after all that she had sown into me becoming the perfect young woman. She couldn't bear the thought of someone tarnishing that image. However, it's funny to me how she completely forgot about her own challenges in her own marriage with Dad. I remember times she'd lock herself in her room, and wouldn't come out. She would stay in bed for hours. My guess is she was sick from heartache after hearing about Daddy's "dealings" with some other woman. I guess that's part of being a parent. You love your children so much that at times you try and shield them from all pain. Even though you know a certain amount of pain is inevitable in their lives. She doesn't remember right now, but I remember what she taught me about going through tough times in relationships.

She'd say, "Shari, when the heartache happens, don't run from it.

Face it.
Embrace it.
You will cry. It will hurt.
But don't run from it.

There is always wisdom to be gained from the experience. There are other ways, but pain can sometimes be a way God is trying to teach us something. If not about ourselves, then about the other person, like how to help them through. Let maturation (or patience) have its perfect work. You'll want to scream and throw things. You may even want to commit murder, at times. Exercise self-control, and you'll find the good in it all."

She was teaching me that it was never ok to allow circumstances to control my life. I had listened and decided to follow her advice exactly as she'd instructed. Yes, it bothered me that my own parents had to witness my husband being bad. It bothered me, big time. I was angry. First off, I trust my parents more than anyone else. They have never steered me wrong. They've always been in my corner through everything, even when I was at fault. It shamed me to say the least, because not even a friend came to me… but my own parents!? What could Tony have been thinking; taking other women around town where we all frequent. I mean is he crazy, or what? I thought I better calm down so I could speak peaceably to him without losing it. Mom had to leave Tiffany's. She was meeting a friend at another friend's little antique shop in West University. She collected antique furniture and knick knacks as a hobby, and would often place items on consignment with her buddies. They never resisted her charm, and always gave her a good deal.

It was Saturday afternoon and I still had shopping to do. I had seen a fur shawl in W Magazine and the caption on the picture said I could find it at Neiman's. It was an absolute must have. It was a creme brown wrap around, with speckles of different colors throughout the fur.

"R-ring," my cell went off.

"Shari, come home quickly!" It was Tony. He sounded frantic.

"What is it, Tony? Are you ok?"

"Yes, baby. I need you to get here fast. Come home. No time to talk. I'll see you when you get here."

"Ok, I'm on my way."

I backed out of the Neiman's parking lot and drove home as quickly as I could. My house was ten minutes away from the Galleria, with traffic lights included. I arrived home in 9 minutes flat. I swerved into the drive and noticed Tony's silver Range Rover in the four-way. I ran past his car, and up through the garage entrance to the house. I zoomed past the washroom and the butler's pantry into the kitchen, screaming for Tony.

"Tony! Babe, where are you?"

I dropped my keys on the kitchen countertop and continued running through the house while looking for my husband. Finally, I ran into our bedroom, through the master bath, and past the Roman shower.

He had suddenly jumped out of his closet stark naked. He quickly grabbed me from behind.

"Tony! Ooh, you startled me."

"Yes, exactly what I meant to do." He grabbed me, and yanked my body to his.

"It was an emergency, baby. I just had to have you."

"But, Tony, I rushed home thinking..."

"Shh. Don't talk," he interrupted, placing his hand over my mouth.

"But, baby..."

"Ahp...I said don't talk. Am I gonna have to gag you, woman? You know I'll do it."

He took his hand off my mouth. He quickly, but gently, placed his left index finger on my tongue. I sucked it. While staring up at him, I sucked harder, in resistance to him slowly releasing his finger from my mouth. He then began to undress me, until I was standing there naked, and trembling. He suddenly fell to his knees. He quickly turned me 180 degrees, forcing my legs wider apart. As I was standing there, he slid in between my legs, head-first, while looking up at me. As I looked down I could see his face, positioned perfectly underneath my crotch. Our eyes locked. My auto-response was to squat down just enough to meet his mouth. He began licking and suckling, from the top of my vagina to the back, and beyond, all while keeping the eye-contact as long as he could. Oh God, the ecstasy...

"Umm, Shari, you never tasted so good."

Whoa, the rest is unmentionable. We made love all afternoon, and night long. After making love that night, we lay in the bed, he at the head, and me at the foot, while facing each other in a 69. He smiled at me like only he can. He caressed my feet, again, like only he can. He placed my big toe into his mouth, and licked, then gently sucked it with his tongue. I was in heaven. I'd completely forgotten about the talk with Mom earlier that day. I laid there listening to the fire crackle in the fireplace.

"You have an incredible sex drive, do you know that?" I asked him.

"Why, yes. I'm aware that my sex is driven, for you."

We both lay there with a look of utter and complete satisfaction on our faces. In that moment, I remembered what Mom had reported earlier about Tony. What a robber, my Mom was. With that thought, I got out of the bed, and walked into the bathroom to draw a bath in my Jacuzzi tub.

"Where you running off to, woman?"

"I gotta take a bath. You're all over me, right now." I told him.

When the water was ready, I slowly placed my left foot inside, and then the right. I had tucked away some dried rose petals, that had been soaked in Shea butter oil and gingered-lime, in a glass jar on the bathroom shelf. I put them, along with some unscented bath fizz, into the tub. The combination of things mixed together gave the perfect scent of sweet and fresh clean I always loved. I sunk deep down into the tub, until the top of my head had hit the bath pillow. I deeply inhaled the beautiful mixture of scents. I laid there thinking how I was gonna approach Tony with a discussion about the Asian woman. I flat-out dreaded confronting him about it. I didn't want to make waves, especially after having such a good time. But the thoughts kept raging. I had to address it. I couldn't hear a sound coming from the bedroom. Apparently he was asleep from the exhaustion of putting in such incredible work on my body.

"Tony," I said softly from the bathroom tub.

"Ma mentioned that Dad saw you having lunch the other day with an Asian woman."

"Yeah. I was hosting one of our sister company employees from Japan. Mikima. She represents a couple Japanese baseball players, and needed some specific advice regarding fee negotiations on the player's behalf. The firm pegged me for the job, since no one else is as savvy in Japanese sports law as I am."

"Dad also said you two seemed too close for comfort."

"Sweetheart, what the...? I wasn't very close to her. She and I joke around sometimes about how much more intimate Americans are with each other in public settings, than the Japanese. But nothing inappropriate happened. Why? Did your Dad say anything else?"

"Naw, Tony. He just mentioned that you looked like a very happy, couple," I said, while exaggerating.

"No, Shari, we weren't personal at all. That would've been the ultimate unprofessional behavior."

I could sense the frustration in his voice. He was probably upset that he now had to prove himself to me, against my parent's better judgment. I'm certain he never wanted to make me choose between his word, and my parent's. Surely he knew he would lose. He was aware of how close my parents and I, were. That's why I was shocked when I heard his next words.

"Shari, are you accusing me of something I said I didn't do? I mean, I thought I married you, and not your parents."

At this point I was really glad I wasn't in front of his face looking at him. I didn't want him to see my facial expressions, and to appear weak in battle. I looked frightened. Had I been playing poker, I would've lost my hand. Anger and humiliation were about my countenance.

"Tony, I haven't accused you of anything. I'm simply asking you about something my parents said. Let's not turn this into a thing. I knew you were a flirt when I met you. I believe your interaction with Mikima was harmless. My parents are not accustomed to you the way that I am. Honey, really, I'm ok."

I had stressed the word "parents" as if to insinuate the shame I was feeling behind them witnessing their son-in-law's infidelity. Yes. I'd already decided to believe my parents. They had no reason to lie to me. There was nothing deceptive going on with them. I was sure my parents liked Tony and they'd originally trusted my pick in a husband. I believed THEM.

However, I was dealing with the fact that I didn't want to slip into the preemptive pain of having to face the truth about the love of my life. The truth that my knight in shining armor had cheated on me, with yet another woman. I didn't want to swallow that giant horse pill, again. I somehow had to soften the blow to myself. I needed to protect myself from the hurt of accepting the truth. And then, there was the whole woman-to-woman competition thing. I'm a fighter, always have been, a silent one, at that; someone who fights with everything other than violence to win. I decided that as soon as I could make time, I would strategize a way to let Mikima know that she couldn't have him. I began to meditate on a combat. Tony was still saying he didn't do anything wrong. He doesn't get it. Little did he know, I'd already accepted what he did, had processed the plan of action to execute the remedy, and was already on the road to forgiveness, all because I'd do anything for him, and that included forgiving his weaknesses. Tony is the love of my life. I'll not give this up without a fight, and that's that. Besides, who else on earth can make me feel uninhibited, like Tony? He'd enlightened me sexually in ways that I didn't know could be done. And yes, it too was well worth fighting for. Damnit.

"Shari," Tony calls while walking into the bathroom. "Woman, I ain't crazy. You think I'm trying to mess up my good thing here at home? You might be right about your parents. Even though I'm not the flirt you suggest, I'll admit I do possess a charisma that attracts women. However, I know when to draw the line. Now, all this charm belongs to you, dear, and only you. Maybe they thought I was cozy with Mikima at the restaurant. When really that was me working it like I do," he said, while giving me a cocky smile.

I looked up at this fool, and of course had humored him. I gave him my usual sweet, "I'll go along with this shit" smile, to make him think he was actually saying something I believed. Besides, we'd only been married for two years. We were still honeymooning, and I wasn't ready to end it.

I had it all under control, I thought. I weighed him out, and just like last time, his good outweighed this situation. So I squashed it, let it go, let it slide, and decided to move on. I was getting good at this sort of thing. I had unconsciously taught myself to turn away from the pain. However, the thought of this incident lingered in my mind. I wondered if I'd ever forget it. Why did I have to have this conversation right after such a wonderful time of making love? Couldn't I have waited to ask?

About a month later, and on the way to the spa for my bi-weekly spa treatment, I became nauseous. I felt lightheaded and dizzy. I thought maybe I'd caught a whiff of something coming from the exhaust in the jeep. So much so, that I wasn't sure I could continue driving. I immediately pulled over at an industrial business center, just to gather my wits and to make sure I'd be ok to continue driving. Instead, it rapidly worsened. I stepped out of the jeep, bent over, and vomited alongside the road. Fortunately, I had pulled up next to a curb. I was glad that I wasn't forced to throw-up in the middle of the street. I sat back in the jeep, and wiped my mouth with a cloth. Then, just as I had finished cleaning up, it happened again. I opened the door and let the curb have it. 'I had a light breakfast, and lunch,' I thought to myself. I didn't know what was happening to me. When I finally collected myself, I slammed the door shut, got back on the road, and decided to drive home. 'What was up?' I thought. As soon as I arrived in the driveway of my home, I jumped out the jeep and ran to the nearest bathroom inside the house. I threw-up in the toilet, and this time, it was more violent than the others. I could feel a headache coming on. I washed my face with cool water. I staggered back out to the jeep, and grabbed my things to bring inside. I dropped my briefcase in the home office, (I'd planned to get some work done while at the spa), and placed my purse on the coffee table in the great room. I thought to call Tony's name out loud, but remembered he was working late that evening. I walked to my bedroom suite and fell on the bed. I couldn't move. It felt like I had malaria. My stomach was erupting. Before I knew it, I'd fallen fast asleep at 6:20pm. I heard the phone ring an hour later.

"Hello," I whispered.

"Hey, babe. What you cooking for dinner tonight? I'm starved." Tony had called while driving home.

"Honey, you'll have to pick up dinner. I suddenly seem to be under the weather."

"Ok. Can I get you anything?"

"No. I'm not hungry. I'll see you when you get here," I said, then hung up.

Tony came in about forty-five minutes after that. I heard him shuffling bags in the kitchen. He came into the bedroom and sat on the bed, beside me.

"Shari," he said gently. He touched my forehead checking for a fever. "Are you ok? Your head feels fine. Is there any pain?"

"Tony, my stomach is in knots. I feel like I ate bad sushi or something."

"What have you eaten today?"

"I had a banana and oat bran for breakfast, and an avocado salad for lunch."

"You think the avocado might have been bad?"

"No. It tasted fresh to me. I don't know..." At that moment I gagged, got out of bed, and ran to the bathroom. This time all that came up was yellow stomach acid.

"Oh, honey. I feel terrible!" I yelled from the bathroom.

"You want to go to the doctor?" He was very concerned.

"No, not yet. Let's just wait and see if it passes. I might feel better tomorrow."

"Ok. If you continue the violent vomiting I'm driving you to West Houston Medical, myself."

I gagged again while he was talking. "On second thought, call Dr. Aiyalah."

Tony called the doctor and learned she had some time to see us that evening. We drove to the doctor's office, with Tony speeding like a race car driver thru all the lights and stop signs. I was too sick to yell at him for it. He drove so fast that, what was normally a 25 minute drive thru traffic and lights, had only taken 13 minutes. We arrived, left the car with the valet, and hurriedly dashed into the doctor's office. Startled, Dr. Aiyalah gestured for us to sit in one of her patient rooms until she could see us. After about five minutes, she came in, took my temperature and blood pressure, drew some blood, and asked me to provide a urine sample; then left to care for her other patients. Twelve minutes later she returned.

"KoShari, everything checks out. Your blood is good. There is no sign of any infection in your blood. All organs are fine. You're the perfect picture of health," said Dr. Aiyalah.

"Doctor, this can't be. I feel like crap."

Tony stood there next to me while I was in the bed, just as confused as I was.

"Yeah, well, most pregnant women do."

"PREGNANT!! What!?" I asked, shockingly.

"Yes, KoShari. You and Tony are going to have a baby."

"Oh my God," I gasped.

I looked at Tony with both hands on my mouth. He looked back, just as stunned. We hadn't planned for a baby at that time. Kids weren't on our agenda for at least another three years, at least. I was shocked. I immediately thought back to my birth control methods. I'd been taking the pill, which seemed to work well, up till then. I remembered forgetting to take them, seven consecutive days a few months ago, and also for five straight days, 1 month ago. Bingo. That must've been when it happened.

"Tony," I said, as we were driving home from the hospital.

"You remember that home emergency we had a little over a month ago? Well, I guess this is our lil' 911. I knew I was late for my cycle. But I've been as long as a month late before, and wasn't pregnant. I didn't think anything of it," I told him.

Tony had a blank stare on his face. It scared me. He said nothing, while sitting there frozen, like a statue.

"Tony, you alright?" I was concerned about his lack of expression.

"Yeah, babe. This is quite a surprise. I wouldn't have expected this. I thought you were on the pill?"

"I am, Tony. Believe me, sweetheart. I was not trying to get pregnant. I'm too busy for that. I don't think I'm ready for kids, yet."

I noticed our conversation started to take a turn. I thought maybe he might have been happy to hear about it, after the shock, of course. He and I had discussed having children before. We both said we'd have three kids when we were ready. I wasn't expecting it to happen when it did. The blessing came a little sooner, is all. Instead of Tony seeing it as a blessing, he looked totally disappointed. I was shocked to hear about the pregnancy, but I was even more shocked at his reaction to the news. However, I had to respect his honesty, even if he seemed extremely let down.

"So Tony... Would you like to discuss our options?"

I wanted to feel him out. Abortion would be unheard of in my mind, but I wanted to learn where his mind was. All I know is, if he was in favor of an abortion, I had been royally deceived when I married him. I wouldn't know who that numskull was.

"Options? Shari, are you talking abortion? I can't believe you would ask me that. What's your problem?" He asked, with a frown.

"Tony I don't have a problem. You don't seem like the happy father-to-be, right now. I expected you to be shocked, but you look downright scared. You're acting as though you don't want it."

"I'm sorry, Shari. A flood of issues just popped into my head, at once. I was thinking about my career, and whether or not I should give it up for something more stable, where I don't have to travel as much. I can't possibly keep traveling with you at home pregnant."

"Tony, we'll work thru those issues later. Right now I want you to be happy. I don't take this sort of thing, lightly. Bringing a child into the world is serious business. A child is your opportunity to make your mark on humanity. You have to shape and mold their little minds, take care of them and love them. It definitely comes first, in my book. Everything else takes a backseat. Even my career may be placed on hold, if there is too much conflict."

"KoShari, I'm not sure I'm ready to put my career aside for an extended family. I've worked hard to make it this far, to build my name over the years."

"And just what kind of name are you building? Playboy of the year? You act like you're losing nobility, or something. This is our child. I'm not positive I like your responses."

"Baby, I'm honest. I see this becoming a hindrance in the future."

"Tony, what will our child hinder you from? You know what, lets end this conversation before I say something I'll regret. I cannot believe what I'm hearing. Please hurry and get me home. I'm getting sick just being in the same space with you, right now. I feel betrayed. The mere fact that it's "our" child should excite you. I can't believe the total opposite has occurred."

"Shari, I don't mean to upset you. I guess I could be more supportive. I'm sorry, honey. I didn't mean to be ugly about such a beautiful thing. I made a mistake. I apologize."

I didn't say anything else to him on the way home, after that. I wanted to tell the sucker it was too late for an apology. He'd already given his first reaction. The first impression is always the lasting one. Had I been a hothead, I would've left his ass, right then and there. However, I had to respect his honesty. Instead, I chose to let it go, and to begin thinking on plans for my next book club meeting with the girls in the next six months. It was coming up soon, and I hadn't had the house gentle-cleaned enough for my taste before inviting guests over. The type of gentle-clean I wanted, included re-landscaping both the front and back yards, with the freshest seasonal garden and shrubbery; re-painting the shutters on the windows all along the outside of the home; cleaning all attics; cleaning the shed, out back; updating the décor on the entire first floor of the home; exterminating the inside and outside; re tiling both the pool and Jacuzzi; re-furnishing the guest house; and buying new dishes, pots, and pans, etc. Six months was barely enough time to schedule all that needed to get done, especially with my constant work schedule, including business travel, as well as my prior philanthropy and social commitments.

Chapter Ten

"KoShari, I couldn't read the book at night. Each time I did, I'd become as horny as a bitch in heat. I got no man at home, like you. It was unhealthy for me. I'd call every man in my black book on the available list for a midnight booty call. The sex scenes in this book are steaming," said Miranda. She fanned herself just thinking about it.

Miranda was a cool girlfriend. She was my friendly bad conscience. Always into something other than her own business, but was a riot to hang out with. Me and the girls who frequently met at Zha Zha's while we were in law school, decided to turn our get-togethers into something more meaningful, like a full-fledged book club.

It was my turn to host the meeting that quarter. I decided to hold it at my home in the backyard, out on the veranda. Lord knows I didn't want all those women sitting inside my home for too long, in case anyone had negative energy. I didn't want residue from bad energy lingering once they had left. Mom said I was paranoid for thinking this way. I believed I was being smart.

"I especially liked the part when Jake was deliberating whether or not to give in to Terra's strong advances, and to have an affair with her, knowing his wife was her long time and trusted business partner. That burns me up how most men are so totally driven by lust these days. This situation is typical, and happens all too often," said Ursula.

Miranda and I give each other a look of concern like, 'Oh God, here we go....'

"A man meets who he calls the woman of his dreams. He's caught on a day when he and his woman are fighting. He looks up to see a desperate young thotty who will let him lay his head in-between her two exaggerated fake breasts, precisely at the moment when his life is out of alignment. He starts dating her, and then he scores, and ends up leaving his wife for a piece-of-ass. Happens the same way each time. I'm not bitter. Truly, I'm not. However, I DO NOT lie when I say it happens ALL too often," Ursula concluded.

Ursula Patterson was an introverted Irish brunette, who had a truckload of man issues. She trusted no one, since her divorce from her husband of twelve years. Unfortunately, he had left Ursula for some plastic Barbie who wore big hats at the derby, which happens to be where he met the skank. If anyone would bring attention to extramarital affairs, it would've been Ursula. I never understood her, though. She was a mystery to me. She was a pro at separating the business from the personal. On the same day, after catching her husband with this other woman, she had seamlessly closed one of the largest corporate mergers in Texas history. She was the consummate professional corporate attorney. That's why she needed the book club. It was the only female exhale experience she allowed herself to have. However, at the time, she vehemently refused our condolences to the situation. When the divorce was final, she didn't return any of our phone calls. Instead, she jetted off to South Asia for a vacation. I heard she got laid everyday by this wild surfer boy she met in Sri Lanka, and also received violent body-massages by the locals every 48 hours during her stay. Upon her return, she was abnormally healthy emotionally, and even more vicious in the boardroom.

"I share your opinion, Ursula. The story is as old as dirt. Men still get lured away with seduction. They are so easy. All of them. Not one of them can be trusted one hundred percent," said Rosie, while randomly pointing her index finger to emphasize the point. Ironically her finger ended-up pointed in my direction.

Rosie tucked her feet underneath her hips in the patio chair to get more comfortable. She was holding her tea in the one hand, and had placed the other on her hip. Her movements were fluid, like a ballerina.

"So what's a girl like me to do?" She asks with a shrug of her shoulders. "I figure I might as well join em'. I believe couples in this country are becoming more and more like some Asian couples I heard about in Japan. The way I hear it, it's not uncommon for men to have wives and girlfriends, who are more traditionally called "concubines," at the same time. The women actually accept this behavior as normal. Prostitution is legal there, so it's nothing for a man to have a family life and a hired mistress, both living in peace and harmony, together. It makes me think about whether I'd be happier as the wife, or the mistress," she concluded.

Rosie Cavrone was half Puerto Rican and half Italian. She was one of the sexiest women in the group. Her skin was the silkiest I'd ever seen, next to mine of course. She had a Caribbean complexion; dark, and freshly-baked light brown in color. She also had a seductive sex appeal about her, that caught the attention of every man in a room. She wasn't pouty, but she had those Prince (artist formally known as) eyes. She was sexy, both inside and out. I made it a point to watch her closely around my Tony…

"You'd make a good mistress, Rosie," said Miranda, with a laugh.

Rosie's response was not catty, but she looked at Miranda with those huge Prince eyes while sipping her hot tea. She had a bit of a devilish grin on her face, definitely a side-eye.

"SO!" I said spritely, to interrupt the awkward moment.

"Anybody else here think all men are animals in heat? It's obvious this book has shed light on emotional issues with some of us. I'm glad Jake came to his senses after almost losing it all, for Terra. He realized the whore wasn't worth the risk. Yep, I guess he decided that a piece of ass, is just a piece of ass. But there's a reason I made my wife, my wife. Personally, I'd much rather bear the "wife" title than the "mistress" title, Rosie. Mistresses always get the raw end of the deal. Sure, they may get his time, and his lust. But the wife gets the whole man, the part of himself he's most proud of. She gets the respect, the recognition, the long term commitment, and the money, should anything happen to him. The wife gets the friendship, the love, and the deep, deep, gut deep, soul connection during lovemaking, that is indescribable, and incomprehensible to a desperate ass, mistress." I was speaking to everyone in the group, but my comments were directed at Rosie.

"Yes, Shari, but many men leave their wives for the mistress. Maybe they believe the mistress fulfills a need that the wife cannot," replied Rosie.

"True, very true. Some men do leave their wives for a mistress, but the men always regret it. Consider the fact that anything God didn't put together ain't gone last. In the book, Terra knew Jake was married and in a fragile state-of-mind when they met. She should've backed off and allowed him time to collect himself. But no, the bitch was so desperate, she took advantage of Jake's fragility, and manipulated the situation to her advantage, regardless of his family life that was at stake. Fuck the kids, fuck the family; Jake was to be hers, henceforth. These desperate witch whores of today just don't give a fuck. You couldn't have paid me to be careless like that, especially when there were kids involved. She should've given him the space he needed, whether he knew he needed it or not, until after he was certain of how he wanted to move forward. A fuck is just a fuck to a man, and that's all it will ever be, whether they marry the fuck, or not. Terra tried to turn that into love, knowing that it wasn't. Sooner or later Jake, and men like him, will wake up one day, and realize they made the biggest mistake of their fucking lives. Sometimes, unfortunately, it's too late when they do."

I looked Rosie dead in her big beautiful eyes with a strong fierceness. If my eyes could speak, they would say, "Don't fuck with me, bitch."

She challenged me. She didn't look away. That heifer meant what she said. I still wasn't sure if she was referring to my Tony. I remember his face had lit up the day he mentioned he'd be working with her. My conscious told me he was taken by her beauty. However, I wasn't worried. Not now, anyways.

I looked around to gather the other's responses to my words. Many of them were whispering to each other and chuckling while I was talking. I wasn't distracted from my diatribe.

"As has always been the case, mistresses are seen as whores, whether they become wives, or not. It's about typification. Quality versus cheap. A queen cannot be compared to a commoner, you know? " I said.

I noticed Rosie's strong non-verbal response to the statement. She was offended by my comment, very uncomfortable. I admit I laid in on pretty thick. I was six months pregnant, cute as a peach, and as bold as a lion. I didn't think my words would offend anyone at the meeting. I mean, who would've gotten offended unless they were already living a mistress role?

I scooted back in my seat with both arms stretched out, and both hands clinching each of the chair's arm rests. I cockily crossed my legs and looked at each person, daring the next remark.

"Whores maybe, but remember it's the whores that have all the fun," said Ursula. Everyone broke into a controlled laughter.

"Yes, ladies. Well, we'll have to come back to that. I believe the little one is calling for Mommy to take her afternoon nap," I said, as I gently rubbed my belly.

Everyone began leaving the veranda and headed to the kitchen before their departure.

"Miranda, I'll send you a special book club link to Amazon.com. You can send it to everyone else, for voting on the next read."

"Sure, hun."

I wobbled into the kitchen.

"Hmm. There's something I never thought I'd see. KoShari Alexander Bryant wobbling around as a pregnant lady," said Miranda.

"Well honey, you just wait. Your turn is coming. I'll be laughing at you someday."

"We'll have to see about that, Shari. I might decide to wear the mistress role for the rest of my life. Ha Ha." We both laughed.

"Ok, sweetie. See ya in three months," said Miranda, on her way out of the front door.

"Bye, babe. You're a lovely friend. See you later. Take care." I told her.

Mom had walked up as she was leaving.

"Hi, darling. I was in the neighborhood."

"In the neighborhood? Ma, you missed the meeting." I was upset she hadn't called to say that she would be late.

"Oh, Shari. I had to do something with your Dad. Sorry, dear. I'll make it up to you. You know I always do." Mom proceeded to walk inside the house. "Shari, when are they leaving? Isn't the meeting over?" She asked, referring to a few of the girls who were still chit-chatting inside, and were slow to leave.

"I know, Ma. I'm tired, too. Can you dismiss them for me? I'd appreciate it. I'm gonna go lie down. "

"Certainly, honey. Ok Ladies! We must clear the place. KoShari is a tired and fat pregnant lady. You know she needs to sleep. In other words, you don't have to go home...But I think you know the rest. (Clap, clap) Ok. It's been real…" Ma yelled.

Of course Mom took care of it. My place was quiet within the next ten minutes. She was nice to stay and clean everything for me after the book club meeting. It's the least she could do since she had missed it. She must've felt bad. I think that's why she decided to come by even after missing the meeting, or was it…

I was still lying in bed fresh from my nap when I heard Mom and Tony talking. He must have made it back from the Astros baseball game sooner than expected. He'd try and make the Astros home games during baseball season on the Saturdays he was in town.

"So Tony, how is business? I hear your firm's client base is growing," Mom asked Tony, with a coffee mug in the one hand, and the Wall Street

Journal in the other.

"Business is great, Janis. We're about to take on the Brazilian Futball Association as a client. They're interested in forming an additional sports entity, a spin-off, and wanted us to transact the incorporation. Did you know there's a new team born every 7 years over there? South America is big on their Futball," he proudly replied. He walked over to the fridge for an apple and bottled water.

"Yeah, Tony. Sounds like you've got a busy schedule. You finding any time for KoShari in that busy schedule of yours? I haven't told her much, but I hear how you parade around at these strip clubs like you're a single man, and all." She had walked up close to him and stood about a foot's distance away. She looked him up and down slowly, all up in his face, like she was sizing him. "Who the hell do you think you are, Tony? Do you expect that she'll never find out?" She asked. Mom was angry. Tony tried to interrupt, but Mom wasn't having it.

"Now you listen to me, you ugly ass, bastard. I will not tolerate you cheating on Shari like she means absolutely nothing to you. We welcomed you into this family despite not meeting your mother, and other family members. Since you were so established with an excellent career and all, you appeared to have it all together. You seemed to treat her well. We thought you two were in love, based on appearances. Henry and I decided against hiring a private investigator to check you out before giving you our blessing. Tony, you've gotten out of hand. I'm hearing too much about you with other women. Are you bipolar, or something? Asshole…" She strangely looked up at Tony, as if to say, your response better be good, because I'm plotting for your death.

"Janis, I resent your hostility. I do believe I'm married to Shari, and not to her parents. Trust me, she's a big girl, she can handle herself. I don't think I've done anything to shame my family. If you've heard something, you should stop gossiping so much. Please, let's not force her to choose, here."

"Choose, what?" I asked. I felt the steam from their heated conversation when I walked into the kitchen.

"Honey, choose where you want to build the nursery," Tony said. He smiled and rubbed my stomach. I noticed Mom's face. She was not amused.

"Shari, dear, I'm leaving now. Everything's been cleaned and put away. I'll call you tomorrow, ok?" Ma gave a gentle kiss on my face.

"Ok, Ma. Thanks for everything. I'll talk with you later."

I looked at her and knew something weird had just happened. As soon as she left, I asked Tony about what had transpired.

"Tony, what's up with my Mom? Is she alright? Did you say something to upset her?"

"Shari I can't believe you would ask me that, and in front of your mother."

"She's gone," I replied.

"Personally, I don't know what's wrong with your mother. If you ask me, she never really cared for me. She might think I'm too tall, or something. Who knows? I don't care, because I got cha'. I got you. I got my little man. And I won't allow anyone to ruin it." He pulled me closer to him.

"So, Tony... You think my family is trying to come between us? Why?" I asked, bluntly.

"I didn't say that," he said, while moving away from me.

"Sometimes, I think your Mom has it in for me. That woman can give a cold look that could freeze time. Back when we first started dating, I swore your Mom had me investigated, to see if I was fit for her precious Shari."

"Hold-up Tony," I said while catching his arm to keep him from walking away.

"You're pushing it. That's my Mom. I'm closer to her and my Dad than anyone else on the planet. You know that."

"Oh, yeah? More than anyone, huh?" He shrugs, as though he was offended I didn't say I was closer to him.

"Tony, I could never think ill of my family. It's how I was raised. I love them more than anything, and..."

"MORE THAN ME?" He had cut me off.

"You're my husband. What do you expect me to say? What are we, teenagers, and you're trying to get me to put-out on prom night by giving me some, "you're a big girl now," speech? Babe, we're beyond that. We don't have to go there. Of course you're priority in my life."

I couldn't believe he was actually attempting to force me to choose between he and my parents. This is what it had come to. 'Let's see, how am I gonna deal with it?' I thought to myself. I wasn't going against my family. I never have, and I never will. But I must smooth things over with him. After all, I do live with the man. I walked into the great room and headed for my favorite comfy chair. I continued to make attempts at melting the tension, by beckoning him to allow me to console him.

"Woman I know how much you love me. I just, you know. Even me, I needed to hear it in this moment, that's all."

I reached out to him. "Come here, baby. Let me rub your neck."

He walked to me and sat on the eudemon of my favorite chair. I massaged his shoulders and neck.

Surely he knew I was aware of the game he was playing. Why was he trying to get me to choose between he and my family? Is it so that I would disregard any further reports I might get from them? Maybe he thinks I'm naïve, and that I don't know what he's doing behind my back. I hadn't figured it out yet. I hadn't gathered why the game was necessary to him. Yes, I could see through it all. I saw that his willingness to play the game told off on his guilt. He is guilty. I had determined it from his actions and lies, that were demonstrated on that day alone.

Common human behaviors are so predictable. In relationships, you can always read when a person has something to hide. They normally follow the same three step process: (1), they do not change facial expressions when confronted with an accusation. It's important for their level of immaturity to remain hidden. The poker face makes them feel they have the upper hand, like they're successful at hiding the truth. (2), they try to pry you away from everything familiar. This modus operandi secludes the victim, making them defenseless in a situation. And (3), they rapidly keep the focus off themselves by reminding you of how imperfect you are. This technique keeps you off their backs, so that they're free to do as they please, regardless of what you already know about their convictions. All this, just to play a stupid game. It makes you wonder what the game is all about. My take on this particular situation, is Tony had some issues, because as I've read many times, it is true that hurt people, in fact, do hurt other people.

I consider myself to be a good people-reader, and I can easily see through Tony's lies. It would be one thing if I was a jealous and accusatory woman, but I wasn't. I've studied human behavior, which I credit to the Psychology minor in undergrad. I pray and have a relationship with God, whom I believe speaks to my spirit about matters of the heart. All these things together cause me to see clearly down through to someone's soul. I can see through Tony. I didn't like all that I saw. But I continued to maintain that his good out-shined the bad. It actually overshadowed it. And who knows? I'm not his creator. All the things I see, the good and the bad, may be what makes him the man God needs him to become in his life. So then, who am I to puff myself up over Tony and his issues that just so happened to affect me, his wife? Not to mention, he is the only man that's ever weakened my knees, ever. I see he needs some work. But he's worth it. I think. I know what he needs. And I have the depth of understanding it takes to hang in there, to sacrifice my own feelings, until he gets it. I wanted to believe I could do this kind of sacrificing for my husband.

Chapter Eleven

"Hey, Mama's boy! How are you, little one? I love you, yes I do. Aren't you the most precious thing God ever sent down from heaven!? I love you. Kiss, kiss. Oh, Mommy loves you," I said while cooing at my baby boy. My three month old little boy was the most precious thing I'd ever laid eyes on. I sat there on the floor of my great room with my legs crossed. I was holding my baby boy up in mid-air just above my head. He was such a happy baby, cheesing, giggling, showing his gums as though they were fully loaded with teeth. His legs wiggled back and forth. He was as sweet as a juicy Asian Bartlett pear. I'd fallen deeply in love with him. In fact, I was delirious. Deliriously happy. Antonio Bryant, II was the most adorable little human being on the face of the earth. I felt for him something awful. Little Tony, is what we called him.

I remember when giving birth, Tony had insisted he participate in every part of the birthing process. He claimed he'd never seen a baby born into the world before, and wanted a front seat to the action. To my surprise, Tony was happier than I'd ever seen him when lil Tony was born. So happy, in fact, that he cried. It was the first time I'd seen him show such strong and genuine emotion. The alpha male hardness he'd carried had melted the moment lil' Tony arrived. There was a point when the doctors had to use strong language to remove him from the delivery room to continue their job, successfully. Actually, Tony had played doctor before they came in, to deliver the baby. I was in labor for a long twelve hours. He coached me thru, and did exactly as the head nurse had instructed he do, before dilation. He even held my hand and counted my breathing while telling me to push. We could've delivered the baby on our own had the nurse not walked in to see that the baby was almost here. He watched the baby's head come out and got extremely excited. I saw another side of Tony that day. I'd witnessed the side of him that reassured my commitment to stay with him. His inner light shone brightly that day, so much so, that I could sense our love strengthening.

"R-ring!" The phone rang and had interrupted my bliss. I ignored the first few rings, hoping it would stop, but of course it didn't. I placed lil Tony in his jumper on the floor to answer the phone.

"Hello," I answered.

"Hi, Mommy!" It was my girl, Courtney calling from the airplane while flying in from New York City to visit the baby.

"How's my baby! I can't wait to see him."

"He's wonderful, Courtney. His mommy is doing great too, you know."

"Oh mommy, don't get jelly. I can't wait to see you both. Listen, my plane's landing in a couple hours. I should arrive in Houston by 8:00pm tonight."

"Ok. Call me if you have trouble getting a ride. I'm available if you need me. Girl, I've got so much to tell you."

"Not nearly as much as I have to tell you, hot stuff," said Courtney.

"Well, I'll talk to you when you get here. Bye, hun."

I hung up the phone. Just as I did, Tony had walked in from work. He had a somber look on his face, like he'd had a busier than usual day at the office. The firm depended on him, greatly. They placed a lot of pressure on his position. Ordinarily he was good at not bringing work home, but tonight his frustrations were visible.

"Hi, Tony," I said with a smile trying to ease him.

"Oh hey, Shari. I didn't see you when I first walked in. How are you sweetheart?" He asked. He kissed my forehead.

"We're fine. Lil Tony's been perfect all day long. He's such a good baby."

Tony reached over and kissed me again, but this time on the lips.

"Did you know he has your nose? It's the most handsome nose I've ever seen."

I reached up to kiss Tony on his nose. I grabbed his neck and rubbed it.

"Honey, I love you," said Tony.

"Umm, thank you, babe," I replied seductively while laying my head on his chest. "I love you, too."

"Hey, did I tell you Courtney's on her way in town to spend a day with me and the baby? She decided to take a day off to spend with us since she was busy during the Christening. I thought that was sweet of her. I haven't seen her, in like, three years. It'll be great to hook-up with her again."

I noticed Tony suddenly get nervous. I could feel the increase in his heart rate.

"Oh, yeah? How is she doing? It's been a minute since I last saw that girl."

"Yes, she's flying in tonight. We're meeting up tomorrow for breakfast at Brennan's, then going to the spa afterwards. To tell you the truth, the "woman-to-woman" will do me some good. I've been so focused on lil Tony, I haven't taken much time for myself."

"I agree, baby. You haven't had much time to yourself, lately." Tony gently rubbed my face. I closed my eyes and melted in his touch.

"You're right. I haven't." My crouch ran hot, and I knew exactly what that meant.

"Hold-up, babe," I said, as I tried pulling away from him. "I'll meet you in the bedroom."

Just then, right there in the great room, and while lil Tony was seated in his jumper, he reached down and pulled my shirt over my head. With his fingertips he pulled down the front of my bra and licked my right nipple. He slowly moved his hands along my waist, then my hips, then back around to the front of my stomach, while gently touching just below my belly button, along the hairline. That one spot, when touched the right way, gave a feeling of falling. The butterflies in my stomach were on steroids. I stood there with my eyes closed. Both my hands were clenching his biceps. He made me wet. With my eyes still closed and while high from his euphoria, I told him that I'd call Lucy, my new French speaking live-in, to take the baby for the rest of the evening. Somehow, I managed to slip my shirt back on before calling for Lucy. The thing I liked most about Lucy, was that she minded her own business. She gave us the space we needed to live a normal family life, without the worry of an uncomfortable audience, closely watching our day-to-day interactions.

"Lucy, please take the baby for the rest of the evening," I said over the house intercom.

"Oui, Mrs. Bry-ant," she said while coming to get the baby. Just as she arrived I had one more message for her.

"Lucy, Mr. Bryant and I do not wish to be disturbed for the remainder of the evening."

"Sure, Mrs. Bry-ant. I have everything under control. No worries for you. Please, enjoy the remainder of your evening."

Tony had made his way to our bedroom while I was on the intercom with Lucy. By the time I entered the bedroom, he was already in the shower. I walked in and locked the bedroom door behind me. I decided to join him. Before joining him in the shower, I put on some sexy music, dimmed the lights, and flicked on the automatic candles. I stripped down and joined him in the shower. He was lathered, and smelled of some scrumptious lemon and sugar scent. The shower was steamy. I walked in and closed the foggy door behind me. He turned around and immediately picked me up, pinned me up against the wall, and placed my legs around his waist. He began licking my breasts, then sucking them. Damn it felt good. I thought to myself, 'I'm glad my milk dried up, or he'd be getting a mouthful right about now.' He kept sucking gently, slowly, and consistently. He grabbed my waist and slowly placed himself inside me. He went in deep from that position. I grabbed his shoulders, and rode him. I started out slow, but the groove was so good it caused me to speed up, naturally. The water was running, steaming hot, and pounding onto the both of us. I got lost in it all. I rode more vigorously with each one of his uncontrollable moans. Boy, did we sex well together...

The harmony, the love, the madness, the desire, the animal magnetism, the emotion, it was all there. Somehow, our connection seemed even deeper than the previous years. It had taken on another form. Sex was even better than the love we made the very first times. It was more meaningful. More defined. He tried, poor thing, he'd slow down when he felt it coming on, and then speed up, then slow down again, but he came after seven minutes of fighting it to the death. Our love making was always memorable. That time went into the archives as the secret shower chronicles.

The next morning…

"R-ring," our bedroom line rang early that morning.

"Good morning, Mrs. Bry-ant. The baby is ready for his morning feeding. Would you like me to feed him?"

"Sure. Please, yes," I said, while still groggy from a deep sleep. "In fact, you will be caring for him the remainder of the day. Courtney and I are going for breakfast, and will be out until the afternoon."

"Ok, Mrs. Bry-ant. Have a wonderful day."

He laid like a rock next to me. I could imagine how tired he was. Good sex sure can provide a magnificent workout if its done right, and with the right person.

"Tony, what time are you going into the office today?" I asked.

"By 8:00am."

"Honey, its 6:43am. You might want to get up. Courtney and I are having breakfast at 9am, she should be here soon." I still wasn't ready to get out of bed.

"K, babe," he replied. He got out of bed and went into the shower just as the phone rang, again. This time I let it roll over to voice mail.

"KoShari wake ya ass up, diva. It's time for our day!" Courtney was leaving a message.

"I'll arrive at your house at 8:30am. Be ready. It's been so long. I have much to discuss. I've missed you girl! Get up, now! BYE."

I'd given my private bedroom number to Courtney so she could reach me directly. Her message was my alarm clock. Soon as Tony left the shower, I got out of bed, showered, and hurriedly got dressed. I remember winking at Tony as we passed in the hallway. He rushed past the kitchen and grabbed a muffin that was sitting on the kitchen island from the muffin platter Lucy had prepared that morning. He was on his way out the back door, leaving for work.

"Mrs. Bry-ant, Courtney is here," said Lucy on the intercom after answering the front door.

"Show her in, Lucy. I'll be right out."

I put the finishing touches on myself, walked out of my bedroom suite, and down the private corridor to the main foyer. I found Courtney in the formal living room with the baby, holding him up over her head.

"You look just like your Daddy, little boy. Aren't you handsome? And sweet, too. Oh, you're so cute. I can't believe how cute you are. You're gonna give em' trouble, little man. I can see you as quite the little heart breaker when you grow up," said Courtney, while smiling at lil Tony.

"Courtney, girl, you still look the same!"

"KoShari Alexander! Oops, I mean Bryant!" We both burst into laughter.

"Come give me a hug, girl. It's been a long time," I told her. Lucy took the baby as Courtney and I embraced.

"Ooh girl, look at you. What are you into, yoga or something? What's your secret," I asked Courtney.

"Shari, it's only been three years. You still look good, as well."

"I know, right. You remember our promise? We would never, eva, let ourselves go. We must always look good. That was a requirement for hanging out with each other," I reminded her.

"That's right, girl. And you know the first person who's kicked out of the club?"

"Who?" I asked, surprisingly.

"Alicia. Alicia is as big as a house."

"Oh, no. Really?"

"Yes, ma'am. Listen, our reservations are for 9:00am we better get going. You ready?" Asked, Courtney.

I kissed the baby, gave him a big hug, then Courtney and I headed out in my jeep. Along the ride to Brennan's the day was sunny, and bright. It seemed to feed into my mood. I was so happy to be hanging with my girl, Courtney, again. Although… I couldn't help but wonder if she'd heard anything about Tony and I up in New York. I wanted to know if his indiscretions had reached that far with our friends, there. Of course Courtney would have heard about it. She hears everything. No matter where you are in the world, she'd find the dirt on you. Courtney, like my Mom, always was, a gossiper. She knew every single thing there was to know, about anyone in her life. She was a bit of a skeptic. Maybe a good screw with a man could help her to keep to her own business. I started thinking who I could set her up with…

After getting all caught up on her family, and my time away from the office to care for the baby, we left Brennan's and headed to the spa. The plan was to start with the Swedish massages, then a seaweed wrap, acupuncture, colon hydrotherapy, and finally a red-mud exfoliate, plus lunch when we were done. Everything together should've taken half the day. We had plenty of time to catch up. We were in the middle of our Swedish massages when I sparked up a conversation.

"So Courtney, what's going on with the career?"

"KoShari, its been great. As you know, I was promoted to Sr. Counsel of Time Warner's New Corporate Contract Division. All I do is manage the groups that create the new contracts, while using the latest form books, mixed with my own corporate genius, to ensure legality. It's tedious, but a very important position. If anything gets omitted from those contracts, it's my ass, and not my direct reports, you know? It's actually very different from the last job I had, there. Last time, I partied my ass off. Now, going to contract conferences is the extent of my outlet. It's good though, I can't complain. They're paying me twice my old base salary, $318,500 annually. The salary is certainly cause for an anytime celebration. I look at it this way... I create their new corporate contracts all year long, and then I jet-off to Antigua or Rio or wherever I want. Sometimes I'll plan big parties in The City just for the heck of it."

"The City, huh? You sound like a true New Yorker, now. No one refers to New York as "The City" unless they're from there." I was being sarcastic.

"Well honey, they must've made me a bona fide honorary citizen, because I'm there to stay. KoShari, you used to want to travel to New York and make your life there. What happened?"

"I did. But after I didn't get accepted into the LLM programs I wanted, I gave up hopes of living there. It's fine, I can visit whenever I want. After I took the job with Dad, I decided to stay and make Houston my home. I grew up here, so it can't be all that bad."

"KoShari, are you sure you didn't change your mind about moving to New York, to keep Tony from being tempted around all those beautiful and powerful women there?" Courtney asked.

"Ha. You mean, beautiful and powerful women, like me?" I could sense our conversation taking an unwelcomed turn.

"I won't lie, Shari. I've heard some crazy shit about Tony. It's all about certain circles that he's fooling around on you, so hard that, for example, by the time you find out, the woman will have had his baby, put it up for adoption, and the child would be good and settled into a new family, all before you'd ever even learn about it."

"WHAT!? Courtney, you mean to tell me Tony's reputation is that bad? Is someone saying he's got an illegitimate child in New York?"

"No, dear. I'm telling you Tony is cheating, point blank, and period. And it makes you look bad. Everything is happening right in front of your face. Can you believe this news traveled to you all the way from New York City?"

"Courtney," I called to her while the attendant placed cucumbers over our eyes.

"That is a subjective opinion. I fell in love with Tony. That makes all the difference in the world. There is absolutely no one on this earth like my Tony."

"Shari, you sound like the quintessential fool in love, if I've ever heard one."

"You just wait. When it happens for you you'll say the same things."

"Na-ahh! Not if I'm being treated like crap!"

"Now you're going a bit too far, damnit. What the hell have you heard, specifically? Shoot… I cannot and WILL NOT be talked to as though I'm an invalid." I was beginning to get angry at her strong language.

"Shari, baby, then quit acting like one. Some of my friends in The City claim they've tasted Tony Bryant from Houston. Girl, they went on about how the man was so fine, that once wasn't enough. One girl said he rocked her world so hard she went to Houston on a whim looking for him, and found out about you. She said she was so strung out that she parked outside his house."

"My house?" I interrupted.

"Yes dear, your house. She parked for hours contemplating whether or not to knock on your door and tell you about her. And this one had only been intimate with him twice!"

"How do you know it was my Tony they were talking about?"

"Several clues. For instance, I remember you calling me two weeks prior to Tony's business trip asking me to look out for him when he comes. Also, Theresa, that's her name, mentioned attending the same sports law conference as his firm. I think that's where they met. Come on, Shari. How many black Tony Bryant's with class and money live here in Houston? Let's get real, girlfriend. Don't worry. I didn't tell her about our friendship. I didn't want her to stop communicating with me in case they continued to see each other. KoShari, I ain't trying to rain on your parade or nothing, but girl your man ain't right. I simply do not have a girlfriend who's with a guy that is not cheating on her. Not one of my high-profile girlfriends is dating a faithful man. Now Shari, that's sad. Whatever happened to good men? My bad! I don't think they ever existed! Men have been cheating since forever, even in the Bible. Look at David and his sons. What a shame. It seems our black men cheat more than anyone, though. Do you think it's just our men that fall super weak, or what?"

"No. Believe me, girlfriend. Dogs come in all shapes, sizes, and colors. It's not just our men that cheat, alot. Trust me."

"Yeah, well, that's why I've decided to give women a try. I'm expanding my options."

"WOMEN!!" I shouted.

"Shari, don't go acting all surprised. Yes, women. I haven't found anyone to settle with yet, but I've experimented a few times with some beautiful women. It wasn't bad, shit, not at all. Not. At. All. In fact, I really enjoyed the sex. Sometimes I miss the masculinity of a man, but women communicate better. The soft touches in just the right spots, will surprise you."

"Ok, who's hurt you? You done gone up to New York and lost your ever-loving mind! Courtney don't get me wrong, I have nothing against homosexuals, I'm not homophobic. But I know you, and have known you for quite some time. You LOVE men, Courtney. Always have."

"You're right, Shari. Someone did hurt me. I dated this guy, Bryce. I fell in love; at least I thought I had. He was an associate professor at the Columbia University Graduate School of Journalism. Shari, I was so awe struck behind him. After six months of dating, I found out he was married. His wife is a photographer for the Times. She had been on assignment in Israel. As soon as she returned, he dropped me like a hot potato. All along he had been telling me how crazy he was about me, and how he couldn't see himself without me. Heck, I was planning to take him home to meet my family!" She said, with shakiness in her voice. She was about to cry.

"You dated him for six months. How could you not have known he was married?"

"He never wore a wedding ring. Remember, at the time, I was new to The City. There really wasn't anyone I trusted to give me the 411 on him. Isn't that a shame? You almost have to get an FBI background check on the guys you meet these days."

"You absolutely, do. And even after you marry their asses, too." I replied.

"KoShari I'm sure this female dating thing will pass. I know it's just a phase. But the experience is enlightening."

"I guess. I already know I must have a man to hold onto. You'll get over Bryce. You piss one of those lesbians off and you've got to deal with a jealous lover, forever. Most of them, and us as women in general, already have forgiveness issues. This could be why women who choose lesbianism choose the lifestyle in the first place. Pile your rejection on top of those unforgiveness roots, and you add dynamite to an explosive mine."

"Yeah, well enough about me. What are you gonna do about the Don Juan you're living with?" She asked. She let out a slight chuckle.

"First off, don't call him that, he's no Don Juan, OK? Secondly, Courtney, I see marriage as something sacred. Each time I experience a less-than-perfect act by Tony, I'm reminded of standing there taking those vows in the presence of God, and all those witnesses. You know me well enough to know that if the man walked me down the aisle he must be pretty damned special. I'm too picky to settle. I said I DO knowing somewhere down the road he would hurt me, and/or I would hurt him. He's human. I knew if I wanted him so badly that someone else would, too. Who wants a man that nobody else wants? I believe there is no one I'd rather journey thru this life with, other than him. He is my soul mate. I don't think we can choose who we fall in love with. I'm not saying it will happen only once. I'm just saying we don't choose who those people become. So then, why not try and make it work with the love of your life? You couldn't deny what you felt for Bryce. It was real. From the moment you met him, you did things that consented to you and he continuing to see each other. You liked being in his presence. So you see, even if you limited the time spent with him, you still couldn't change the fact that you "wanted" to be with him. Eventually you spent enough time together for you to fall in love with him. At that point you were locked-in. As for me, I'm woman enough to realize this early on, when I discovered that I'd fallen for Tony. No matter what Tony does, I still want to be with him, because I'm in love. The desire to be with Tony is very strong. I believe in having what I want, especially when it already belongs to me."

"So Shari, are you telling me you're willing to stay with Tony even after he's screwed you over, numerous times? That's just freaking dysfunctional,

I ain't even gone lie. From the moment I learned about Bryce's wife, I told him to kick rocks. I don't give a damn how much I loved his ass. I couldn't allow myself to stay in love with a fool."

"No, dear. What's dysfunctional is the fact that he has the love of his life at home, but still feels the need to mess around. There is no doubt in my mind that Tony loves me. I know in my heart he'd kill for me. What I don't know is why he's doing what he does."

"Cause he CAN, that's why! KoShari you've changed. The woman I knew in law school would never have put up with no shit like this."

"Courtney, I'm a grown woman dealing with real, grown woman, issues. I can't just bail on him like a girlfriend can. I'm his wife. By covenant I'm forced to work through this with him."

"Sounds like the covenant is giving you an excuse to be stupid. After it's all said and done, what if he doesn't want to work it out with you? What if his intent is to get his wiggles and thrills and be mischievous, for no good reason at all? What if his nature as a human being is different than yours, and that's why he doesn't hold to his vows the way you do? What if he doesn't change?" She asked, bluntly.

"What if he does, Courtney?" I asked back.

"Well, I never thought of it that way. I guess if he did change you would've missed out on the improved product had you left."

"Now you're thinking like a married woman."

"I guess. I'm not so sure I'd be as mature about it. He doesn't give a damn about you right now. If you're willing to wait on something that may or may not happen, more power to you. If you like it, I love it. Just don't come running to me when the sucker leaves you for some fleusy."

"Courtney, that's not fair. You've got so much to learn."

"I guess I do. It will never be ok for someone to drag my name through mud just for the heck of it." She was angry with me for not being more protective of myself about the situation.

"Courtney just hang in with me, my friend. You're gonna see a transformation take place before your very eyes. When God's done with him, he'll be a totally different man. And I'm going to be standing right there beside him when he does, with open arms."

"KoShari you're either a very strong woman, or a very stupid one."

Strong or stupid. There's something to think about. I was so confused when I told Courtney that. On the surface, I knew I appeared to be emotionally sound, and to have it all figured out. Underneath, I was uncertain. There was absolutely no surety Tony even wanted to change. After all, he is quite the free spirit. He probably doesn't believe he's doing anything wrong. There was tremendous conflict inside me. I was screaming inside, yet on the outside I looked fine.

I wondered what else to say to Courtney. I couldn't tell her about the talks Tony and I had, had. I couldn't let her know that I was already well aware of his adultery. I thought it crazy to tell her about the advice my Mom and Nana had given me about fighting for my marriage, God's way. Courtney wouldn't understand. I know she loves me, and I've always appeared to have it all together around her. I couldn't let her know about my apparent weaknesses, that I was fighting for my man, even though I shouldn't have to. Courtney knew there were numerous quality guys who would love to be with me, and that I didn't have to put up with what I was going thru.

Independent and professional women like us are never to stoop to such a low level, at least with anyone finding out about it. We don't have to put up with the drama like other women whose sole purpose in life is to please their man. No, not us. We don't need men. We use men as toys, extras, lagniappes. Without realizing, the difference between myself and what I had described as an "other" woman was fading fast. How many times have my friends and I discussed the uselessness in a woman trying to change a man? We all concluded men will not change for a woman. Some cataclysmic event would have to occur in his life, one that would cause him to finally look in the mirror and realize he's being a dick, and that he should change his behavior, or risk losing all that truly matters.

I kept reminding myself of the last fishing trip Ma, Nana, and I went on. After my talk with Courtney, the memory of our trip helped to settle my heart:

"KoShari," my mother called to me, as she began baiting a hook in the dark on that cold and foggy Friday morning. "You've got some serious decisions to make. I want you to be reminded of one thing. Tony is just a man. You are just a woman. Meaning, we are all human, and capable of making mistakes. Tony has some deep rooted unresolved issues that cause him to commit adultery on you. Now, you can choose to leave him and move on with your life. You will be fine. Everything will be ok. You'll meet someone else and possibly find a love like Tony again. But if you love Tony, deeply, like I know you do, you can choose to fight for him. By fight, I don't mean you fist fight all the women he encounters. You fight for your marriage, spiritually. Nana gave me this same speech when you're Dad started acting up."

Nana's fishing pole was in the water. She yanked on it a little, to reposition the line. All the while, she was listening to our conversation. Suddenly, she chimed in.

"Yes, KoShari. And your mother was much feistier than you. She DID fist fight any woman she heard was even looking at your Dad. Ha, Ha." She laughed and shook her head at the thought of her own talks with Mom.

"KoShari, I don't particularly care for Tony," Ma continued. "But I place my love for you higher than my anger at him. I know you love that man something awful, and don't want to give him up. So I'm going to tell you what to do to get him to change. The first thing you do is fall to your knees and ask God to fix your relationship. He is the only one who can change Tony. You'll find that on your own you will not be able to get him to change. I don't care how much screaming you do. Tony will write you off as a nag. You can fight him, but he's stronger and he'll win. You can manipulate him, but he'd catch on, because he'll consider himself the master manipulator. Remember he's the one fooling around. You can try revenge by dating someone else. But in the end, you'll feel terrible, because you did it out of spite, and not because you really liked the guy. Baby, your only choices are either to leave, or to stay and do it God's way. And who knows, in the process, you might even learn a couple things about yourself that need work. I'm sure if Tony were interviewed about why he cheats he'd have something to say about you contributing to the problems, whether they'd be true or not. You know you're not perfect, Shari. You've pretty much been used to having your way, your whole life. You're very bossy. Some men have a real problem with strong women like you. They see a strong woman as a power struggle waiting to happen. It can be hard, but sometimes we can stand to do a little changing ourselves."

"Ma, if Tony is intimidated by my strength, then he needs to leave me. I'm not walking on egg shells for that man, or any man for that matter. I would hope he accepts me the way that I am, like I accept him. If not, then we'll forever have issues."

"Yes Shari, I can see you have the same fiery streak as your Mama. Sweetheart, listen to me… You married a real leader, an alpha male. Tony has an ego, partly due to his personal life accomplishments, and partly due to the crap his Mom fed him about how special he is. The brother thinks he's all that, and he probably is. The friction comes in the fact that you believe you're all that, as well. There's nothing wrong with it, you two are a power couple. It all boils down to the fact that you've got to allow him to be the man in your relationship. He has to know to some degree that you need him in your life. I'm not saying become manipulative and stroke him all the time, just so he can feel more comfortable about himself. I'm saying do your part as his wife and show him, that indeed, he is your king. Men need to know this. It makes them feel like a real man when we respect them. Now, if you were in a relationship with a woman, you wouldn't have these issues. Women have different needs than men. You should love him enough to give him what he needs from you. That may mean you'll have to yield. Isn't that what love is all about, being willing to forgo your own feelings to help someone else's? Especially if you love them."

"Ma, I love Tony. I don't know if I can modify my personality for him. I shouldn't have to. I certainly didn't believe he was an insecure man, but if he is, that's his problem, not mine. Besides, it doesn't appear that I have to make him feel like a king. Those skanks he screws already do a good job of that. I'm not giving him the royal treatment just so he can go somewhere else, and get more from someone else. That's dumb."

"Yeah, I can see you need some work. That's one of the smuggest things

I've ever heard you say. Baby you've got some maturing to do. Marriage is give and take. Compromise. Purging and merging of oneself. Obviously, the fact that he needs to go outside the marriage after you've given him star treatment at home tells you there's some bad mental issues going on up there, (she said, while tapping the right side of her head.) You can leave him if you like, but you don't have to. You can stay and work this out, KoShari. If you do, and once he wakes up from his jaded thinking, he'll love you all the more for staying by his side during his dumb days. Listen honey, I'm proposing to tell you how to work on your marriage, God's way. This is unconventional, and will go against everything you think you should do. Are you interested, or not?"

When she asked me that, I looked at her like she was crazy. "What!?" I asked.

"Shari, do you want to save your marriage, or not?" She asked again.

"Ma, I want to castrate him!" I yelled.

"Yeah, yeah. Well since we all know that won't be happening, do you want him, or don't you?"

I let out a long sigh. "Yes, I do."

"Trust me, the pain you're feeling will indeed go away after a while. You won't always want to castrate him, dear. Shari, I'm not wasting my time. If you don't want my advice, or if you aren't serious about fighting for your marriage, then we can go home."

Nana looked at me with raised eyebrows when Mom posed the question. I let out another huge sigh, and even added an eye-roll, or two.

"Ma, I love Tony. I'll do whatever it takes."

"Alright, then. Here's what you gotta do…"

That day out on the lake, Mom proceeded to tell me what to do to turn this thing around. I agreed to do it and all, but that still didn't change me wanting to strangle Tony for cheating on me, repeatedly. He was totally not thinking of me. He could care less. Mom explained that there is a lot of pressure on him as a handsome black man in Corporate America. Even though companies say there is no discrimination, the people we work with will still treat us stereotypically. In Mom's opinion, a handsome black man in Corporate America, despite how smart and successful he may be, has to bare the reputation of a gigolo if he wants to get anywhere. I wasn't sure I agreed with her. In fact, I thought she was bonkers for saying so, but I continued to listen. She said Tony could be feeling a lot of pressure on his job in that regard, and may be attempting to position himself for advancement. She said I have to be understanding and not crash on him all the time. She suggested I get a hobby to keep me from thinking about him being with other women during this whole process. She mentioned between the baby and my own active lifestyle, I should be able to keep busy. I already knew this. I had already begun to take on some extra responsibilities. I continued to pray for him, and to believe my prayers were answered, just as she had instructed. I found biblical scripture, 1 Peter 3, and read it all the time, to remind myself that God is faithful, and he was gonna fix this in his own time.

> 1 Peter 3: Wives, in the same way submit yourselves to your own
> husbands so that, if any of them do not believe the word, they may
> be won over without words by the behavior of their wives, [2]when
> they see the purity and reverence of your lives. [3]Your beauty should
> not come from outward adornment, such as elaborate hairstyles and
> the wearing of gold jewelry or fine clothes. [4]Rather, it should be that
> of your inner self, the unfading beauty of a gentle and quiet spirit,
> which is of great worth in God's sight. [5]For this is the way the holy
> women of the past who put their hope in God used to adorn them-
> selves. They submitted themselves to their own husbands, [6]like Sarah,
> who obeyed Abraham and called him her lord. You are her daughters
> if you do what is right and do not give way to fear.
>
> [7]Husbands, in the same way be considerate as you live with your
> wives, and treat them with respect as the weaker partner and as heirs
> with you of the gracious gift of life, so that nothing will hinder your

prayers.

[8]Finally, all of you, be like-minded, be sympathetic, love one another, be compassionate and humble. [9]Do not repay evil with evil or
insult with insult. On the contrary, repay evil with blessing, because
to this you were called so that you may inherit a blessing. [10]For,

"Whoever would love life
and see good days
must keep their tongue from evil
and their lips from deceitful speech.
[11]They must turn from evil and do good;
they must seek peace and pursue it.
[12]For the eyes of the Lord are on the righteous
and his ears are attentive to their prayer,
but the face of the Lord is against those who do evil."

[13]Who is going to harm you if you are eager to do good? [14]But
even if you should suffer for what is right, you are blessed. "Do not
fear their threats; do not be frightened." [15]But in your hearts revere
Christ as Lord. Always be prepared to give an answer to everyone
who asks you to give the reason for the hope that you have. But do
this with gentleness and respect, [16]keeping a clear conscience, so that
those who speak maliciously against your good behavior in Christ
may be ashamed of their slander. [17]For it is better, if it is God's will,
to suffer for doing good than for doing evil. [18]For Christ also suffered
once for sins, the righteous for the unrighteous, to bring you to God.
He was put to death in the body but made alive in the Spirit. [19]After
being made alive, he went and made proclamation to the imprisoned
spirits— [20]to those who were disobedient long ago when God waited

> patiently in the days of Noah while the ark was being built. In it
> only a few people, eight in all, were saved through water, [21]and this
> water symbolizes baptism that now saves you also—not the removal
> of dirt from the body but the pledge of a clear conscience toward
> God. It saves you by the resurrection of Jesus Christ, [22]who has gone
> into heaven and is at God's right hand—with angels, authorities and
> powers in submission to him.

I found it interesting how Sarah obeyed her husband Abraham, in verse 6. Legend has it that Abraham was a timorous leader, meaning, that as a man, he might not have been the strongest branch on the tree, or the most forthright of his peers. Sarah, on the other hand, is rumored to have been a very strong and opinionated woman, one who ran her household and businesses shrewdly, and with great authority. If the rumors are true, how difficult it must have been in her day-to-day life to submit to, and obey a less-authoritative man, such as her husband Abraham, whom she may have felt didn't always do things the way they needed to be done. Yet the scripture says she submitted to, and obeyed him. Well, like Sarah, I too am an opinionated business woman with a strong personality, and I find it very hard to watch my husband not turn away the temptation of having sex with other women, while being married to me. How am I supposed to submit to that?

Verse 4 says a woman's gentle and quiet spirit is of great worth in God's sight, and that the holy women of the past who put their hope in God knew of this great virtue. Not to submit to our husbands the way God instructs, as wayward as they may become at times, is to give way to fear. When we're in fear, we are not in faith, and God cannot work on answering the prayers we've prayed over them. Needless to say, I did not want my prayers to go unanswered, so I agreed to follow this scriptural advice by remaining quiet and gentle while continuing to esteem him in spite of his actions, and to believe God for the changes, no matter how long they would take to become reality.

I believed in this chapter, Peter the disciple was teaching us wives that when you and your marriage are in the will of God, continue praying while submitting to, and respecting your husbands, no matter the circumstances. As unlikely as it may seem, these acts of obedience to God and belief in God, by a wife, can cause positive change in husbands, and in marriages in general. I knew this was not going to be easy. I felt that Tony, although he was the opposite of a timid man, was purposely taking advantage of my submission to him, by cheating on me. Where I didn't get it before, I now understood that what he was doing had absolutely nothing to do with me, that he was just being a selfish man who carried a host of negative life issues, and was probably never taught how to properly deal with all that. Yet, he was still my loving husband and life partner, and I didn't want to lose him, regardless of whether or not infidelity might've been mentioned in the bible as a reason for divorce. Heck, I wanted my marriage, I wanted my husband… So I sat on this scripture and believed that God would move heaven and earth to change things in my favor, and in my marriage.

However, in that moment none of the scriptural analysis quieted the voices in my mind. The voices kept telling me I'm crazy, and stupid. I kept hearing Courtney's tone thinking how I must've appeared to her. One of the things Mom said, was that I had to be ready to get ridiculed by my friends. She said to prepare yourself for some serious persecution. She said my marriage was between me, God, and Tony. They won't understand, and it had nothing to do with them, I must remember that. Besides, she reminded me that no one knows what they would do in a given situation. She was right. I never thought Courtney would get involved with a married man. Yet, she did. I didn't buy that crap about her not knowing he was married. I think she knew all along and compromised anyway. Anyhow, I had my own battles to fight. I worked hard to stay focused. I was determined to trust God for my marriage the way Mom, and Nana, had taught me to do.

Chapter Twelve

It was cool and breezy that Fall night at Vargo's. Vargo's was a beautiful place where there was dinner and dancing in a large glass-windowed ballroom. Outside the ballroom was a full garden of exotic animals and peacocks, freely roaming the property. A few of the peacocks were in full bloom and searching for a mate. In the center of the garden was a lighted red brick waterfall, that flowed into a glowing indigo pond, filled with geese, ducks, and baby ducklings. The stars were out shining brightly in the dark blue sky. Soft and subtle music played in the background. I walked over to the silent auction to view the items on the table. The party was the firm's annual holiday celebration. I appreciated that the money from the auction went to a local charity for homeless children. A senior partner's wife came up with the idea that year to raise money specifically for homeless families.

As I strolled along the table, I'd periodically look up at Tony and Rosie talking. I saw her laugh, and lean on him. I looked away quickly, to keep myself from getting upset at what appeared to be an exchange of mutual affection between them. I was feeling particularly succulent that night, in my sleek and slender, velvety knee-length black semi-formal gown. I had pinned my hair up to put the finishing touches on a sexy, yet professional, look. I had recently broken a life-long commitment not to drink. At one point, I was tipsy from the red wine. Nevertheless, I remained keenly aware of Tony's whereabouts in the room. The awkward feelings about my marriage had caused me to search for an additional form of relaxation, to help calm those antsy nerves. I found wine did the trick on those lonely nights when Tony had said he was working late, but didn't actually get home until the wee hours. However, the drinking was short lived after I started gaining weight from the alcohol. The day I realized I'd gained five pounds from the wine, was the last time I remember thinking of a drink. But watching Tony and Rosie that night was tough, and had caused me to dip back into the bottle. Rosie and Tony had been spending quite a bit of time together working out the kinks of the merger, and all. I couldn't let it bother me, though. I was flattered when I saw other women blushing just from talking with my husband. He certainly had that magical effect. From where I was standing at the party that night, I swear she looked the happiest I'd ever seen her before. During the entire three years we were in law school together, I'd never witnessed her smile so fresh.

Tony is a force of nature. He reminds me of a character I saw in a movie once. The character Tristan, played by actor Brad Pitt in the movie, Legends of the Fall, was an incredibly attractive man with an enthralling personality. Tristan had a super human effect on people. He emanated an overwhelming joy and peace that created an undeniable draw unto him. The air in his presence was pleasant, and sneakily comfortable to others around. Women wanted him, and men wanted to be like him. Tony's social life was very much like that of this movie character. He had an electro-magnetic positive energy, an aura that pulled both male and female to him. I myself had already been consumed by it. I couldn't understand how Tony was able to charm people without feeling a real affinity for them, himself. He's so suave with his flirting, that another woman would think he actually had genuine feelings for her. Well, he didn't feel anything genuine for the other women he flirted with. He only had the genuine feelings for me. I was special to him. I believed this in my gut, because he had chased me, and pursued me. He never did that for anyone else, it was always the other way around for him. Women had opened themselves to pursuing him after an initial encounter. I admit he swept me off my feet the same as he did everyone else. The only difference was his heart had responded to our connection. All the others were hoping and wishing to get to him the way that I had. With me, it came natural. Tony was the bad boy that no one else on this earth could tame, but me; and not even me, without God's help. We truly were each other's soul mates, or so I believed. I love myself a great deal, but somehow this marriage was like kryptonite to my own self-assurance.

I gave Tony and Rosie a couple more minutes together, then decided to join them. I couldn't allow her too much of my man's charm. I eased up behind Tony during he and Rosie's seemingly intimate conversation.

"Hi, baby," I whispered to him.

"Shari. Did you see anything you liked over there?" He asked, referring to the auction table.

"Actually…I did." I muttered.

Just then I looked over at Rosie. She had a horrible look on her face. She looked disgusted, like she'd eaten something sour. Apparently she was disappointed I'd come over. I've never seen her look so upset… but only briefly. She quickly covered it up by fighting a smile.

"Hi KoShari, love that dress," said Rosie. She slowly looked me up and down while holding her wine glass in one hand, the other lay folded around her waist.

"Why, thank you," I told her with a slight curtsy.

"No seriously girl, you're WEARING that dress," she said.

"Don't watch me too hard. You might find a flaw," I said, attempting to reject her flattery. She smiled, cunningly.

"Well, I must go. Tony, always a pleasure. I'll talk with you Monday, as planned," she said.

"That's fine, Rosie. See you Monday," replied Tony.

She seductively looked at him with those big ass googly eyes. I watched her closely. I noticed the whole time as she walked away, neither one took their eyes off of the other. They created a rather lengthy, goodbye. Maybe I should've, but I didn't interrupt their exchange. I was always careful not to come across as prematurely possessive. However, sometimes you've got to raise your head. Sometimes it's a matter of the individual respect you demand for yourself, and dare I say, your property. This was NOT one of those times.

"My, lady. I haven't danced with you once, tonight. Shall we dance?" He held out his hand for mine.

"Certainly, handsome."

I placed my wine glass on the nearest table and allowed him to lead the way to the dance floor. The rest of the night was magical. We danced and we danced and we danced. His lead was gentle, his guidance firm. I wondered in a moment, out there on the dance floor, that as smart as he is, I know he's aware of this little game between us. Yet, he acts as though our relationship is as tight as a vault. This man shows absolutely no response to anything he does. He flirts around anytime he wants, and with whomever he wants. With the flip of a switch, he's all over me, as though I'm his irresistible princess. And I do mean, princess. He genuinely could make me feel ultra-special, like our love was unique and unusual. I don't get it. Is he bipolar, schizoid, or what? How can he so easily flirt with another woman right in front of my face? I was trying, I truly was, to hold on to whatever decency I had left. It's not a part of who I am to clown anyone, especially in public. But it's as if Tony wanted me to let my guard down and lose my mind. I tried not to think about it, because I felt like I was going crazy. I felt like my man was not really on my side, like we're not really the team we portray to everyone. It often seemed like he was working against me. 'Is he a misogynist? Does he hate women? Does he NOT care at all how I might be feeling, while watching my loving husband's attraction to someone else play out right in front of me? Damn, what's wrong with this dude!?' There I went thinking too much again. All I know, is if I'd kept all that bottled up inside, I would've imploded. These thoughts are the precise moments when I must call on supernatural help to maintain my sanity. Ma said, "The battle in the mind is always the toughest, and is when all those negative thoughts about Tony would begin to flood. The moment those thoughts attack your mind, you are currently enthralled in the middle of combat warfare. When this happens you need to open up your mouth and speak God's powerful word, in prayer."

After the dance, I excused myself to the bathroom. I made sure no one else was in there along with me, and while sitting on top of a toilet in a stall, I began to pray:

> "God, I praise you, because there is no one higher than you. I thank you that no weapon formed against me will prosper. I thank you that you know what I need and want before I even ask. I believe you've already surveyed my marriage and you know where we are right now. You know the pain I'm feeling, the deep hurt that creeps into my soul, and the thoughts that weigh heavily on my mind, because of my husband's philandering ways. But Jesus died for all my pain over 2000 years ago on the cross. Therefore, I receive the peace of the cross, the mercy of the cross, the compassion of the cross, the grace of the cross, and I command these evil thoughts about my husband to cease. I call my husband a blessed man of God who leads by your guidance, and who recognizes the gift you've given him, in me. I know this pain will not last always. So I give you the glory right now for the work you're doing in my marriage, in my husband, and in me. In Jesus' name I pray, Amen."

I honestly admit my belief in the prayers made me feel much better. Suddenly I felt empowered. My Mom had taught me well, step-by-step, how to save my marriage. But God's work in my marriage started with a choice to remain and fight for it. Each time I prayed, my mind cleared like dark clouds rapidly parting to a sunny sky. I was given more grace to handle the pain. After praying, I'd be reminded of my to-do lists. Like, order the baby pictures, have the window treatments cleaned, call Ava at the civic association about the fundraiser I had agreed to chair, meet with my personal trainer... I was indeed busy. Too busy to be running behind Tony trying to trace his every step. I also found that each time I would pray after being flooded with the thoughts of his infidelity, Tony would suffer in the tiniest, but most effective ways. Once, I remember he was supposed to come home early one night. I had been dressed in my finest lingerie and was anxiously awaiting his return. He ended up doing God knows what.

That night was torture for me until he returned home. He fed me some sorry excuse that I didn't buy, and then he fell crashing onto the bed. One can imagine my frustration, anger, and disappointment. Of course those thoughts begin to set in. I said nothing to him, as Ma had instructed me to do. Instead, I prayed for him, and for God to remove my angst. That next morning his car wouldn't start, and he was late for work on a very important day. He showed up to court unprepared, (which is a horrible thing for him. We both had set high standards for ourselves, professionally). That day was an altogether bad day in the life of Tony Bryant. His bad luck was a small example, but I believe if we yield, there's no problem too big, no ant hole too small that God cannot fix, as long as it's within His will to do so. I'm proof that these words are true.

I've never been a religious person. I've always acknowledged God and have known him, but I didn't go to church or anything. I learned about having a relationship with God through my parents, primarily my mother. She's the one who made me aware that my faith in God is what will give me an edge in life. Mom was right. I believe life lessons are always pivotal. If I activate my belief system in God, I'll navigate easier through life's journey. Come to think of it, I don't believe Tony was aware of my faith-filled life. We'd never discussed it. I think he was aware of my good girl image and my value system. Maybe he had an inkling, but for the most part he was clueless about the spiritual battles he was currently, and unknowingly, participating in. He was totally oblivious to God's ultimate control over our lives. I did have to submit, though. Submission…Now that was my hardest lesson. Submission to a husband was "kissing-ass" to me. Was I prepared to kiss his ass, after all he had done and was doing? Was he even worth it? The distractions of this marriage on my life were beginning to take a serious mental toll.

Chapter Thirteen

After constantly dealing with the stress of my marriage, I decided to go on a girl's night out with Miranda and a couple of her friends. We went to a club called, "Crystal's" located in The Heights near downtown Houston. It was an upscale place where Miranda and her co-workers would hang out at times. Miranda got drunk, and did karaoke all night. It was a funny picture; a blond-headed white girl singing, "C'mon, let me see you shake a tail feather..." old school Tina Turner. Miranda was goofy when drunk. With all the confusion going on in my marriage at home, it was good for me to get out and laugh with that good girlfriend of mine.

I returned home that night around 1:45am. The baby was with Mom for the weekend, I had given the nanny the weekend off. Tony said he had to work late that night. Since that usually meant him not returning till around 2:30am, I expected to beat him home. I was shocked when I drove up and noticed the light in our backyard shed was on. I held off on pulling into the garage. I didn't want the garage door opener to startle a crook, if there was one. I turned off the car, got out, and quietly closed its door. I had a taser in my purse and was not afraid to use it. I began walking over to the shed, taser in hand, and tip-toeing along the way. I was a mixture of scared, and angry, that someone might've tried to break into my home. This was totally unexpected. Our neighborhood was well off the beaten path, and was monitored often by police and our neighborhood watchmen. Since first moving into the neighborhood, no one had experienced criminal activity in the difficult-to-find, and hidden area. Nevertheless, I walked up to the shed without making a sound. I opened the half-opened door, and walked inside as quiet as a mouse. I couldn't believe what I saw and heard. I was desperately hoping these two senses were deceiving me. There was Tony, sitting atop my craft shelf, while some skank was on her knees giving him a blow job. She didn't hear me come in. I walked in, and she just kept right on bobbing her head back and forth while making loud slurping noises. He finally looked up and saw me.

"Shari, Oh God, No!"

I completely lost it. Without realizing, I'd picked up a 15lb half empty can of paint, and threw it upside his head. The can hit him, hard, just above the left eye. He fell to the floor, out cold. The skank was some Latin chick with a bad body shape. As soon as he hit the floor, she jumped up, grabbed her clothes, and took off running down the street. Periodically she'd stop and put on a piece of clothing, then start back running again. Poor thing, she had no transportation. I didn't care. She could've been a hooker for all I knew. In fact, I think she was. The nerve of that man, bringing some whore to my house. What if some of our neighbors had witnessed this scene? How humiliating would that have been? 'Oh its official, this sucker is crazy,' I thought. I walked away from Tony, leaving him there to die.

I think my throwing the can was a release of months, and now years of silence about his cheating. For years, I'd been quiet about his adultery. I'd been praying and confessing God's word each time something happened. I got peace when I prayed, no doubt. But I think the human in me would lodge the pain somewhere deep into my subconscious, even though I'd chosen to forgive him, time, and time again. Something inside me had latched onto a wincing mechanism; as if I'd wince internally each time I realized he was being unfaithful. And I always knew each time he was unfaithful. It was like I'd suddenly become psychic, and intuitively would know it, when he was emotionally detaching himself from me, to attach to someone else. Most women say they always know when their man is cheating. How we always know without any clear evidence, is somewhat of a mystery. We seem to just feel it when our men become interested in someone other than us. Indeed it is a scary feeling, to feel your man slipping away from you, and knowing you can't do anything to stop it.

The emotionally healthy ones, like I consider myself to be, will play it smart and won't try and stop him. We know that to complain would really push him over the edge. Pushing him over the edge was not my goal. My goal was to let on to the fact that if he did decide to leave, I would be his loss.

Guys don't know how to react to nonchalant. If they cheat in the first place they do it expecting their woman to pitch a hissy. To some, it can give a boost to the ego, as though their fragile ego needed to feel their woman's anger, as a reassurance of her love. Why my husband, who is handsome and has a brilliant mind, has time for the games, I couldn't understand. All I knew, was he would have quite the headache in the morning when he woke up… if he woke up. I decided I better pray to God that I didn't kill him. Preventing a homicide was the extent of my prayers on the marriage after that particular incident.

That night, as he lay in the shed knocked-out cold, I decided to go to bed and sleep it off. Maybe it didn't actually happen. Maybe it was all a dream.

The next morning my alarm clock went off at 6:00am. I decided to go for a three mile run at Memorial Park. Notwithstanding the events that had occurred the night before, I got up, got dressed, and headed out. I thought for a moment he might've still been out-of-it in the shed, and lying there unconscious. Surprisingly, I didn't care. I went running, anyways. When I returned at around 7:45am, Tony was upstairs in our den reading the Sunday paper.

Breakfast for me that morning was fresh strawberries, one scrambled egg with fresh avocado, and thin slices of crunchy red bell pepper, along with two strips of iced gingerbread biscotti. It was a light meal of energy foods, which I needed, to ensure I'd remain focused and calm during my confrontation. I knew he was ashamed, and would not become the initiator of a conversation with me. I walked upstairs, somewhat reluctant, but well aware of the potential for his shameful temperament, and that he might've anticipated tension, with my sitting there next to him. But I was wrong. The sucker acted as though he wasn't the least bit ashamed of anything at all.

"KoShari, babe, I'm upstairs. Can you come here for a second, sweetheart?"

"Hold on, I'm on my way," I muttered, as I walked up the stairs to the den, where he was comfortably lounged on the chaise with paper in-hand.

"I see you survived the hit," I said while standing at the top of the stairwell with my hands on my hips.

"Yeah. I have a small gnash on my left temple. There was swelling. After an ice pack and a couple BC powders, I'm ok."

"I will not apologize for last night. Who was that?"

He let out a big sigh. "No one, Shari."

"Tony, I've been a good wife through all your madness, wouldn't you agree? Look. All I ask is that you leave that junk out there. Don't bring it into our home." He looked at me with a blank stare as I was talking.

"Shari, I..." he said, but I quickly interrupted.

"No, no. Don't respond. Not yet. I don't know what you think about me taking all this shit off a' you. So let me tell you what to think. Don't think at all, cause it ain't about you."

"KoShari, why do you always cut me off like that? I'm trying to talk to you, and you won't listen to what I have to say. What if I have something important to say?"

"Tony, you jerk! You can kiss my ass! What the hell could you possibly have to say to me, right now? Screw you!" I told him, and then I walked away.

I could feel him staring at me as I headed back downstairs.

That was my time to let him have it. I could've ripped into him something awful. He would've felt about two feet tall. I was good at this sort of thing. I could rip a person into tiny shreds with my words, then recklessly throw them to alligators. But I didn't go nearly as hard as I could have. Instead, I heard Ma's voice in my head:

"Shari you will come to rely on God through Christ at the very moments you want to give up. It's often the hottest when He is making all the real changes in your heart, as well as in Tony's. But don't give up. In fact, force yourself to do exactly the opposite of what you want to do. Don't scream. Don't blow your top. Stay calm. Let God be God, and you sit back and go through the process He has for you. If you hold on, Shari, you'll find the changes will most likely be made within you."

I remembered what Mom had also said about respecting Tony when he didn't deserve it. I suppose she was right on that one. However, he sure is hell wasn't getting any respect from me that day. Let's just say that particular time I had struck out when stepping up to the plate. I later realized that there was no power in me going off on him the way that I had. No progress had been made in the situation. No effective communication occurred between us on the matter, which probably would've been a good thing. We might've made some sort of progress had my responses been different. Admittedly, I wasn't there yet, but had decided to work on responding more maturely during discussions that had been inflamed by his infidelity.

That day I decided not to give any more time to the particular issue. I had lil Tony to think about, and a calendar to create for the civic association. I decided to take on the responsibility of designing a civic association calendar after a member had visited my home once, and saw my self-designed jewelry boxes in the upstairs closet. I guess she thought I was creative, and figured I'd be good at designing the calendar to raise money for their annual March of Dimes Fundraiser. I agreed, and said I'd have samples in a month. That was a week ago. I figured I needed to jump on it right away.

Lil Tony and I were laying in my bed playing airplane, when Tony walked in more chipper than usual.

"Hey, woman," he said as he swiftly took lil Tony and threw him up into the air.

"How's my boy. How's my little man!" Lil Tony laughed out loud and stretched out his limbs with each high toss up in the air. He loved horseplay with his dad. Theirs was a warm connection.

"Hello, Tony. Did you smooth things over with the Japanese client? I remember you were supposed to meet with them this week."

Tony heard my questions and treated them like bad distractions from playing with the baby. He cut his eyes at me as his smile waned. He placed lil Tony on the floor, let out a deep sigh, and rubbed his hands from the top of his face, down to his chin.

"Actually, no KoShari... The meeting went wrong. All wrong. Apparently my idea for pitching the Japanese baseball players to Major League Baseball wasn't good enough. The firm claimed it lacked universality, and relevancy. They said it was boring and common. Boring and common... Can you believe that? After all the clients I've nailed for them. After all my innovation in the past. All that I've amounted to, is boring and common! That's ridiculous."

My asking the question was a major mistake in timing. I remember when I'd come home from a hectic day at the office. I never wanted him to ask me about it. I hated that. After a challenging day at the office, the first thing anyone wants to hear when they walk in, is a peaceful personality and pleasant conversation, that had nothing to do with work. I assumed it was ok to ask him about work since he appeared to be in such a good mood, but that was an incorrect assumption. He was probably just happy to see his family, which could've explained his initial cheer. Nevertheless, I'll never assume that again. I vowed that, next time, I'd welcome him home correctly. I'd want that if I were in his shoes. I didn't interrupt while he spoke. I said nothing. I wanted him to say all he wanted to say, without offering any feedback. This was a fragile moment for him, and I wanted to listen more than anything. I think that's what he needed most, again, placing myself in his shoes, realizing that I would've wanted the same.

"KoShari, I walked out of there. I quit right there on the spot." Ok, I had tried, but I couldn't hold my peace any longer…

"Tony don't you think that was a bit rash? Honey, you've put so much into this job. Why would you walk away so quickly? That doesn't sound like you."

"So who does it sound like, Shari? You think I'm a dummy? An idiot who makes snap decisions without thinking first? Surely you know me better than that." He said, as he began slowly pacing back and forth.

"KoShari, my quitting has been a long time coming. I've felt tension between Eric (his boss) and myself, ever since we acquired the Japanese client. From the start, I never felt he was comfortable with me leading the team on this one. I think he's wanted it all along. It's been one year since I was given head counsel on this transaction. One year, of constantly watching over my shoulder, checking for knives in my back, and whatever else. He's been on me all this time, never having the confidence that I'd do well, despite the fact that I've brought millions to the firm since I started seven years ago. I never complained, not once. I didn't threaten to go to Alkstein, Inchk, & Slovak's, or Platinum Entertainment, though they both offered to pay me at least forty percent more in base salary, and an additional six percent consultant fee on the business I generate, but no."

I gestured for him to calm down while in front of our son. Lil Tony didn't need to be around the negative energy. In that moment, he ignored me as he continued.

"Now suddenly I'm boring and common." He toned down after noticing lil Tony. "That's a blow, KoShari, a real blow…"

"Yes, Tony, I can imagine it was."

I walked over to him and touched him on the neck to calm him. After, I placed my hands on his waist and began to gently rub up and down his torso.

"We have no worries. Financially, we'll be fine until you work this out, or find another job. Sometimes things happen for a reason. Maybe it's time for you to move on. Seven years is a good life with a firm. The timing could be right for something better. Maybe you are being positioned for something else."

I so had to grit my teeth to be encouraging. What I wanted to say, was the real reason you lost your job, you asshole, is because you're living like a fool! Your personal life is spilling over into your professional life. You've lost a good sense of reasoning, because you've given over to a reprobate state of mind. You're not living right, and that's why you're unhappy right now. You will never be fulfilled if you keep fooling around on me! I was angry. I wanted to burst. But I restrained myself as best I could. Whatever work God was doing in him, I didn't want to interrupt it. Underneath it all, I still loved him, and didn't want him to have to suffer through it alone. Besides, who else was he gonna talk to, if it wasn't me? I didn't realize it, but a tremendous work was being done in me too, during that time.

Anyhow, I don't know how I did it, but I managed to calm him ok. I talked him into taking a week's vacation with me to Catalina Island, a secluded little place off the coast of California. I thought it was a necessary trip, to help clear our heads after the devastation of losing his job. It would also give us the chance to get re-acclimated with each other's sensibilities. We needed some spontaneous time away, together. Maybe it would remind us of the reasons we fell in love in the first place. Mom was real good about telling me to focus on Tony's good, rather than his bad. Certainly the time away would cause me to remember all those reasons.

Sometime in the next month, we took a flight from Houston's Bush Intercontinental Airport, to John Wayne airport in Santa Ana, CA. A cab drove us to Long Beach, where we hopped a sunset cruise to Catalina Island. Scores of other couples were on the large yacht along with us. It was very much a party atmosphere, with everyone sitting on an open deck, while a group of waiters bounced around with trays of drinks, and hors d'oeuvres.

We arrived at the west side of the island just before sunset. I remember thinking on the yacht ride over to the Island, that it was a picturesque sky-light; to see the sun setting, and to feel as though you were diving over the horizon along with it… California sunsets are the best.

Tony and I decided to take a run along the Island beach, to warm-up for the vacation, or rather in preparation for the sex later that evening. He ran in running shorts and a tank, while I wore a pair of leggings and a sports bra. It was special to be running in the cool of the night, amongst the open dark blue sky, and the millions upon millions of stars. We ran one mile without a word. We were both pushing it, and running at a fast pace. I'd look over at him a couple times to gather his energy. He'd be seriously looking straight ahead as though he was trying to beat his own time. He ran hard. I could imagine the extra exertion in the open outdoor environment did him some good. There's no better muscle relaxer than a brisk run, followed by a good massage and robust sex, afterwards.

The run left me breathing heavily, like a horse. We decided to eat at an all-night café located near the marina. I loved the fried lime cod with sweet potato wedges at this place. Tonight I was careful not to bring up anything about work. This was a get-a-way, and I wanted Tony to sense that it was.

"What a lovely night. My chest is wide open after that run. I love taking in this wonderful cool air, directly off the water. This place is beautiful, as usual," I told him.

I was hoping that my smile and charm would help him focus on us, and not on his worries. I was right. He finally smiled.

"Yeah, it's pretty fantastic. I'm glad you suggested this, KoShari."

Suddenly I heard soft jazz, that seemed to blow out of the wind. "Tony, let's dance."

I grabbed his hand for him to follow me to a small dance floor, located at a bar next to the cafe. He stopped me, and grabbed my hand to take over and lead the rest of the way. I realized he was being his usual take-charge self, and I loved it. Of course I followed along at the satisfaction that he was fully invested in the evening with me. That night, we danced our worries away without many words at all. We danced to our own unique rhythm. I grabbed his arms firmly, but not too tightly. I closed my eyes and laid my head on his chest. It felt like my place, like I was supposed to be in those arms, on that particular chest, for the rest of my life. And then I felt it, again. It was as if his love had permeated into my soul, directly from the pores on his skin, and into mine. I found it difficult to break free from receiving the sensation. A tremendous magnet was pulling us into one another, like we were physically becoming one in that very moment. Moments like this cannot really be explained. The feeling is beyond words. I knew it was heavenly. It was a feeling that can only be felt once you've gone through strong turbulence, and had landed on the other side. However, this was strange. I'd felt the bliss, but we hadn't gotten over the hump. I knew that we hadn't arrived, yet. The feeling of satisfaction and total forgiveness of Tony's cheating hadn't come. Tony hadn't completely changed, yet. I was still struggling with the pain he had caused me. How could I be feeling the satisfaction of the end result, before reaching the end? The only explanation for this is genuine, unconditional, and pure, true love. I knew that if I'd left him, I wouldn't have felt it. I knew that had we argued and argued about his behavior, I wouldn't have felt this way. I'd allowed my heart to forgive, and God had blessed me by granting the heavenly feeling of a pure spiritual connection with another human being. I believed it was from God. Nothing else would've given me something this harmonious. No drug, no alcohol, no Middle Eastern meditation practice, this was straight from God himself, through Christ. I know, because there was an indescribable freedom in what I felt. There were no inhibitions, no bondage. It was unpolluted, and quiet. Another miracle was that Tony seemed to also be masking in the bliss. To love, is a gift. To also be loved by the one you love, is divine. It is total synergy.

Tony sprang a big one on me in first class on the plane ride home. I was reading a Vogue magazine, while propping my feet on the foot stand, when Tony called my name…

"Shari, I forgot to tell you. My mother is coming to town. She's coming from Paris in about five months. She said she'd like to see her grandchild and she misses me," he said, in all smiles.

"Oh, what a surprise, Tony. How long is she staying, this time?"

HIS MOM!! You mean the woman who was forty-five minutes late to our wedding? He refused to start the wedding without her. This woman was pure evil. She was the most conniving and manipulative thing I'd ever met in my entire life. I wondered what she'd come for. She was so incredibly mean. Everything this woman did had an ulterior motive. Not to mention she took pity parties to a whole other level. She blamed everyone else for anything wrong in her life. She was an anal-retentive control freak, that made a career out of trying to steer her son's life into all of HER directions. Her only son, I might add. Oh, and did I mention how she hated me? This woman HATED me with an unhindered hate. I tried to please her and found early on that she didn't give a damn about how she made me feel. I didn't want her coming back from Paris. Ever. She could've decided to live there till death, for all I cared.

"Not sure, sweetheart. It'll be nice to see her, it's been a while." Said, Tony.

Chapter Fourteen

"Bon Jour, Cheri! Bon Jour! Oh Mademoiselle is so gorgeous, today. I try to encourage her often," said Lillian, Tony's mother. She was speaking to her transvestite friend Eva, who had walking by while she was having lunch at her favorite Bistro in Paris.

"I figure if anyone is confused about their gender they should need a great deal of encouragement just to make it through the day, don't you think? Ha Ha, Haaa." She asked her friend, Ardour, as she laughed. Ardour was seated alongside her at the small round table.

"Oui ma'dam, I agree." Ardour, responded.

Ardour was a pet of a man to Tony's mother. He was one of those suck-up-people, who gained self-confidence simply from being in the same company as the rich. He was her butler, car-washer, masseuse, dog-walker, Brazilian wax man, and lover on-call, all whenever she wanted. That day he was merely being her hang-out buddy, and tea-time pal. The fact that she would need all that in a person should provide an in to her personality type. Lillian Bryant was a diva with a capital "D." She was careless to the rest of the world. The only thing she cared about was herself. She used to have a very nice and giving spirit. Everyone says she was quite the philanthropist back in the day. If there was a big socialite event, she was the first there. If there was a gala, count on seeing Lillian Bryant in full effect and looking dazzling. She made a career out of being stunning, and the life of the party, at every affair she attended. The way I heard it, she was so deeply in love with Tony's father, that she flipped when he died.

Charles Bryant, Tony's father, was a different story. He was a quiet man who kept most of his personal life to himself. He rarely accompanied his wife to the galas and public functions. He was an investment banker, and a great provider for his family. According to Tony, he and his Dad became very close while his Mom was away at her functions. Most weekends while his Mom was out with her friends, Tony and his Dad would spend time together fishing, night-hunting, or going to movies in Germany. He mentioned that him and his Dad put together many a model airplane and ship, back in the day. Charles loved to fly. He had a pilot's license and would take Tony to all the major air shows around the world. Tony said he only flew with his Dad about three times total, because his Dad was very careful not to allow Tony to fly often at an early age. I'd say Tony's Dad sounded like a saint. After meeting his mother, I wondered how his Mom and Dad had ended up together. Charles Bryant seemed too good to want such a superficial woman like Lillian. The two of them couldn't have been more different. Now that I think of it, they were probably perfect for each other. Where she was weak, he was strong, and vice-versa. I know she had a deep love for him, because nothing else can make a person change the way she apparently did, for Tony's Dad. I realized they worked hard together, both for themselves, and for Tony. But something had gone drastically wrong with her along the way. Tony and his parents lived in Germany until his father died when he was eleven. Following the death of his father, Tony and his mother moved to Garden City, New York, where Tony lived out the rest of his teenage years. After law school at Harvard, Tony's job had placed him in Houston. He liked it, so he stayed.

This woman acted so incredibly over-protective of Tony. Maybe she hadn't properly dealt with the death of his Dad, and was over-protective for that reason, not quite sure. All I know, is she is one conniving middle-aged, BITCH. At least that's how she behaved towards me. She had tried numerous times to come between our marriage. I personally had never given her any reason to hate me, she just did. I think she would've hated whomever married her son, especially if they hadn't bowed down to her first, like I simply refused to do. In my opinion, she is in desperate need of some serious psychological therapy. She hated me so badly, that she resorted to things like witchcraft and black magic to break us up. I don't think Tony ever believed it. However, each time I'd ask him about it, he'd clam up, and would quickly change the subject. Whether or not his mom was a practicing witch, he didn't like talking about her, ever. I'd ask him simple questions about her, like, "I wonder what types of flowers your Mom prefers?" He'd respond, short and quick… "Why? I don't think she likes flowers. Don't bother getting them for her." I could always sense the hostility of his mother towards me, through him. After a phone conversation with her, he'd treat me like an unwanted groupie or something, not his wife. I can imagine how she'd bad mouth me over the phone. Tony was like an extremely obedient puppy dog around her. He obeyed her every command, even if it was at my expense. The way he mistreated me after interacting with her, was a major challenge in our marriage. I found it very hard to stay humble in this area.

I remember one time he came home after visiting with her. He found me dressed in a red teddy, laying spread eagle on our bed, with a bowl of melted milk chocolate, and whipped cream placed in between my legs. Tony walked right passed me, barely noticing. He'd been so poisoned against me by his mother, that he saw me, this beautiful woman who longed for his kisses and his touch, and thought I was the ugliest woman on the planet. How could I compete with that? I often tried to appease her, but it was to no avail. She simply hated me because I was the love of her son's life. One would think with all his accomplishments, she'd be proud of her son, and supportive of his efforts. This simply was not the case. In fact, he'd try so hard to please her, that each time he'd lose himself in the process. After experiencing her repeated rejection, he'd escape to the nearest strip club, or adult movie house, for a quick release from his super-controlling mother. He never admitted it, but I'd watch him very closely. Most times after he'd get off the phone with his mother, after she'd put all kinds of lies into his head about me, and made him feel really small, he'd go out and do his thing, anything to get a fast stress relief. Some folks deal with this type of stress by doing hard drugs. Tony's release was of the sexual nature. I never complained to him. I didn't want to add insult to injury. After talking with his mother, the poor man really didn't need me pouncing on him even more. I just recognized the relationship between he and his mother was delicate because of me, and never discussed it with him. I figured I could be the escape he needed to get away from her tantrums. However, things would began to get even worse. The harder I'd try to support him during his rocky relationship with her, the more crap she'd feed him about me. Therefore his attitude towards me, when he was around her, was always disrespectful, and unloving. She must've really painted a horrible picture of me, to him. I realize the relationship between a mother and son is special, and theirs was no exception. Her opinions are very powerful over him. Too powerful, if you ask me. She made him pay, sorely, if he dared to stand up for me in her presence. When I talked to my Mom about Tony's estranged relationship with his mother, she'd say, "I feel sorry for her. She sounds like a woman who's in a lot of pain, and is diverting all of that onto her son." Mom said she's incredibly jealous of Tony's happiness, and wanted nothing more than for me to leave him, so she could have company along with her misery. Mom also said the best defense is a good offense. She said I should treat her like the special case she is, and to never fall into her traps, never allow her antics to get to me. As extremely difficult as that had been, I still followed Mom's advice. After all, I'm not married to Lillian, I'm married to her son. I don't have to live with her. Because she's a traveler, I don't see her often. Our current monster-in-law arrangement made my job being the daughter-in-law of a mental patient, that much easier.

All in all, I had to gear up for her visit. I was sure to do some serious meditation in God's word a full week before her visit. I'd also say some very specific and special prayers for her, as well. I'd pray for her several times a day for a week before she arrived. It's somewhat comical, but all this was necessary before being around that woman. I had to re-anoint my home, especially the guest house where she'd be staying. I became holier than a nun each time Lillian came to visit my house.

I remember when Mom tried to school me on how to deal with folks with bad intentions. Someone on a TV show had been betrayed. She used that as an opportunity to explain away wickedness. We were watching a show where a woman came home one day and caught her best friend in bed with her fiancée. She'd say, "Now see, look at that. This is the perfect example of what not to do. This woman went off, too quickly. The best thing to do in that situation, is to see them in bed and walk out, leaving them to wonder about your next move. When you do that, the best friend won't know what to think, and the fiancée will want you even more. He'll want you because he notices your confidence. Because you didn't let him see you lose it, he'll admire your maturity, and actually fall deeper in love with you."

"But what if you decide you don't want to be with a cheater, mom?" I'd ask.

"If you don't want him anymore, fuck him," she'd say. Sage advice.

I can imagine Mom might've been right, but her sage advice was hard to follow, even for herself. I later discovered I wouldn't respond that way. The time I caught Tony in the backyard shed reminded me of just how any person can lose it if pushed over the edge, regardless of one's upbringing. I believe the deeper you allow yourself to fall, the harder it is to come back from the pain of being hurt; that is, if you try and handle it by yourself, without God's help. Also, I was starting to doubt what I had been taught. After both the jeep and backyard shed incidents, over time, I noticed Tony become even more cocky and ruthless. He didn't run out and do something else right away, but I could tell, he felt he'd buckled a couple more notches on his belt, proverbially speaking, when I didn't leave after his cheating. Contrary to what Mom had said about him wanting me more, after noticing my confidence from not reacting to his cheating, Tony loved to see me vulnerable. It had become a goal of his. He often wanted me to fight back in anger. He liked to see me lose it. He'd seen me work hard to be a rock hard pillar of strength, who'd always responded the correct way to everything, yet he wallowed in watching my moments of weakness. From the day I noticed his pleasure from my pain, I never let him see me sweat ever again. Ever. I'd declared war. Whatever was working in him, was not going to get the best of me, ever again. I had begun to see that the apple didn't fall far from the tree. His mother used the same exact tactics. She would go to outrageous lengths, just to piss me off, all for no good reason.

My issues with Tony's mother were particularly difficult because Lillian had inserted herself into the space that is reserved for the bonding between a husband, and his wife. In her warped thinking, she believed it her right to keep her son from bonding with another woman, other than herself. She had forced her son to bond only with her, while using tactics that ruined his resolve, as a man. This type of parental interference in a marriage, is ungodly, and evil. It means that Lillian's insecurities run so deep, that she'd decided to snatch-up her son's soul, and to hold it hostage to her, like an old lady clinching her purse, while holding it close to her chest, fearing that others would steal it away. This was imprisonment, bondage, and entrapment, for Tony. Each time he'd try and break free, so-to-speak, Lillian would threaten him with suicide, or by constantly nagging him until he relented to her desires. Her problems are quite textbook, actually. However common her problems, the mental suffering that she would impose on him, was tremendous. So much so, that he would seek desperate means of escapism. The things he would do to escape the stress of their relationship, would cause problems between he and I. The experiences of marital interference became cyclical, patternistic, and never-ending, with Lillian. No wonder the Bible says that when a man gets married, he is to cleave to his wife, and away from his family. I believe Tony's best efforts at this were always thwarted by his mother. Needless to say, she's a piece of work. I had heard of controlling mothers, before. But this one, was a very rare, and special case. Marriage is hard enough without the interference of a pestering parent. A marriage with parental interference, is almost doomed for failure from the start.

Because I pity Lillian, I'm prevented from wanting to strangle her when she's around, even though she treats me like shit. That, and all the prayer and meditation in God's word kept me from losing it on that old BITCH…

"Lillian! Oh how wonderful to see you. You look marvelous, as usual." I told her, with the fakest smile anyone had ever flashed across their face.

"Bon Jour, Mi Shari, Bon Jour. Ha, Ha. Hello lovely darling. Look at you," she said, while looking me up and down. Where'd all your baby weight, go? Seems to have disappeared, fast."

She arrived as scheduled, and on-time. I couldn't have been more disappointed. I could tell she was envious that I'd lost the weight so quickly after the baby. Had I been chunky or overweight, she was sure to fix Tony up with one of her younger chain-smoking girlfriends.

"Where's my little Antonio? Is he asleep? If so, go wake him! Tell him Grandma is here!"

"He's actually out with the nanny right now. She's taking him for a stroll around the neighborhood."

"You should be careful. Don't be so quick to trust right away. How much do you know about your help? I'd hate for her to take my baby."

She hurriedly looked at me for my reaction. Instead of watch her ignore me, while I explain the extensive background check the nanny underwent prior to working for us, I chose to smile it off. I knew she was attempting to plant seeds of doubt about Lucy. She was good at being extremely negative. I could imagine the horrid and debilitating thoughts that frequented that mind of hers.

"Oh well, dear. Where's my handsome son? Tony, Tony where are you!?" She yelled, while looking around the house and calling for him. Her yelling was very annoying.

Tony finally came downstairs.

"Hey there, Mom." They both smiled and embraced each other warmly.

"Oh, son," she boasted. She kissed and hugged him tightly.

"How've you been, my dear? You look marvelous. Aren't you two a vibrant couple? I bet the sex between you is wonderful. Ha, Ha!" She laughs.

I thought it highly inappropriate for this woman to mention my sex life, like it was a mockery. But she knew she was being offensive, and took great pleasure in doing so. I wasn't bothered. I'd been through this crap with her before. Plus, I was all prayed up. I kept my cool, even though I wanted to go crazy, on her ass. Going crazy is exactly what I knew she wanted me to do. I wasn't about to give her the satisfaction. I decided to let her look the fool all by herself, by not responding. It was challenging to do this. At the time, I hadn't known anyone, any of my friends or family members, or even any associates, who would withstand being treated the way she treated me, as her daughter-in-law. I wondered how many hours they would allow me to volunteer during the daytime at the civic center. I desperately needed an escape from this lady.

Tony had taken off. He'd scheduled a golf game with some of his pro-football buddies. I wanted to strangle him for leaving me there alone with that woman.

Before long, Lillian had gotten settled into the guest house.

"Hi, Mom, I made it," said Lillian. She'd called her mother, Tony's grandmother, letting her know that she was in town.

"I'm here at Tony's. You know these kids have a lovely home. It's so damned cozy it makes me sick. I'm telling you, there's so much love up in here, all I want to do is sleep, it's so boring," she said.

"Yes, mother dear, I was in touch with cousin Florence in Paris. I have to admit, I was very busy. I didn't have a chance to make a visit…

Oh mother, stop your fussing. I'll call her when I return. I promise to visit her, then…

Mother, how's Dad?

Mother, don't start…I'm sure you're over-reacting…O-ok mother. I gotta go…Mother... Bye, Mother…I love you, BYE!" She said, then abruptly hung up the phone.

The conversation with her mother had frustrated her. After her phone call in the guest house, she decided to walk downstairs to the kitchen to grab a glass, and a bottle of wine. Apparently, she had seen me working in the backyard through the kitchen window and had decided to join me, uninvitedly, of course.

I was out on the veranda sorting cloth swatches for the calendar project. God, I could feel her walking over from the guest house, like a dark rolling fog…

Classical music was playing softly at a low volume on the home intercom system. The music could be heard in every room of the house and throughout the backyard. Lillian had taken off her shoes, and was barefoot walking along the paved and plush landscaping in the backyard. She had gotten quite comfortable. Somehow, I continued working without allowing myself to be distracted. I braced myself for her pessimism.

"Ah dear, classical music soothes the soul," she said, while walking over. My stuff had been scattered all over the table. Sometimes I liked to work there. Normally, I'd do my craft work in the shed. It was a pleasant day out, that day. I had decided to work in my backyard, instead.

"KoShari, did I ever comment on how absolutely lovely your home is? I just love the atmosphere, here. It feels like you all are just one big happy family. So comfy, cozy…"

I looked at her and smiled, then quickly looked away while continuing to work.

"I never would've guessed that Tony would adjust well to the home life."

'Oh Lord...' I thought.

"He traveled for the most part of his young adult life. Most of the girls he dated were, shall I say, very much like me. Worldly and fabulous, Ha-ha! I will be honest; I didn't think he'd marry a black girl. I could've sworn he'd marry an Asian, or a Latina, even an Italian. I remember this little Italian girl he dated back in New York, a pretty little thing. She left to study commercial trade back home in Italy. Her family owned wine vineyards, along the Italian countryside. She was beautiful. How I miss her, so. Annabelle. That was her name. Huh. Anyhow, he settled for you, instead."

She looked down at her glass and poured the wine. I tried to be quiet and not lash back, but I wasn't successful.

"Well, Lillian, maybe Tony fell for me because I am nothing like you."

It had slipped out like the words were anxiously waiting to escape the prison that was my lips. However, I was calm, I didn't raise my voice, nor did I have a sarcastic facial expression. I kept right on working on the calendar. I didn't stop working once, while talking to her; didn't even look at her.

"Yes dear, you would say that. Truth is, Tony had been groomed for a cultured, and a worldly woman."

She was speaking to me as though I wasn't cultured, or worldly. My parents spent lots of money to send me across the world, to Switzerland one year, and to Kenya the next. If my Mom had only heard her insulting me, I know she would've popped Lillian in the mouth, right then and there.

"Lillian, Tony and I are very happy together, very happy."

"Well, that's not what I hear, sweetie. I hear he's the consummate whore. I hear he's running around on you with all sorts of women. All different colors, I might add. Looks like he's trying to get back to his roots, ha-ha."

Oh no she didn't. My God... How do I respond to that? I had no idea she knew, but she was right. I stopped sorting the swatches and looked at her, with yet another nice/nasty smile.

"Lillian, I love my husband, and he loves me. Whatever is wrong, we'll fix it. We'll work through it, together. I'm not leaving my husband, for you, or anyone else."

"Ha, ha. Aren't you a sweetheart. And you're such a devoted little wife. How sweet, pretty, peachy, perfect of you, Shari."

"Yep, that's me. Sweet, pretty, peachy, and perfect. I support my husband, no matter what. I think he needs that."

"Sure, he does. But remember that's MY son, and I know him well."

"And I don't? Tony is no longer your son, he's now my husband. He's a man. My man. And we'll be fine. Here, why don't we do this... Why don't you tell me what I can do to make your stay here more comfortable. I'd love to take you shopping."

I was strongly trying to force a turn in the subject matter, but she ignored me. What was with this woman?!

"Oh Shari, dear. Tony was my son long before he ever decided to become your husband. I know him, and what I know about him hasn't changed. I really hope you have what it takes to keep him. To be honest, I don't think you do. You seem too churchy for him," she said, right before taking a swig of her wine.

"Well Lillian, seems Tony never cared much about what you've thought. Your son seems to think you've needed professional help for quite some time. He said you had some unresolved mental issues."

I stood there looking her in the eye while leaning back on the top of my patio chair. I didn't need a drink. I had no nervous energy. This old heifer wanted to see what I was made of, so I showed her. How my Mom ignored this kind of person was beyond me. However, I did regret my nastiness after our conversation. I could see her sinking deeper and deeper into a scared little girl, with each one of my subtle insults. Powerful is the tongue of a woman scorned. In this case, two scorned women were going at it, at a highly distressed level.

"To be frank, Lillian, once you've been labeled as fragile, no one takes you seriously, thereafter. I never take you seriously, anymore. Sorry. That is what you've strived to be all your life, right… to be taken seriously? It's hard, seeing as all you've ever done was try to ruin our marriage. Your motive has always been to disrupt our happy home. Could it have been because you're envious of our love? Are you possibly…dare I say… jealous?"

"KoShari, you're taking it a bit too far, don't you think? Tony made a mistake in marrying you."

"A, mistake? Lady, you're hopeless. I won't fall into your trap. Obviously Tony and I have a love that you simply cannot comprehend, and that you envy. You know what; all those issues are yours, not ours. You'll be returning back to Paris soon. Tony and I will be getting on with our lives, just as we did before you came to visit. Do what you will to try and come between us, while you're here. You'll be forgotten after you're gone. Personally, I think it's a waste of your own energy to try so hard to interfere in someone else's married life."

"Not just someone, Tony's my baby. He'll always be my baby, till I die. You won't change that. And I'll do whatever it takes to ensure his happiness. Whatever."

Just then, Tony walked through the back door from the detached garage.

"Hello, ladies. Hey, I'd love to take you two out to dinner tonight. What'd ya say?" He asked with a smile on his face. He was a sweet man, always thinking of ways to impress his mom.

"Well, Tony, I don't know. I'm not very hungry. I don't think I'm feeling well right now. Can I get a rain check?" Asked, Lillian.

"Um, ok, if you want. I thought it would be nice, but I guess the three of us can do it some other time."

"What about you, baby?" He asked. He walked over to me, I stood up, and he grabbed me, then pulled me to him. He began kissing my neck, while rocking me back and forth.

"I have this quaint little Thai place, in mind." He kissed my ear, while making a sucking noise. By this time, the fact that I love it, is on my face. I was blushing red, and laughing. It tickled.

"You know what, on second thought, I think I will come along. Thai sounds good. I'd love a good Thai soup for dinner. You two make it seem so irresistible. Just look at you, the consummate love birds," she said.

Listen at her...Jealous, ass. She wanted to be a killjoy. That heifer…I didn't want her going to dinner with us, but for his sake I swallowed my frustration and decided to tolerate her. We went to dinner that night, and just as I thought, it was uneventful. As usual, she said things to remind Tony of his insecurities. People like her will pull you down to pump themselves up. It got on my nerves, and I'm sure it got on his, too. But we put up with it anyways, because, after all, that is his mother. He might not have said anything to her, but he knew his mother very well. He knew all about the facades she would display. For the sake of peace, he'd go along with them. He probably thought she had so many issues, that it's not worth it to play therapist and confront her. Or maybe he was downright afraid of her. Come to think of it, Tony shuns all types of confrontation. He didn't like to rock the boat. And with a mother like his, I can't say that I blame him. I thought to myself how tortuous it must've been to be raised by a woman with such a troubled mind. No wonder he had issues fooling around with other women. The man hasn't ever felt in control of his own life. I believe his lack of being in control has led him to overindulge in whatever he thinks he has control over. Apparently, he's always been a ladies' man, and a winner in the sack. He's had so much success with it, that he must feel he has great command and control over his sex life. With a mother like Lillian, he's starving for it, self-respect that is. So he keeps doing it, and doing it, as some sort of pseudo-sense of being in control of his own life. This theory seems far-fetched, but, after watching his own humanity shrink yet again, after being around his mother, I thought that I was on to something.

This is classic. Young man grows up with control-freak mom. He never gets to properly explore his own manhood because his mom, the man eater, never allowed him to be the brilliant man he was created to be. She stunted his growth, because of her own personal fears. He felt out of place and lost most of his life, because he never really felt in control of anything, ever. That explains why he's gun shy, overly so, with allowing me to exercise my right, as his wife, to demand a faithful husband. He's determined that no one will ever demand anything from him, and get it, certainly not another woman. She controlled him for so long, that she ruined his resolve, and shattered his self-esteem. Not to mention, the love that Tony and I share, in her mind, surpasses the love between her and Tony, as though she envies the fact that he places me, his wife, in a higher prong than he does, her. This threatens her, in some weird crazy momma-shit, fashion. She didn't know any better, I doubt she did any of it, intentionally. I think she did the best she could, with what she knew. This was deep. I can't yell and scream at him for what he does. His ego is extremely sensitive and fragile, due to the interaction with his mother. He doesn't cheat because he wants to be a dog. He cheats because he feels in control when he does so. Now I see why it's so important for me to support him, no matter what, I've got to be a rock. He's just now starting to fight for the right to run his own life. I must be there for him. For the sake of helping to restore this man, whom I love with all my heart, back to being the ultimate man that he was created to be. I have to yield, so that he can grow.

Does that mean I allow him to walk all over me? I'd rather look at it this way… I believe God by standing on his word, that Tony will come around and heal, at some point. Because I now realize the source of his pain, I'm not going to allow my personal feelings to interfere with the healing process. His mom messed him up, pretty badly. My leaving him won't help him heal. And I do love him too much not to help see him through this. Yes, I love myself. But rather than focus on submitting to Tony, I focus my submission on my wedding vows, and to the promise I made to God that I would stay with him, till death do us part. I want to see him feel better about himself as a man. If that means I should switch my focus off his current actions for a time, then that's what I'll do. The fact is, I'm brave enough to hang in and believe God for my husband to change, rather than to become a statistic, divorce him, and give up on my faith. Either God can do anything, or he can do nothing. If he can do anything, he can fix my broken husband and marriage, no doubt. I just happened to believe that nothing is impossible with God. Nothing. Not even, Tony. Tony's problems are typical. Tony just happens to be married to a very non-typical woman. Many men cheat on their wives for various reasons. I want my marriage, and now that I see why he's broken, I'm absolutely not leaving him. Did this mean I was trying to change my husband? I certainly didn't see it that way. I wasn't doing anything other than praying for my marriage, and my husband. God was the one responsible for changing his heart, not me.

> "Dear God, I'm glad I can finally see all this. I thank you for the wisdom. I realize it didn't come until after five years, but that's ok. I guess you needed to observe that I was gonna hang in there by trusting you and

your word, before you answered the whys. I do so love my husband, with a deep passion. I now understand why he does what he does. I get it. I'll hold on until the change comes. I promise. In Jesus name, I pray. Amen."

Chapter Fifteen

"Courtney, are you gonna be ready for our shopping weekend?"

I'd called her since she'd sent an email asking if I was interested in attending a fashion show in Milan. She liked to go to the parties, and she also liked the men. After the fashion show, she wanted to fly back to New York for some shopping in the fashion district.

"Did you contact Alicia?" I asked Courtney, while waiting for the baby to get his massage at the baby salon.

"Shari, Alicia is busy dealing with the details of her divorce. I doubt she'll want to come."

"If she's going through all that, she needs a girlfriend weekend. This would be a great get-a-way for her. Plus, I haven't seen her in a while. Tell her it's about time we all got together. It's been too long."

"You can call her if you want, KoShari. Maybe she'll listen to you."

"Courtney, you know how busy I am. You call her. You guys are closer than she and I, anyways."

"And I'm not busy? I'll try. Kiss my baby. I'm off to my meeting. Toodles!" I truly hoped Alicia could make it. I really missed her.

Lucy and I had our usual discussion about lil Tony, and my plans for him while I was away. I shared my plans with Tony, and he gave a green light. I didn't know what I'd do if I didn't have my girlfriend weekends. My recent mood swings suggested it was in Tony's best interest that I get-away from the everyday, for a few days. Also, my Mom ended up canceling her Martha's Vineyard plans due to some sudden function with Dad. I was disappointed when she did that, but at the same time, elated, because I was now free to spend time with my girls in New York without the burden of caring for my Mom while there. Basically, I could hit them New York streets without Mom judging me. I was super-excited about that.

I arrived in New York at 6:00pm, Thursday evening. Courtney sent a driver to pick me up from the airport. She owned a beautiful two story apartment on the Upper East Side, right in the heart of Manhattan. She was living the life, but didn't realize it. She was lonely, inside. I could sense it without her saying. I arrived at Courtney's, walked up, and rang the bell. Alicia answered. I was so surprised, and happy to hear her voice. Alicia instructed the door man to escort me up to Courtney's apartment.

"Alicia! Oh my God! You came!" I said, while getting off the elevator, which led directly into Courtney's apartment.

"Shari, sweetie, I've missed you. Give me a hug! Girl I hear you got the baby, the career, the husband, the house, the whole nine yards. Aren't you a regular suburban wanna-be!"

"No, dear," I laughed. "I'm not the suburban type."

"Well, come on in. We've got to catch up. Courtney isn't back yet, she had some major contract review tonight. Just leave your bags. I'll have her housekeeper take them to your room."

"Shari, you must tell me all about your wonderful life. What's up with you?"

We walked into Courtney's living room, where Alicia had poured us both a cup of hot green tea to sip while catching up.

"Alicia, I'm good. I'm still beautiful. I'm in shape. My baby is healthy. My husband is fine, as fuck…"

"Fine, huh? I hear he runs around on you. Girl you shouldn't let him do that to you. You gotta divorce him. Don't let him dog you out like that. Ralph started showing himself. I had to cut him loose."

"Alicia, but you two seemed so in love. I just knew you'd be together forever. I didn't think you'd let anything come between you two. Nothing."

"Yeah, well that was the fairy tale. Real life kicked in, and I found out how weak he was. I just lost interest. I told him if he had a better offer on the table, to take it. So he did. Some chick who worked at his health club. I told him that his loss would be someone else's gain. Wouldn't you know it, my divorce isn't even final yet, and that tramp is already telling him she's pregnant? You'd think he saw it coming. Oh well, what a waste." She looked away at the thought of him, while taking a sip of her tea.

"Anyways, I've already got a new man. This guy I work with, named, Seth."

"Seth? What kinda name is that?"

"I know, right? I think it's cool. He says he was named for one of the angels in the Bible. And Shari, he IS an angel! I mean, he takes me on midnight escapades… he surprises me with jewelry… we go on sexual scavenger hunts… I dig him. Plus, he's a head partner at my new firm in LA. I'd say my future with him is bright, girl!" She laughs.

"But how does he make you feel?"

"Ok, Shari. I see you're still little Ms. Analyzer. Shari, I know what I'm feeling isn't love, just yet, but I'm having a damned good time with the man."

"How do you know he's not already with someone else, or several other people? Chances are, if he treats you that special and spontaneous, he's probably doing the same for someone else."

"What a cynic, you are. Maybe he is, and maybe he's not. I don't care. As I said, I'm not in love. I tried love and it flat-out didn't work. I see nothing wrong with a little bump and grind. Besides, why are you so staunch? Isn't your man cheating on you?"

I was embarrassed to say yes and feel like a fool. So I didn't allow myself to…

"Alicia, honey… I've decided to gather the courage to stay with my man. I refuse to become another statistic. I know Tony is still very much in love with me. I've decided to fight for our love, God's way."

"God's way?? So what, you've gone churchy on me, now?" What was with this word, "churchy?" Lillian had said the same thing, before.

"No dear, I'm not churchy. I don't even go to church. I've decided to believe God to change Tony."

"I don't know what you've heard, but my pastor says even God cannot change a person if they don't want to change, and I believe that. Ralph and I were both in church when he decided to leave me for his personal trainer. I prayed for Ralph all the time, but nothing happened."

"Really? Well, I just don't believe God can fail."

"No one is calling God a failure. I know there were things I was supposed to do. I just couldn't see myself doing them. I was not about to turn into some weakling that allowed her man to walk all over her. I didn't understand why God wanted me to lay over and play the good submissive wife, while Ralph was sexing up some other woman. I just couldn't do it."

"Sounds to me like you've got it backwards. It's easy to walk away when he's acting up. What's hard, is to stay and do what God says to do. Seems to me the weak one leaves, and the stronger one stays and obeys God. I think it takes an unbelievable amount of strength and faith to stay, pray, and wait for the man, or whomever to come around. Who knows, there may have been changes you needed to make, Alicia. Unless you've matured past it, you had no problems reading a person quickly, and making them feel like your opinion is the only one that matters. If you were that way with Ralph, maybe that's why he sought someone else, that he thought would listen. Alicia things are not always so cut and dry."

"Who you tellin? Yeah. Maybe counseling would've helped to save us. Anyways, it's too late, now. What about you? I remember you being the sweetest one of us all. Why do you think I've always called you, sweetie? You never had those kinds of issues, Shari. What's Tony's problem?"

"Alicia I'm not perfect, but you're right. I don't see there is anything I'm doing to make Tony stray. I think he had some issues growing up with his mother."

"What issues? You don't think she was crazy, do you?"

"Well... I think his mom was a control freak, and basically zapped his manhood early on. I believe he cheats to try and get that manhood back."

"Wait-a-minute, not Tony! You mean, Mr. Suave, and debonair, Tony? He appears to be emotionally in-tact."

"Yeah, well. Looks can be deceiving."

"You're my girl, and I love you, no matter what I hear about your man in these streets. You let me know how this thing with God works out, ok?" She said with a smile.

"Sure, I will. And as for you, once Ralph wakes up from his daze, he'll realize the jewel he left behind."

"Huh. I wouldn't bet on it, but whatever..."

Just then, Courtney walked in. We gave each other a huge, lengthy threesome hug.

The next morning we caught a red-eye to Milan, Italy, after hours of staying up and having fun in true girlfriend-pajama party style. While both tired and sleepy, we arrived at the airport at 4:00am that morning, overflowing with anticipation about the coming days, together.

The fashion show's production was first class. The clothes were attractive, some eclectic, and some were just plain trashy. We sat at our table laughing and joking about the crappy rags, and applauded the quality stuff. We couldn't help but compare the healthy, versus unhealthy models. Some looked like walking sticks, and death warmed over, but others were incredible.

While about the business of enjoying ourselves, suddenly from out of nowhere, three white roses appeared. A waiter had brought them to our table, and said they were from the table in the corner. He pointed to a single gentleman sitting alone at a small table near one of the exit doors. From what I could see, the man was striking. He had thick and refined curly hair, was tall, and was dressed to the nine. He was in a light gray silk shirt, covered by a long-sleeved white linen Armani jacket, and jeans; as fine as they come. The gentleman raised his glass when he caught our acknowledgment. We raised ours in thanks, then swiftly went back to our shenanigans.

I was watching the show when I noticed, out the corner of my eye, the generous man who sent us the flowers. I remember thinking how handsome he was. He looked to be an Italian man in his early forties, with a little salt in his hair, and go-tee. Indeed he looked my kinda sexy.

I'd heard of fascinating things happening with Italian men at the fashion show after-parties. With the music egging me on in the background, my mind began to wonder. I imagined us walking along the beach barefoot, with wine glasses in our hands. I saw him take me into his arms, and gently lay me down into the sand. Just then, thoughts of Tony and what he might be doing abruptly interrupted the blissful fantasy. God only knew where he was, or who he was with. It had seemed the fantasy of spending time with this man, felt justified, until…

"Excuse me, madam. The gentleman would like a word with you," said the waiter, to Courtney. I was shocked. I had wanted him to be interested in me.

"Ask him if he would be so kind as to come over and speak with me in person," she told the waiter.

"Very well," he said before walking away to deliver the message.

Five minutes later…

"Hello, ladies. Might I comment on your beauty tonight? You are all gorgeous women. I particularly noticed you, Madam." He gently took Courtney's hand and kissed it, while gazing into her eyes. Courtney could not look away. She was in a trance, mesmerized. He grabbed her hand even tighter, and led her away from the table.

"There she goes," I whispered to Alicia.

I believe Italian, Middle Eastern, and Israeli men, are some of the most handsome men in the world. They possess the most beautiful dark olive skin, and thick and luscious wavy and curly hair, I'd ever seen. I guess I have a thing for thick hair, and good skin… I admit, I was disappointed he hadn't come for me. Maybe it was a good thing he hadn't. I'm sure I would have done something I'd later regret. I know that sounds silly with all that

Tony had done. I'd be repressed to have any regrets, after all of his cheating. But I've never had that carelessness thing working. I simply could not cheat on him with another man. If so, I was sure to feel ugly inside. The conviction would be intense, and conviction outweighed temptation in my eyes. I thought the opposite was true for Tony. For him, temptation outweighed conviction. Anyways, I was secretly sad to myself that day when the gentleman didn't come for me.

Later that night, Alicia and I were asleep in our hotel room. We'd gotten a plush three bedroom suite with a large living room. The bedrooms were outfitted with immaculate Italian designs, and had unique Italian silk and lace curtains, in deep hombre colors of red, silver, and charcoal. Each room had its own bathroom.

Courtney came bursting through the doors at 1:00am. "Wake up you homebodies! You can sleep back home! I think I'm in love. Again!"

I came outside my bedroom door, straggling over to the couch. I was tired. Alicia followed.

"Ladies, have you two gotten old? What is it with you! You're missing the highlight of our trip. The big after party is downstairs. Come on you guys. I got this suite because it's near the party scene. Get up, you old hags!"

"Courtney, unless you're drunk you can clearly see with your eyes, that we're awake. Can't you see that, dear?" I said.

"I'm from the city that never sleeps. A good party is worth a little crow's feet! Besides, I gotta talk about this wonderful man. His name is DiMaggio, and he, is, a, DREAM!"

"First of all, you are not from the city that never sleeps. Stop claiming New York, hun." I said. Alicia fell to the floor in laughter.

We carried on like teenagers, like giddy school girls who were discussing their first crushes.

"He is so kind. And get this, he's crazy about me! He said he's never seen such beauty in his life, said it was love at first sight. No man has ever said that to me before. And to think, my love was waiting in Italy all along! God is awesome!"

"Uh oh… she brought spirituality into it. She must be feeling something strong," I told Alicia.

Alicia responded by holding her head down and looking up at me from the top of her glasses.

"The weird thing is, I feel it too. It's mutual. You guys, I think I'm really in love," she told us. She fell back onto the couch and let out a big sigh.

"Well, Courtney. What will you tell your girlfriend back in New York, Ha Ha," laughed Alicia.

"Alicia, you know that was just a phase. I'm over the lesbian thing. But Shari, you were right. There ain't nothing like some good old-fashioned one hundred percent pure dick, to get you through a cold night. DiMaggio and I are meeting for breakfast in the morning. He wanted to have a late dinner with me tonight, but I thought that was a bit forward."

"Girl, go for it. I know you will," I told her.

I was secretly envious of her and DiMaggio, but I got over it after seeing how satisfied she seemed. It made me happy that she was able to feel the high that comes from meeting someone special.

Courtney had convinced us to get dressed, and after a few foamy Italian espressos, we left the room and headed to the party downstairs. It was wild. People were dancing everywhere, up on tables, in the balconies, on the bars. Truly I hadn't partied that hard since before I got married. Twas some much needed fun with my girls.

After accomplishing what we'd set out to do on our trip to Italy, we slept on the entire plane ride back to New York. We made it back to Courtney's around noon. I thought about Tony and lil Tony, and decided to call them. I so hoped someone would answer the house phone because, to my surprise, I'd missed my husband and baby, and couldn't wait to get home to the both of them.

"Hello," that damned Lillian had answered our phone when I called.

"Hi, Lillian. What a surprise. How are you?" What I really wanted to know was, what the hell was she still doing in town, and furthermore, why was she answering my house phone?

"Wonderful. Couldn't be better. I decided to stay over and have a couple visits with my family before heading back to Paris. Are you enjoying yourself? How are the girls? Better yet, how was Milan?"

"Milan was the best. We're all having a great time. Is Tony or Lucy around?"

"No, dear. Tony had a lunch date, and lil Antonio is out with Lucy."

'Lunch DATE?' I thought to myself. I was quickly reminded of the person I was speaking to, and decided not to entertain her with any further questions, in case she was purposely attempting to send my mind racing about Tony's lunch date.

"Ok. Tell them I called, and I'll be home tomorrow. Continue making yourself at home, there. I'll talk with you later. Goodbye, Lillian."

"Goodbye, dear."

Boy, that was shocking. I hadn't expected Lillian to still be in town, especially since she had mentioned needing to return to Paris for an important meeting that had been scheduled months in advance. I thought about calling Tony on his cell, but thought again. I didn't want to alarm him of any unnecessary worries about Lillian while I was away; that would have made him uncomfortable. I also had lots, and lots of serious shopping to do the day before heading back. There was no need to continue trying to reach him just for a hello, and check-in.

Alicia and I went shopping in Manhattan that day. Courtney?? Oh Miss Courtney remained in Milan for one more day to be with DiMaggio. She had quickly abandoned us. Getting together was her brilliant idea, and yet she wasn't around much. Oh well, she must've really fallen for the guy. I'd never heard or seen Courtney respond that way to any man. Even the married guy, Bryce, had to chase her a lot longer than DiMaggio had. I couldn't say her actions were unheard-of. I was well aware of the process of falling in love. I was very happy for her, that she was able to experience the life-altering feeling of falling in love. I thought I'd be the one to end up with the older man. It was Courtney who actually did.

We walked the streets of Manhattan after leaving Bergdorf's. Alicia had found a must-have scarf, and a pair of female golden cuff links in the shape of bees. I bought a beautiful white cotton flare skirt, veiled by a thin turquoise silk covering. It had an off-white petty coat underneath. I also bought a tight sleeveless tan and light brown Gucci t-shirt. My next mission, was to find a pair of peach colored snake skin three inch wedges, the kind that strap up the leg, to go along with the skirt.

We were approaching the Coach store, when I noticed this handsome guy getting out of a cab, and walking our way. At first glance, the guy looked as handsome as Denzel Washington. His complexion was the color of rich, smooth, black coffee. He was about 6'3", slim, and buff in the pecs. His hair was dark and clean cut. He had thick eyebrows, and very defining facial features. And then, he smiled. I've always been a sucker for a man with a nice smile. When I saw his smile, I immediately thought of Tony's warm smile. However, the thought was quickly replaced with the image of Tony and the woman in the craft shed that dreadful day I caught him. Therefore, I quickly refocused my attention back on the guy. I noticed there was no wedding ring on the left ring finger. I had studied this guy down to the detail. His look alone was luring, and had warranted the examination. After gaping him down for about three minutes, he noticed me watching him. There's a glance that passes between a man and a woman that communicates louder than words. This fleeting look is instantly familiar to both men and women. He knew he had captured my attention, and I knew I had captured his. He watched me until our eyes met. He cut his phone conversation short, and started walking towards me. Alicia was busy checking out the purses in the Louie Vuitton store window, when he walked up.

"Hi. I'm Ian. I noticed you from across the street. You ladies out shopping today?"

"Yes, we are. I'm KoShari, and this is Alicia."

"Nice to meet you both."

Alicia looked at me, strangely. She hadn't noticed the connection Ian and I had made before he approached us. She didn't know what to think about the guy. She was baffled at first, and then looked at me, as though she had suddenly caught on to Ian and I's flirtations. Once she figured it out, she gave a look of support, as though she was proud I'd allowed myself to become interested in someone other than Tony.

"Hi Ian, nice to meet you. Uh, Shari I'm gonna price this purse. I'll meet you back at Courtney's. Here are the keys. Check you later, sweetie," said Alicia.

Alicia gave me a corner eye glance, as though she was communicating, 'you go girl, you better jump on that,' with her eyes. I smiled in acknowledgment of the unspoken message.

"Ok Alicia, see ya," I told her, as she walked into the Louie Vuitton shop.

"So Ian, I like your name. It's different. You live in Manhattan?"

"Yes. I moved here last year from Arizona, on an extended consulting assignment, in The City."

We began walking down the street together. I was as forward as I've ever been with a man. Before I realized it, I'd welcomed this man into a dallying match with me, while I was still wearing my wedding ring, I might add. Who knows what he was thinking. Maybe he thought I was looking for a one night stand, or an escort. The more I thought about it, as Ian and I walked down the street, the stupider I felt about being so anxious to toy with him in the first place.

"So KoShari, what are you doing in Manhattan?"

By this time I was feeling regret, and was thinking I must have looked desperate. I tried to turn him off by mentioning my husband and son, hoping he'd go away before realizing just how spacey and confused I actually was.

"I'm visiting friends. I live in Houston with my husband and six month old son."

"So, you're getting a much needed vacation, then. I can understand that. Tell you what… Some friends and I are getting together tonight at Londel's in Harlem for some dinner and jazz. Why don't you grab a couple friends and come join us. We like meeting new people. It should be fun."

"Sure. I'm in town until tomorrow. I'll check with my girls. They won't mind. I think it'll be great. How often do you meet people on the streets in one hour, and go to dinner with them the next? You seem cool enough. You don't look like a serial killer, ha ha."

"I meet people all the time in these streets. Then it's settled, hope to see you tonight. Again, it was nice meeting you."

"You, too. Londel's in Harlem at 8:00pm. Got it. See you there."

I watched as he walked away. He was sexy like a super model. He struck me as the type who knew it, too. I liked those lips, all luscious and all. I headed into the Louis Vuitton store to find Alicia and give her the big news.

"Alicia, he was cute, huh?"

I interrupted her eying a sunset yellow Louis Vuitton purse that she had been salivating over.

"Yes, Shari. A real cutie. What's his story?"

"He's an Information Technology consultant temporarily here on assignment. He invited us for dinner tonight at Londel's in Harlem, said he and some friends are getting together. You got plans? I thought it would be nice, for our last night here, to get out with some new people. Plus, Courtney should be back by now. You know how she loves that sort of thing. I'll call her and see if she's interested."

"Sure Shari, sounds like fun."

"Ma'am, I'd like to see the Indigo blue wallet that matches this purse," Alicia told the store clerk.

Courtney, Alicia, and I arrived at Londel's at 8:20pm, a tad late for dinner, but really, right on time. Ian spotted us walking through the door, and gestured for us to come over to their table. I saw him telling the waiter to add chairs for us. A very lively jazz band was playing Chuck Magione in the back drop. The lights were low, and there were a few couples dancing on the small dance floor. The place was decorated with soft hues and candlelight, which made the ambiance urbane, and chill. I could smell the scent of cinnamon and lamb chops. It was subtle, and it didn't overwhelm my taste buds, or clash with the music and light dancing. As we approached the table, we saw that there were four men seated altogether; everyone taking on the personality of the stronger man at the table, which was clearly Ian.

"KoShari, is it?" Asked Ian, hesitantly.

"Yes. Hi, Ian. I believe you met Alicia earlier. This is Courtney," I told him, while pointing Courtney's way. Of course she smiled and spoke to everyone. One thing I prided myself on, was how friendly my crew and I, were. We never appeared stuck-up when meeting new people, especially when we were all together. Well, at least not at first.

"Hi Courtney, nice to meet you," said Ian. He scanned her body, admiring her perfect shape, and naturally long curly hair.

"Ladies this is Luke, Greg, and that's Ahmad."

After everyone said their hellos, we sat down at the table. Ian was sure to seat himself next to me.

"What are you ladies drinking, tonight?" Asked, Ian.

"I'll have a red wine," said Courtney.

"I'll take one of those," said Alicia.

"I'm ok. I'm watching my weight. I'll take a water with lime," I said.

"Watching your weight? Girl, you fine!" Said, Greg.

"Well, thank you."

"Anytime, sweetheart. Say...What's your workout plan? I'm looking for something new to do, at the gym. I've been doing Pilates and strength training for a while. I'm ready for something different."

"Well, I'm afraid I can't help you. I don't work out much, just running. I meet with a speed coach every once in a while. I mainly watch what I eat. However, I've heard about a new soul cycle gym here in Harlem. I hear it's lots of fun."

"Oh, yeah? I'll have to check it out," said Ahmad.

"Dude, please. I can't see you cycling at the gym. Who are you, Lance Armstrong?" Said, Luke. Everyone at the table let out a controlled chuckle.

After the band finished, the DJ laid an up-tempo track. I was swaying side-to-side in my seat.

"You look like you want to dance. Would you like to?" Ian, asked.

"Sure."

He grabbed my hand and led the way to the dance floor. Ian reminded me of an Islander I met once while vacationing with my parents in Cabo San Lucas, when I was fourteen years old. There was this teenager, Jock. He had a pocket full of energy, and wasn't so stingy with it. He pulled me into a limbo contest, that I was too shy to participate in on my own. He was all smiles, all the time. He knew just what to do to make you enjoy yourself around him. He had nothing but compliments and optimism for the vacationers he met. Likewise, Ian too was all smiles and full of fun-loving energy. On the dance floor, he became a jester. Laughing and joking about my dance moves. In one moment, he'd say, "you go girl, groove on." Then next, he'd ask, "Ok now, what was that? Don't get too wild on me," with a laugh.

That night I forgot all about Tony and my problems back home. It felt like I had been lifted in levitation about 70 feet off the ground, and was caught up in the amazement of it all. We all left Londel's in loud laughter. I noticed how not one of us was ready for the night to end. Even though we'd all just met, we walked the streets of Harlem like old friends, side-by-side, cackling away. Sure we all might've had our own baggage, but it didn't matter that night. We'd all forgotten about our own life challenges, and just enjoyed each other among thirty-something friends.

No one threw out strong advances to anyone else. We'd had one big, great and careless, good time. Ian had talked us into walking to Greg's place, which was a couple blocks from Londel's. Along the way he began telling us a story about a friend of theirs who, after being bored one night, decided to make crank calls to all of his buddies. Luke, Greg, and Ahmad told of how Ian was caught up and got carried away with who he thought was a club bouncer, that he'd pissed off one night at a club. Ian was so frightened, they all thought he was gonna call the police. Apparently Ian had gotten so scared, thinking the guy had found his address, that he called Greg crying like a baby, terrified the bouncer was coming to get him.

We were crying from laughter. In fact, our stomach muscles were so tight from all the laughter, we could barely walk to Greg's brownstone. The girls and I spent another hour at Greg's. After that, we called a cab to take us back to Courtney's.

Before I left, Ian was sure to exchange contact information with me. He said he couldn't remember the last time he'd had so much platonic fun in a group setting. He suggested we all take a trip together, maybe a cruise to the Caribbean, or to the newly travel-friendly, Cuba. I didn't gawk at the idea. I admitted something magical had occurred between us all, that night. I couldn't deny it. It felt rare. Of course I agreed, and had keyed my contact information into his phone. I wanted to remember our time together, and would've jumped at the chance to do it all again.

My flight arrived on-time in Houston, that Saturday afternoon. The weather was humid, sticky, and cloudy, with a peep of sunshine, typical Houston climate. I was tired from the night before, but there were absolutely no regrets. It was the perfect ending to a lovely, lovely, extended weekend with good friends. I caught a cab to the house. I wanted to surprise Tony, and lil Tony. I was all set to show off the rested and refreshed version of myself. They would reap the benefits of my good mood. I couldn't wait to wrap my arms, first, around my husband, and then, my baby. I was sure to drown them both in non-stop kisses. I was struggling to get my keys in the front door, when the nanny opened it for me.

"Hello Mrs. Bry-ant welcome home," said Lucy.

"Hi, Lucy. Where's Mr. Bryant?"

I heard Lillian talking in the formal dining room. To my surprise, there was Tony, Lillian, and some woman I'd never seen before, seated at my dining table. She looked a little young to be one of Lillian's friends.

"Hello, Shari. Welcome home, dear. Come on in. I want you to meet someone. KoShari, this is Annabelle. Annabelle this is KoShari," said Lillian. Lillian had a huge grin on her face about the size of Texas.

"Hello, Annabelle. Nice to meet you. I've heard great things about you, from Lillian."

Tony sat alongside Annabelle, looking aloof.

'What the hell?' I, thought. Apparently, Lillian had invited Annabelle to my home while I was away. I was still high from the vacation and didn't even bat an eyelash at her disrespect. I was so accustomed to her behavior by now, one could say that I'd become desensitized to her crap. What a bitch, and for no good reason at all. 'Fuck, Lillian,' I thought to myself. I proceeded to treat Annabelle like any other welcomed guest in our home.

Chapter Sixteen

The grass was damp while walking to the burial grounds. Tony was close, walking alongside me, with one arm around my shoulders, and the other holding up the large umbrella over us and the baby, whom I was pushing the stroller. Grief had its grip on me. I tried very hard to hide the tears streaming down my face under a low brimmed black hat, with a small lace veil. I noticed Mom and Dad walking several feet ahead of us. Mom could barely walk upright. If Dad wasn't there to hold her up, surely she would've fallen to the ground. I saw her pain, and it was deep. She hardly cried. She was in a state of serious shock. Her head hung low, looking straight towards the ground, as though it was too heavy for her neck to uphold. I wanted to be strong for her, but I doubted that I could. We approached the grave site and took our seats on the front row. The tented seats filled awfully fast, within the first five minutes. Those without seats had to crowd around the tent, with umbrellas, to shield themselves from the hard pouring rain. There were at least two hundred people in attendance at Nana's funeral, a healthy crowd.

"As we gather around to celebrate the life of Ethel Lynn Dubaki, we are reminded of the fight in her. Indeed she was a warrior. A fighter, not in the sense of a physical fighter like, Muhammad Ali. No. She was well aware of the spiritual world. She did her warring in the spirit realm. Whenever she came around, all hell would run. That woman knew who she was in our Lord and Savior Jesus Christ. God said in his Word to cast out demons, heal the sick, cleanse the leper, and bring sight to the blind. Ethel used her faith in the Lord to do all she could, to make a difference in this world. Jesus also said to love one another, as He has loved us. This, she did with all of her heart, to everyone she encountered. It was her love for others and each one of us that has caused so many of us to pay our respects here, today. Never in all my years, have I witnessed a life lived out loud and in color, so vibrant and purposeful, the way Ethel lived," said the pastor.

Several people in the crowd affirmed his words in agreement with groanings of confirmation.

He continued, "So before we place her body into the ground to go back to that from which it came, we'd like to hear from some of you on how she's impacted your life. Please keep it brief, there are many of you."

I looked at Mom to see if she wanted to speak. She made no eye contact. She was rocking back and forth while staring into mid-air. After I realized she couldn't do it, I hopped up to be the first to give remarks. I gathered myself, and looked out into the audience.

"To me, Nana was a rock. Someone I could depend on to give me Godly advice. Life can be hard, we all know that." I looked at Tony. He couldn't get himself to make eye contact with me. I continued looking at him, while speaking.

"Yes, life can position us to make some tough choices. Somehow during those tough times in my life, Nana would call out of the blue to check on me. Not fully knowing all that might've been going wrong, she would encourage me not to ever quit, or to give up. She said there's always hope in Jesus Christ. She would tell me, when all else fails, find peace in listening to your heart. And then obey it."

I began to look at the others in the crowd.

"What courageous advice. That was my Nana, the most courageous person I've ever known. I am glad that her strength lives on in me, and in my mother. Nana is the happiest she's ever been, right now. She's in heaven with her Lord. Realizing this, makes her home going bearable."

I looked up to the sky as if to speak directly at Nana, herself…

"Nana," I smiled. "I hope you catch all the fish in heaven. Thank you for always being there. I love you, forever."

As I finished my speech I noticed tears streaming down Mom's face. There was no facial expression, only tears, flowing and falling, onto her dress. It hurt me to see my mother so sorrowful. I knew she and Nana had been as close as any mother and daughter ever were. Nana meant the world to Ma. She was a very powerful force that Ma had grown attached to over the years. They spoke on the phone, daily. They even had private fishing trips, that I only heard about from time to time. I don't think there was ever anyone on this earth that Ma trusted, as much as she did my Nana. Not even Dad had a shot at that one. Nana had pushed Ma to become the best at whatever she did. As a result, Ma attributed all of her success to her faith in God, and to Nana. Though she suffered in grief that day, I knew in time she would recover successfully. There is always recovery from any kind of pain. After my speech, I walked to my mother and gave her a long and endearing hug. I was hoping to remind her how strong Nana had always taught us to be. My goal was to prevent her from slipping into a deep depression. Somehow, she drew some strength from my hug. We looked into each other's eyes, and smiled.

Everyone met at Nana's house after the burial. Nana lived in North MacGregor, a subdivision in the third ward of Houston. She had outright refused to leave her three story mansion in the historical black neighborhood. She loved her home, her friends and neighbors, and her close-knit community. Ma tried several times to get Nana to move in with her. She constantly refused. She'd say, she couldn't leave her garden, or her bridge club girlfriends. Nana maintained an immaculate home. Selling it would be no problem at all. Initially, we all took pause about placing it on the market right away after her death. It carried all of Ma's childhood memories, and mine as well. However, the decision was made to sell the house within the year, and to use the money to reinvest it into Dubaki-Alexander Chandeliers, and into the 3rd ward community revitalization projects.

Ma and I arrived thirty minutes prior to everyone else to prepare the food. Dad and Tony stood outside, greeting the guests as they began to trickle in. By now, the rain began to subside, and the sun had come out over the clouds.

Ma was in the kitchen preparing food. She had gone through a drawer looking for a serving spoon, when she came across a note from Nana that was addressed to her. Puzzled, she looked at the note and wondered what it could be about.

"Shari, come here," she called out to me.

"Yes. What is it?"

"Look at this. What do you think it's about?"

"Don't know," I said. I wiped my hands in the cup towel. Ma slowly unfolded the hand-written note that was written on Nana's script letterhead.

"I'm happy now Janis, happier than ever before. Please don't cry for too long. I'll see you again, someday. I love you so much, my dear."

Ma began to tear-up. She placed her fingers over her mouth as she continued reading:

"Take good care of your family. Love them as I've loved you, and your father. Teach KoShari all the secrets I've taught you about life. Tell her when she's ready to learn, just as I did you. Teach her not to let go of her husband. Their relationship is God's will. I made you something. Go to my bedroom and get the freshly crocheted blanket from the chest that sits at the foot of my bed. I secretly worked on it for two years. Just finished it last week. Enjoy, my love. Till we meet again, Mom."

My mother both laughed and cried at the same time. She put down the note and ran upstairs to find her surprise. I ran behind her, following along.

She opened Nana's bedroom door, and got the brightly colored blanket out of the chest that was located at the foot of Nana's bed, just as the note had specified. The blanket was in brilliant shades of pink, peach, white, lime green and light blue. Ma fully unfolded the blanket. To her surprise, Nana had crocheted a picture of the two of them hugging, cheek-to-cheek and with big smiles, in the center of the blanket. Ma laughed out loud.

"Shari, look at this! The woman never ceases to amaze me. Even after death she still has a way of getting to the best of me. Oh, mother," said Ma, with a big sigh.

"Buzz!!" Just then an alarm clock went off in Nana's bedroom. Ma and I jumped and gasped in amazement. The noise had startled us both. We glanced at the clock, and then back at one another. We burst into a loud and uncontrollable laughter. Without saying, we both knew that was Nana. Nana never liked missing out on laughing with the two of us. That buzz was Nana's way of letting us know she is still, and always will be, with us.

Sometime, like maybe four months after the funeral, I decided to run at Hermann Park on a particular Sunday afternoon. My usual was Memorial Park. I hadn't run at Hermann in a while. I decided on the different scenery, as well as a run through the Japanese Gardens there at Hermann. I'd also remembered a local jazz band was performing at the Miller Outdoor Theatre for one of their "Sunday in the Park" performances. I thought it would be nice to have a run all to myself, and then enjoy a jazzy Sunday afternoon in the park afterwards.

Going on those much needed self-day retreats had given me great peace of mind, I always looked forward to them. I arrived at Hermann Park around noon. I parked in the front parking lot of the Museum of Natural Sciences. The parking lot was directly adjacent to the Miller Outdoor Theatre, and was a convenient place to easily return to the car, after the run. The park was packed full, with families and lovers walking everywhere. All were enjoying the semi-overcast day. I noticed a huge Hispanic family having a bar-b-cue at one of the public grills in the back of the theatre. The theatre sat sunken in the dell of a tall and steep hill. At the top of the hill were tall oak trees, and picnic benches with matching waste cans standing beside them. There was beautiful greenery, and gardens all around. Fifty yards west of the theatre was a duck pond that was sized a little bit larger than a football field. The ducks were several different colors, and had fat bellies from the illegal feedings they received on a daily basis. They wade in the water slowly and unassuming, appearing content in their little lives.

Yes, I'd say it was a perfect day out. I decided to run down the hill to check out the concert in the sunken theatre. There were people everywhere in the theatre area. They were dancing in the grass, and cueing in the pits that were strategically placed about seventy five yards from the theatre seats. I was enjoying the moment when I spotted Tony with some old co-workers from afar. That day, Tony had told me he needed to do some research at the bookstore. He said he'd be there all afternoon. I was surprised to find him at the park, and appearing to be having such a great time. He was walking towards a group of women with a Heineken in one hand, while gesturing with the other. When he arrived at the group of women, he grabbed one from behind. It was Rosie, ole' hypnotic-eyed, Rosie. He grabbed her and began to nibble on her neck while holding her. Of course she stood there receiving his scrumptious goodness with her eyes closed, while smiling from ear-to-ear. He'd wrapped one arm around her tiny twenty-two inch waist, and the other, the one holding the Heineken, around her neck. She placed both her hands on his forearm, the one that was around her neck. They began to slowly rock side-to-side like two infatuated lovers. Man, was her face gleaming. Apparently, he knew she was blushing up a storm, and loving every minute of it. He had a look of gloated confidence on his face, as if to say, "I got this woman, and I know it." I was shocked and ashamed that my husband was all over this other woman, in front of so many people who knew we were still married, and living together.

"What is wrong with this fool?" I said out loud, while staring at him with my hands on my hips. I was too angry to confront him. Not now, I'd convinced myself. Instead, I decided to continue my run, as painful as it was, to do so. My rational mind had resolved that running was the best thing to do in this situation, and it was right. I ran the two mile track twice, at a nine minute per mile pace, with tears streaming down my face. It didn't matter. Onlookers wouldn't have known if they were tears, or sweat.

The kind of pain I felt, was indescribable. A thought entered my mind to run out into the street in front of a fast-moving train on the rail system. I couldn't believe it, but I wanted to die on that gorgeous Sunday afternoon. Somehow, the pain had ignited a desire to no longer want to live. It was excruciating. After the hard run, I slowed and finally stopped. I stooped over, placing my hands on my knees while breathing heavily. When I caught my breath, I fell to my knees with my head down. Fortunately I was in a shaded area with not many onlookers. I imagined that I must've looked pretty pitiful to the people around me.

"OH, GOD!" I yelled while breathing heavily.

"I can't do this! This is too much!" I screamed, while crying hard, and uncontrollably.

"Take this away, please! Don't allow this to happen to me! Not like this, not like this," I repeated.

I fell to begin sitting on top of my legs. As my crying slowed and I started sniffling, I was suddenly conscious of the passersby around me. I looked up to the sky searching for answers and relief from the grief. None came. I gathered my composure and wiped my eyes. I arose slowly and walked to the nearest bench to stretch. While stretching, I thought of Ma and what she might've been doing in that moment. She was a comforting thought during that horrid time. I decided to call her on my cell phone on the way back home. After all, now that Nana was gone, she was all I had in the way of a confidant about my issues with Tony.

I found myself driving to her house without thinking. I was unconsciously falling apart, and wasn't doing a very good job of hiding it on the outside. I stopped crying just as I drove up to her house. Thank God she was home that day. I think if she hadn't been home, I would've driven off a cliff or something. Good thing there were no steep cliffs within my reach.

I knew I could leave Tony. I could pack up the baby and go home to my parents. They would've welcomed me with open arms. I knew in this experience that any of my friends would've left in a heartbeat. I didn't know anyone who would put up with what I was going through. I desperately needed my mother's advice. I walked through the back door using my key. I heard my mother talking on the phone with a friend. I dashed past her while she was on the phone. She knew something was seriously wrong with me.

"Let me give you a call back. Shari just stormed in…Ok I'll tell her… Bye. Oh yeah, call Geneva about tomorrow night and remind her to be on time. You know how she's made a career out of being fashionably late. Bye," Ma told her friend.

She hung up the phone and opened the fridge to get a bottle of water, and then let out a large sigh.

"What happened? Is everything ok?"

"Ma, Tony, he's crazy! I figured it out. The guy is straight bipolar! Do you know I saw him at Hermann Park all hugged up with Rosie!"

"Who? That Dominican girl?"

"Yes, and she's Italian and Puerto Rican."

"The girl with the big eyes, who comes to your book club meetings?"

"Yes, Ma. How could I have not known! What am I, blind?"

"No dear, just in love."

"Does that mean I suddenly lose good use of my senses because I've fallen in love? If so, what's the use of falling in love Ma, what's the use?! I could've walked up on him, and he would've kept going. He looked like he really liked her, Ma. Like he preferred being with her. Oh Lord, what have I gotten myself into?"

"Why didn't you confront him?"

"I didn't want to risk looking like a fool in front of all those people. Ma, he was around his old co-workers. People we've known together. I wonder what they're saying. Maybe he told them he's phasing me out, or something. Damn, this is a mess."

Ma took me by the shoulders and looked me square in the face.

"Shari, sweetheart, first, you need to calm down. You're becoming hysterical. Listen here, dear. There is a reason for all of this. I don't know what, but there is. I want to go hang Tony on a plant hook by his testicles. But my spirit guides me to something else. Remember Nana's message to you in her letter after she died? She said you should fight for your marriage because it's God's will for you two to be together."

"Ma, how can that be? Tony acts like he doesn't want me. Clearly he has chosen someone else over me. There were no signs in my marriage that we were headed in this direction. How did it come to this? I don't nag him. We rarely argue. I give him all the kinky sex he can handle."

"Well, apparently he can handle even more. Ha, ha...He's a man, baby. Most of them can never get enough sex."

I rolled my eyes at her as she continued. I knew she was being humorous, but I fought the laughter. Still, her comment somehow managed to lighten my hysteria.

"Shari, what he's doing is not about you. He's obviously hurting for some other reason. You have to be patient enough to go to God and wait for Him to tell you why. Incidents like what happened today are designed to make you give up and leave Tony. You've got to be stronger. You've got to fight this through. Remember, Tony isn't your real enemy."

"But come on now, what would you do? Would you let Dad walk all over you, like this?"

"Shari this fight is yours, and no one else's. You cannot compare yourself to anything I might've done. Personally, knowing what I know now, I would've done whatever God told me to do."

"But how do I know that God is telling me to stay? Maybe it's just me who wants him so badly." I asked her out of desperation, while seeking a comforting response. She removed her hands from my shoulders, and leaned on the kitchen island. She grabbed her bottled water, as she continued.

"Think about your question, dear. With as much pain as you're feeling right now, your first thoughts are telling you to leave him. At this moment, you feel stupid about all of this. There is nothing in you, in your soul, that agrees with remaining married to Tony after what you saw today. Trust me, hunny. IT IS God telling you to stay and fight, my love. NOT YOU."

"Mom, this is hard."

"I know, dear. I know. But anything worth having is worth fighting for. Tony is your husband. YOURS. If you continue to trust God, one way or another, you will win. No doubt. If He's trying to get you to stay with Tony, then Tony will not leave you for anyone else, and stay gone. Your job at this point is not to worry about any of that. You have to trust God, blindly, even if it means he never stops his behavior and leaves you permanently for another woman."

"That is so easy to hear. You make it sound believable, but it's another thing to go through it yourself."

"I know. I know. Baby, I wish I could go through this for you, so you could escape the pain, but there's just no getting around the fight. You have to live in the verb, and actually perform the action of trusting God. Stop stressing because God always provides whenever you are in his perfect will. Always. KoShari, this is exactly what Jesus died for. He died so you wouldn't have to carry this cross without grace. The pain you're feeling is your moment of truth. This is where the Gospel meets your situation. Either you will believe and plead the blood of Jesus over Tony, or you can try and fix things on your own, like most people try to do. The more you try to fix it, the more pain and frustration you'll feel. Have faith in His Word, and He will fix it for you. He'll give you strength you never knew you had."

By this time I was feeling much better. I believed her words about how God provides when we're in his will. I remembered what Nana once said. She said most things God asks us to do are not easy, and most people don't do them. She told me I shouldn't settle for being like everyone else. She said because I've got the same stuff in me, that she had in her, it was already in me to believe God; we were just bold enough to do what others wouldn't. She was right. I am bold enough to withstand the persecution and ridicule, from those who will not understand.

The new perspective, and the emotional drain, as well as the run, had worked up an appetite. I looked in Mom's fridge to see what I could eat.

"So Ma, do you think I should confront him when he gets home?"

"Dear, I don't know. If you do, prepare for an argument. His ego will not allow you to win a fight. He'll resent the fact that you've found out, and will hold it against you. He may even become manipulative and start playing even more games. You know, the ones where he turns everything around on you and makes it all your fault. I think it's funny; the lengths folks will go to remain in control. Stay calm, don't trip, and he'll keep his eyes closely on you while thinking you could go out and cheat on him. He'll believe those lies because he's doing it himself. Besides, you missed your chance, really. You should've confronted him right then and there. Now he can deny it altogether, like it never even happened. Just like with kids, you have to confront them at the moment when the damage is done, not some hours later."

I sunk my head into my shoulders. By this time we're both leaning on the kitchen island.

"Ma, I don't have the energy to go through all this, it's too much. I certainly didn't bargain for this when I met him. Here he is… with a beautiful family, wife, and son. He's secured, financially. What is his damned problem? Doesn't he know? Doesn't he care about losing it all?"

"Not right now, he doesn't. He's taking it all for granted like so many others do. He believes you'll always be there. He's thinking he can focus on doing the right thing some other time."

"Yeah, but what makes a person lose interest in a happy home? One minute he's very happy with us, and the next, I don't know if he likes us at all."

"Baby, he's obviously very unhealthy, emotionally. From what you've told me about his mother, she's contributed to him having some serious issues."

"And that's another thing. I never told you what happened the day I returned from New York, that time."

"No. What happened?"

"Well, you remember his Mom had flown in from Paris for a visit, which was a crazy experience, in and of itself. She's so overbearing. Anyhow, the day I came home she, Tony, and this woman he dated when they lived in New York, were all having a late lunch in my dining room. Apparently she'd contacted the girl, found out where she was, and invited her to come have lunch, at my house, mind you, the day I was scheduled to return home. Ma, she was trying to get Tony to leave me for this woman! Fortunately, her plan didn't work. The woman was happily married herself, with two children. I don't think her being married bothered Lillian one bit. Lillian tried hard to rekindle whatever Annabelle and Tony had felt for each other, in the past. Of course, I walked in, all happy-go-lucky, and didn't let Lillian get to me. At least, she never knew if I had. I was kind to the guest, and introduced myself to her as Tony's wife. Turns out Annabelle and I had a lot in common. We liked each other. That must've burned Lillian to a crisp. Ma, you should've seen her. She would interrupt our conversations, discussing memories of the times Tony and Annabelle were together in New York. It was a sad effort on her part, but we managed to get through it."

"So what did Tony think about all this?"

"When Lillian left, he looked at me and smiled, then shook his head and said, "let's not go there," so we never did. I was ok with not discussing it, once I determined he saw through her tricks. To be honest, I still don't know why she hates me so much. I've done nothing but try and respect her from day one."

"Shari, people like her have jealousy pinned up in their hearts. For her not to like you for no reason tells me she's jealous of your relationship with her son. It's a shame for a mother to be that way, and to hold her son in such bondage. But that's what you're dealing with. If I were you, I'd pray for her."

"Pray!" I yelled. I was shocked that Ma would suggest praying for someone who hated me the way Lillian had.

"Yes, pray for her. That will keep her off your back much better than you ever could. Shari, your Dad and I sure miss you at Dubaki-Alexander Chandeliers. You've got the baby squared away now. Why don't you come back to work? I'm sure Jack won't mind giving you carte blanche over your old position. And even if he did, we'd set him straight. What'd ya say? It would help to get your mind off things."

"Yeah, I guess I can give it some thought. Especially since Tony's not employed right now. I can use the steady flow of income, even if we're ok financially."

"Tell you what...You think about it, and get back to me."

"Ok Ma, I will," I told her. I reached over and gave my Mom a huge hug.

"Thanks, Ma. I love you."

"Awe, honey. Everything's gonna be alright. You'll see."

"I'm gonna go home now. I'll see you later." I got my keys off the key holder on her kitchen wall, and headed home.

I didn't realize it at the time, but God had answered my prayer about taking the pain away. The discussion with my mother placed everything in perspective, and helped to ease the venomous sting I was feeling in my heart. After that last discussion with Mom, I started reading my Bible and praying even more than before. I had to know more about the one and only solution to my problem. It got so, that Tony began to notice my developing relationship with God. He'd catch me praying in the study, and over our son. I can imagine he thought I was becoming a fanatic, because he started acting out even more, like he disapproved of it, or something.

Regarding the situation with Rosie, I decided not to complain about it. I could clearly see him playing the games Ma mentioned after a big argument. I decided to place it in God's hands, and force myself not to mention it, or to go off on Tony. It was like forcing a newly recovered smoker not to smoke a cigarette being waved in their face…REALLY difficult to do. I decided to allow God to help me through it, this time…I wasn't sure how long I could keep it up.

Chapter Seventeen

I was home on a Thursday night playing with the baby when the phone rang.

"Hello."

"Hi KoShari, its Miranda. How are you? How's the baby? Ok, ok. Listen... Chicago's throwing a brown liquor fondue party this weekend at the fondue place downtown. You interested? He asked about you the other night, so I thought to invite you. It won't be a big thing. Just something quaint with close friends. Hey, how's Tony? You should bring him. Couples are encouraged." She said everything all in one big breath. I couldn't get a word in edge wise.

"I'll think about it. Thanks for the invite. Talk to you soon. Bye."

I rushed the conversation with Miranda. I know how close she and Rosie are, they're good friends. Surely she knows about Rosie and Tony. Was she being messy and vindictive by inviting us, or what? I wasn't sure. Anyhow, I knew that once I told Tony about it, he would immediately say no. Therefore, I dropped any ideas about going to the party.

The day Miranda called was Tony and I's sixth wedding anniversary. He and I had planned dinner at the Rainbow Lodge, where we had our first date. Tony had little excitement about it. I was the first to say, "Happy Anniversary" that morning. Normally he'd beat me to it. His day-to-day attitude towards me had changed, drastically. Things had gotten much worse. Where he was usually pleasant, he had become cold and negative. I could feel the tension between us. We'd go shopping for a piece of furniture or a home improvement item as a family with the baby in tow. Normally, he looked forward to our off-time together, but now it had become laborious. He stopped smiling as much. The delightful mannerisms of lil Tony went unnoticed by him. He even became more frustrated than usual at lil Tony's baby mistakes. He was totally turned off by me. Anything I did to try and make it better, made it worse. I wanted him to leave. I would've rathered he left, than to stay with us and be unhappy. It was very painful to watch my marriage crumble before my eyes. He was changing, but that wasn't the worst part. The worst part, was that I couldn't do a damned thing about it. He'd become interested in another woman, and I couldn't make him want me anymore. However, deep, down, I terribly wanted to make my marriage work. I perished the thought of losing my husband to another woman. Losing your husband to another woman is the worst thing possible, in wife world. It's difficult to feel that your husband, whom you love with all your heart, whom you've completely given yourself to, is slipping through your fingertips. Reason doesn't matter at that point. All you care about is doing whatever it takes to make it work. But there was nothing I could do, and nothing I could say, to make him stay if he wanted to leave. I felt myself slipping into hopelessness, falling into despair. Then I remembered my Mom's words. "Anything worth having is worth fighting for."

I prayed for strength and for God to help Tony see through the seductive spell he was under. However, it seemed the more I prayed the worse he got, and the more rejection I felt from him. Tony and I hadn't made love in two months. Even before then, it had become sporadic, and not meaningful. It hadn't happened yet, but I could see Tony leaving me for Rosie. The thought of it made my flesh crawl. During this time, I began remembering how attractive I was. How smart I was. I thought, 'I already possess a high level of confidence that had always been unshakable. Who was he to prefer her over me? What did she have that I didn't? Why did he want her, and not me, anymore?' Obviously there was something wrong with him. And that is what reminded me of the fight to keep him. I knew there were bigger things happening than what I could see. I couldn't abandon the fact that I knew in my belly he loved me.

I wouldn't allow myself to believe he'd fallen out of love, I just wouldn't. I encouraged myself by remembering he was the right one in the beginning, and he is the right one now, no matter what I saw happening in front of me. Sure I thought about how devastated I'd be if he left, but I couldn't give up without a fight. I abruptly caught a vision of me in a boxing ring with gloves. I was jumping around and punching at the air, like a real pro. My opponent was invisible. Suddenly, I heard a bell go off, as though the round had changed. "Ding!" The bell distracted me from my thoughts.

I took lil Tony up to his room. He'd fallen asleep in his cubby, while I was in the kitchen on the phone with Miranda. Upstairs, I reminded Lucy of the date Tony and I had planned for our anniversary.

"We have 7:00pm reservations at the Rainbow Lodge tonight. Not sure if we're coming straight home afterwards," I told Lucy.

She was in lil Tony's nursery folding clothes and placing them on a shelf. She gave me a look of disbelief. I placed lil Tony in his bed. I asked her if she had any questions. She shook her head, and crimped her lips in disappointment. I could tell she had an opinion about our marriage. However, she was the help in my mind, and didn't need to comment on what she saw happening in my house. I realize the woman is human, and can see Tony is messing around on me. She was a good nanny, and had developed an affinity for our family. She'd cared for our son as though he were her own. I trusted her. I just didn't need one more person confirming what I already knew to be true about my husband. It was hard enough putting up with an adulterer, when I didn't want to. I was trying hard to yield to God's will.

That night, Tony and I arrived at 7:00pm sharp for our reservations. I tried to force a good time, even though it was not happening. Tony wasn't feeling it, at all. We were seated at the same table as our first date.

"How romantic, Tony. Can you believe those look like the same ducks that were here seven years ago, ha, ha!?" I said, trying to break the tension that was there underneath it all. He didn't catch the humor.

"So what, Shari… are you an idiot?" He asked, with a serious look on his face. How rude of him. He knew I was joking, but he sharply rejected it.

"Yeah…anyway," he said, as he rolled his eyes. I couldn't believe I was being treated this way, like a used whore.

"Shari, there's something we need to discuss. I've been given a job offer at Alkstein, Inchk, & Slavic's. They want me to head up their South American sports division. I'd be in charge of acquisitions for a couple major sports organizations in Brazil, and Chile. They want a greater presence in those areas. Since I have a lot of experience with foreign sports associations, they're really interested in me for the role."

"Tony, I think that's great. When did you get the offer?"

"About a week ago. They've been trying to recruit me ever since I facilitated the first Japanese alliance. Remember, it was their firm we worked with on the Japan contracts."

I remembered Rosie worked with him for a couple years on that alliance. She's a partner at Alkstein, Inchk, & Slavic's. She must've recommended Tony for the job.

'Shari, don't blow up, don't do it.' I thought to myself. I wanted to ask him if he was going to work with her, so badly, I could taste it, but I didn't.

"So, are you accepting the offer?"

"Don't know yet. I'm still thinking about it. What do you think I should do?"

"I think you should follow your heart. Whatever you feel is gonna make you happy, that's what you should do, Tony."

I was basically talking about the decision regarding me and Rosie. I was hoping he'd allow himself to make the connection with no shame.

"Well, I'd be traveling even more than I do now."

The waiter brought water, and asked to take our orders. Tony gestured that we weren't ready, and he continued talking.

"I'd be out of the country, off and on, for nine months out of the year. They suggested I purchase a home in Brazil where their South American headquarters are located. I told them I'd think about it, and would talk with you first."

"So what do you want to do, Tony? Are you interested in the opportunity?"

"Yes Shari, I am. I'm also interested in some other things we haven't discussed, yet."

"Oh yeah, what's that?" I asked, hesitantly.

"KoShari things haven't been right between us for some time, now. Since I left the firm, I've been doing some thinking about our family. I'm not sure I'm happy here, anymore. I don't know what's going on. I'm not saying it's you. You've been a wonderful wife. I couldn't have asked for anyone better. I've been confused lately, like I'm not very happy with myself right now."

I tried as best I could to have a straight face. I'd trained myself to act out the opposite of how I feel when I'm most angry. Therefore I smiled, and looked away from him. However, I'd lost the battle for keeping the peace. I had gone berserk.

"So you think you want to leave me for Rosie, do you? You think I don't know, Tony? You think I've been in the dark all this time? Each time we're around her together, she looks like she's gonna have a conniption! Have you fallen in love with her?"

"What??"

"I said, are you in love with her the way you fell in love with me? You think I've been asleep all this time? Well, I haven't. I saw you last week, you know."

He attempted to interrupt, but I didn't allow it.

"No, no, no… don't insult me by trying to deny it. I saw you at the Miller Outdoor Theatre, with her. How long, Tony? How long have you been seeing her?"

I paused to give him the opportunity to respond, but he didn't say a word. He sat there stunned, and looked away, as I continued.

"Tony, how did we get here?"

"Shari, I honestly don't know. I think we need some time away from each other. I've been thinking about this for a while now."

"Tony, please, do whatever you feel you need to do. The baby and I will be ok. You go find yourself, or, sow your oats, or, go through your mid-life crisis…or whatever. Antonio and I will be fine. I will be fine. Just fucking FINE."

I looked at him briefly in disgust. He looked remorseful. In fact, he couldn't even look me in the eye. In that moment, it felt like all the honesty that had existed between us for so long, had suddenly disappeared. His eyes were hollow, and glossy. He looked like his soul was in bondage, entrapped by something. Either that, or he had completely morphed into someone I no longer recognized.

"Oh, and by the way. Happy Anniversary, Tony."

I got up to leave. I couldn't sit there any longer. I tried, but I became nauseas when looking at him. The pain from losing him had hit me like a bullet, and I decided it was too much to take. I walked out the front door to ask the valet to hail a cab. I'd forgotten to discuss the details of him leaving. I resolved that we'd work things out later.

I cried all the way home that night. I was deeply heartbroken. In my soul, I felt him drifting away from me. In my heart, I still loved him very much, and still wanted to fight for him. Tony was my husband, not hers. But he had chosen someone else. How could I make someone stay with me that didn't want me? I thought on what I could've done to make him lose interest. It all seemed so bizarre. I couldn't figure out why my prayers hadn't worked. I was battling in my mind. On the one hand, I became disappointed at God. I felt he'd led me to stay with Tony, and then Tony left me. I felt that all my mother and Nana had taught me was wrong. Then, I remembered what Ma said about having to actually fight the great fight of faith. God is not about disappointing me, and letting me down. I knew in my heart that God is faithful, and that he is much bigger than the heartbreak I was feeling. These thoughts encouraged me. Suddenly, I thought about Tony's mother, and how she's treated every man in her life like a little boy. What man can feel respected when all his life he's been treated like a little boy? The most important thing a man needs from the women in his life, is respect. She or they can love him something awful. Even more than love, he needs respect. I thought of the deep wounds Tony must possess from the estranged relationship with his mother, and the lack of respect she'd shown him in adulthood, as a man, and how it has impacted his responses to the pressures in his life. The fact that she didn't like me, and tried terribly to come between us, certainly didn't make him feel any better. It only contributed to his pain. I'd imagined she had something to do with his decision for space from me. He probably had suffered mentally for so long, that he wanted a release from the pain. Lillian knew the type of sweetheart her son was. She knew that if she applied enough pressure on him, he would cave, and would do whatever it took to remove the pressure. In my case, I happened to be the subject that was being removed. That is some kind of bondage to place over someone. Its pitiful, is what it is. Nevertheless, that woman, as clever as she thinks she is, has already lost. Tony and I were gonna be together.

How could I be so sure? Furthermore, Lillian probably didn't say one word to Tony about leaving me. It might've been unfair for me to assume she had anything to do with his decision to leave our marriage.

Nawww... she had put so much pressure on that man his entire life, he was sure to run fast from anything that even resembled the look of a negative emotional experience. It's sort of like being confined to a torture chamber for several years. After getting out, ones entire life and future life decisions have all been impacted by the years of torture endured in the past. A tortured person picks-up certain avoidance behaviors developed while being tortured. Certainly the decision to leave our marriage most likely was developed from a desire to abandon quickly, those things he deemed unpleasant. As confusing and temporary as the unpleasantry may seem, the tortured soul cannot see beyond momentary satisfaction, and therefore chooses to move along quickly, for fear of remaining in a painfully negative sentiment, even if the temporary unpleasantry is a seemingly dead marriage. To a tortured soul, commitment means nothing. Instant gratification defines their very existence. Long suffering, which the Bible says we should all endure, is not made real, but rather a hoax, in which participation doesn't make sense. So then, I took back the notion Lillian might not have had anything to do with Tony's decision to leave our marriage. I wholeheartedly believed that she had. Whether she personally told him to leave me, or not, through the way she treated him, she'd conditioned him to abandon the perplexing things in life when the going got tough, and also to abandon anything that she felt would threaten his love for her, his mother.

Nevertheless, Tony didn't come home that night. The next day he showed up and packed some bags, kissed lil Tony, and said he'd rented an apartment at the Doubletree, Uptown. He said he wasn't sure how long he'd stay there, but that he'd be in touch. That was it. After all the years, the best he could offer me, was I'm leaving you after loving you for so long. When he left I forced myself to choke back the tears. I wouldn't allow myself to cry. I decided to dust my dining room furniture. The maid had dusted two days prior. I had to find something to do with my hands right then, to keep them from yanking my hair out. It was sobering to realize that the man who once described himself as the love of my life, could detach himself so easily from our life together, from our family. Who does that? I mean, is this just a man thing, or what? Maybe I should issue a survey to the masses and ask about how common this experience is. I get that certain folks fall out of love. I get that others can come along and become an attractive diversion from a person's problems in their life, and cause them to stray away from a committed relationship. I had felt that folks who wander away from a good marriage, always had roaming eyes, even before making a lifelong commitment, and that the commitment was merely a front to cover their philandering nature. Serial cheaters could never really remain committed to anyone, except for themselves. I didn't know the answers. I didn't have anything figured out. Should I have abandoned the idea of true love? Does it even still exist? Is anyone of us capable of holding onto a real God-sent relationship, once the other party has decided to go astray, for whatever reason?

I just don't see the reason he decided to leave. I swear I did every, and anything possible, to work on my marriage, and to keep the fire burning between us. Common sense told me the pain was intense because I still very much loved him. I agreed with common sense, and still did not want to give up the fight for our marriage. I continued to pray for him, and his mother, every day. God, it was hard.

Prayer in this regard was a weapon. The way Mom explained it, the prayer disarmed the enemy working through Tony to thwart against me. It wasn't that I was trying to be super compassionate. No, not really. I was praying to rid myself of the wickedness that was trying to pierce into my heart. Anger would not have gotten me anywhere in this situation. His mother would've loved nothing more than for me to get pissed and go off in some ungodly way. I couldn't give anyone that kind of power over me. I'd learned too much, and had come too far.

I decided to take my mother up on her advice and went back to Dubaki-Alexander Chandeliers. She was right. I needed the extra work to keep my mind occupied during all this. I also decided to take Miranda up on her offer to go to Chicago's fondue party. Chicago was a messy scoundrel. I'm sure he'd heard about Tony, Rosie, and I. He knew us all, well. In fact, Tony introduced Chicago to Miranda. He had attempted to date her ever since. She continued to tease him by leading him on, then turning him away, the old 'hot and cold' treatment. I think she likes him, and will give in when she's ready. Anyhow, Chicago loves to be in the thick of things. I heard his major at Berkeley was, Broadcast Journalism. It seems fitting for his motor mouth. I swear, if there was some chaos, he was in the middle of it. If there was a scandal, he knew about it. If there was some instigating to be done, he'd be the instigator. I knew what to expect at his party. In fact, I was sure both Rosie and Tony would be there, together. For that reason alone, I was going. Not only would I show up, but I was gonna make sure I looked damned good. Tony would watch me work the room the way I do when I'm looking like a million bucks. He was going to see that he had not broken me, and that I was still at the top of my game, in public.

I didn't care what it took. That fool was gonna get some karma if I had anything to do with it. That's just it; I didn't have anything to do with it. I wasn't in control, at all. Had I interfered with God's work, I would've come away looking crazy to everyone else. People in our circle at the party would know that I'd be over-reacting, and trying to show Tony up. They know I'd be faking the confidence, appearing to be ok with Tony's choice to leave me for Rosie, all the while facing the harsh reality that I had not been ok with it. I simply didn't care. He was not gonna drive me into some hole to hide out, get addicted to sugar, and get fat behind my troubles, or get hooked on Xanax to numb the pain. Nope, I wasn't going out like that.

Chapter Eighteen

I arrived alone to Chicago's party, and had parked my jeep with the valet. I was determined to show that I didn't need the security of my girls around me. Nope. I wanted everyone to see me arrive, looking hot, of course, like a viper on the prowl. I walked into the place on a mission. I saw a couple familiar faces and acquainted myself. I had a couple laughs with some fondue partners, and danced with a few old friends. Miranda and I chatted for a minute. And then I spotted her… Rosie was coming out of the restroom. She had on a too-tight shiny dark brown skirt that clung down to her ankles, and a deep red short-sleeved t-shirt, with a very large white collar. I won't lie; the girl had it going on. Her hair was a shorter symmetrical cut, and tapered along her neckline. It was a glossy thick and curly cut, with large curls, that were tucked behind her ears. Yes I admit, I had to size up the competition. How could I not? I Immediately scanned the room for Tony. No Tony. He was nowhere to be found. Not even a whiff of his presence. I guess he was too scared to show up. Maybe he wasn't ready to face the clique again. I didn't know where he was, and was becoming frustrated at myself for wondering about it.

"KoShari, hi, how are you?" Asked, Rosie.

She had walked up behind me. No this heifer didn't! That bitch. The nerve of her to approach me after she'd been screwing my husband! Never let em' see you sweat, that's my motto.

"Rosie, oh hi. How are you? You look great." I touched her left shoulder.

"Good, good," she said, while purposely pulling, no yanking, her shoulder away. She slowly looking me up and down.

"I hear Tony is coming to work with us." That bitch was bold.

"Yes, he is," I replied.

"So what do you think about it, KoShari?"

"Oh I think he should do whatever makes him happy, Rosie. We all should. Life is short, you know."

"Right, I agree. Ok. Well, tell him to call me when you see him. Oh, wait, I forgot. He moved out of your house, (she chuckled). On second thought, I'll probably see him before you do. Take care. Kiss the baby for me, would you?"

"Will do, Rosie."

I wanted to slap the slut. I quickly looked around for someone else to talk, or laugh out loud with. I wanted her to see she hadn't ruffled my feathers. She was small potatoes. The best way to prove that, was for her to see me move on as quickly as possible. She should witness me not thinking twice about our conversation. Heifers are vicious. You gotta be prepared to flaunt your strength. Besides, her meaningless relationship with my husband, was only temporary. If anyone was gonna show weakness about Tony, it was gonna be her. Not me.

The next day Mom and I went shopping at the Galleria. Mom had heard about a sale at Saks, and liked to arrive early the first day. She wanted first pickings of the new mark-downs. Of course we were the first to arrive that day. She was a serious shopper, and even more serious about her style of clothing. Mom sifted through the clothes like a scientist studying human cells under a microscope, very fastidiously. I followed behind her, as her help for the day. I held all of her selections, until she was able to try them on.

"I decided I'm gonna go back to work for Dad. I tried calling what's his name… Jack, the other day. I kept getting his secretary. Should I show up to discuss the task transfer?"

"Well, I think you should keep trying him on the phone. Your Dad's already sat him down to discuss the transition. He's aware you're returning. I think it's more respectful to speak with him over the phone, before showing up at the office."

"So do you think he's ok with everything?" I was referring to Jack being ok with me taking my job back.

"Yeah, he's fine. He mentioned that he'd be able to take a vacation now that you're returning."

"So Ma, when did Dad speak with Jack? I JUST NOW told you, I wanted to come back to work."

"Shari, I know you. I knew you'd want to come back. I realize it's no fun going through what you're dealing with at home. You're a smart girl, and I knew you'd make the right choice."

I had placed all her pickings into a basket and held a red dress up to my frame. "Ok. So, this dress would look great on me, don't you think?"

"I think it's cute, honey. Why don't you try it on?"

"Watch my purse, Ma, I'll be right back."

I handed her my purse and went into the dressing room. Along the way, I noticed Ma continuing to sift through the racks looking for that golden outfit. Suddenly, my cell phone rang.

"Ma, can you get that? It could be the nanny," I told her from the dressing room.

"Honey, can't it wait till you get out?" She kept sifting away.

"Ma!"

"Ok, Shari. Dang. Where's the phone. A woman can't get some decent shopping done around here without the phone ringing all the damned time." I heard her mumbling while I was changing clothes.

"Hello," answered Ma.

"KoShari, dear, what the hell is wrong with you! Why do you insist on leaving the baby with that nanny all the time? It's gotten to where each time I call your house, the nanny answers the phone, and tells me you're not there. You need to be home taking care of your men. Maybe then things would be better between you and Tony," said Lillian.

She was calling basically to be a pest with her harsh words, and also to rub it in my face like a grinder, that Tony had left me. Her tone was attacking, and judgmental, all for no good reason, of course. The only thing is, she got my Mom instead of me this time, and Ma wasn't nearly as tactful as I would've been.

"Excuse me! Who is this!" Asked, Ma.

"Like you don't know my voice. KoShari this is Lillian, dear."

"Lillian, oh you must be Tony's mother. This is Janis, KoShari's Mom. Shari is indisposed at the moment. Would you like to leave a message?"

"No dear, I'd like to speak with KoShari. Do you think you can un-dispose her for me?"

"No, I don't. Maybe you didn't understand what I said. I heard you had some loose screws upstairs. Let me slow it down for you, like I would a retard."

She began talking in slow motion."Shari, is, not, able, to, come, to, the, phone, right now. I'll have, her, call, you, back, later."

"No, that won't be necessary. I'm trying to contact Tony. He called me the other day, and I'm trying to return his call. Would you be so kind, Janis?"

"Sure Lillian, I'll tell her to relay the message. Good day."

Ma hung up the phone. I can always leave it to good ole' Janis Alexander to get somebody told just in the knick of time.

"Shari, you were right. She is fragile."

"Yep. Told you she needed some tender loving care, ha, ha." We both burst into a loud belly laugh that lasted about a minute long.

I walked out of the dressing room wearing the red dress. Ma looked me up and down, smiled, and nodded her head in approval.

"So what'd ya think?" I asked Ma.

"Humph. Well then. I'd say that about does it. Sexy, woman. Very sexy."

I slowly turned around 180 degrees so she could see the back, then turned back around to the front again.

"You think I should get it?"

"I do. You've got an incredible figure, honey. You know you take after your Moma, don't you?" She smiled at me.

I shook my head with a laugh and walked back into the dressing room to change.

That night, Tony and Rosie were spotted at an exclusive nightclub in Midtown. He appeared happy, very happy with Rosie. They walked into the club like a couple in love with love. She clung to his arm like she was an extended limb, another part of his body. Tony knew the bouncer at the door, and was able to walk right in, to his special table, he and KoShari's special table. KoShari and Tony had made the table famous, not Tony and Rosie. The setting was silky smooth. There was low lighting and a warm atmosphere. They sat there, gleaming into each other's eyes. Rosie's smile was resilient, bright, and beautiful. She had two large dimples with her smile, and they were deep that night. She appeared free, and definitely in love. She was happy, from the inside out. Indeed, another woman had fallen in love with Tony, the way KoShari had. The big question was, did Tony love Rosie the way that he was still in love with KoShari? The musical artist, "Kem" was the live entertainment for the evening. Tony loved Kem's music. Everyone applauded as Kem prepared for his opening performance. There were whistles and screams coming from everywhere in the intimate room. Tony and Rosie sat there anxiously awaiting to hear his performance.

"Whoa, I love him." Said, Rosie.

And then the music began. Kem opened with a song titled, "I Can't Stop Loving You," a slow and thought-provoking ballad. The song fit the jazzy room and cool environment. Suddenly, Tony drifted into deep thought. The words of the song had permeated. He began to remember lost times with KoShari. They caused him to reflect on lost affections, and how difficult it was to get over losing someone that you longed for. They also reminded him of the die-hard love he still had for KoShari. The burn, the mysterious calling to her, had arrested him. He remembered how they would have dinner in the nude. Times when they would dress-up and go out. How he carried her to the bungalow on their honeymoon to make love. How they'd chase each other around the house. He was officially missing, KoShari. Rosie noticed his trance. Immediately she knew that he was thinking of KoShari. She stared at him for a moment, and then tried to distract him from his thoughts. She grabbed his hand and smiled at him in an attempt to put his mind back on the two of them. She'd failed. She soon realized there was nothing she could do to distract him. Therefore, in the middle of the song, she storms to the restroom, obviously in tears. Tony looked at her briefly, put his head down, and then continued listening to Kem and thinking of KoShari, and their son. Rosie was hoping that Tony would have come after her. She could see from a distance that he was not going to. Her face turned red with envy. She dug a hole into the lining of the wall that she was peeking around. Her teeth were tight. She was angry. Killing angry...

"Ms. Bryant, you have a call on line two," said Rainey, my assistant.

I was in the middle of drafting a patent description document to attach to Dad's latest patent application. He'd traveled to Antarctica and found a rare and natural ice sculpture that he wanted to use as a chandelier design. Upon his return, he had the designers mimic the sculpture to an exact replication, in the form of a crystal chandelier. He wanted it buffed, and hand polished a certain way, that made it even more unique in the industry. He'd envisioned it becoming a hot item in Europe and in the most extravagant parts of the U.S., in locations where Dubaki-Alexander galleries had established a healthy business presence. I figured a patent was the smart route to protect its unique design. In our business, hoarding creativity is a must. Your creations become your own trademark, and establishes your reputation in the industry. I had drafted the patent description document longhand and planned to transfer it to the computer later that day. I had attached several written sticky notes to the document. I was typing away on my laptop keyboard, while biting a pen, when my assistant interrupted again.

"Rainey, I don't wish to be disturbed right now. Please take a message," I told her while typing.

"I tried, Ms. Bryant. He said it's your husband, and he must speak with you at once."

'My husband?' I thought. I immediately stopped typing, and then had gasped from the surprise. Tony and I hadn't spoken in three months. Yes, three months. They were the most tortuous three months of my life. It was painstakingly difficult not to call him. I was miserable being alone all the time. It was especially hard dealing with the fact Tony had left me for another woman. That is a harsh reality no woman will ever want to experience. In fact, many of us do whatever we can to prevent it from happening. In my case, I chose to keep praying for him. Not praying for him to come home, but praying for him to be delivered from past pain, and that his eyes be opened to his mistake in leaving me, and our family. I suppose I could've grown bitter and started to hate all men, but I decided against that. I'd seen what becoming a bitter woman had done to Tony's mother. I didn't want my son to grow up with a control freak mother who was afraid to allow her son to make his own life choices. I couldn't allow that kind of bondage to take over. Instead, I clung to my belief in God, and the fact that I believed He told me to stay and fight for our marriage. I'd repeat to myself that God is faithful. When I'd get lonely at night for Tony, I'd remind myself that God loves me, and wants what's best for me, even if his best meant losing Tony, and moving on to bigger and better things. Still, I'd remind myself that it was only a matter of time before Tony would wake up from his selfish spell. I couldn't let go of the fact that I knew in my bones we were supposed to be together. Not sure how I knew, I just did.

I tried going out a couple times with friends. We'd often meet some really interesting guys. But I'd put up this six inch thick wall, and never allowed myself to feel anything for anyone else. All this with Tony was still too fresh. God, the pain seemed unbearable at times. I remember one time opening my Bible searching for answers or help with the pain. I opened to the book of Job, the twenty-eighth chapter. It mentioned how God grants wisdom to those who allow themselves to walk through the hard places. It discussed the thoughts of Job before God brought him out of his suffering. Job talked about the price of wisdom. He mentioned that no man knows the price of wisdom, or where understanding lies. He discussed how valuable wisdom is, that it is more precious than any jewel or stone on earth. Then he reflected, where does wisdom come from? He said it was hidden, but that only God understood where it was, and how to obtain it. He mentioned that God gave the wind weight and pressure, and he made a decree of the rain by thunder and lightning. Then after God had done all this, He saw wisdom. Job concluded the chapter by saying, 'for man, the fear of the Lord is wisdom, and to depart from evil is understanding.'

And then it hit me… God grants true wisdom to us after we've walked through chaos while obeying him, every single step of the way. I likened "fearing" God, to "obeying" God. I thought about how I only began to understand Tony's issues after each act of obedience to God. There were times when I would sense an urging not to curse Tony, or his Mom. It would always be very difficult to obey. But after I obeyed, he'd show me something else I hadn't known before, that would make it easier to stay and pray for the both of them. God would show me flaws in Tony's character that had little to do with me, and more to do with his painful upbringing. It had caused him to act out in our marriage. I believe that God showed me Tony was comfortable in domestic dysfunction because he had become accustomed to it in his adolescence. And then He gave me a commission. I sensed that God asked me to show Tony the way back to stability. He asked me to show Tony the way back to Him, by loving him through the heartache. I couldn't believe it, but I'd answered yes. Yes, that I would help God, and God would help me. These types of thoughts and conversations between God and I kept me holding on. Not to mention my deep, impassioned love for Tony, which I believe God had placed inside my heart. I couldn't deny that I'd allowed myself to fall in love with Tony, and I still wasn't ready to let go. I was thankful that I'd developed a relationship with God through this tough time. I needed all the help I could get, to hold on to my enchanted love. I suppose most women would walk away from it all, but I'd been given too much information to do that. Besides, I wasn't in the mood to become another statistic. Everyone goes that way, and I never wanted to be like everyone else. I didn't care what folks would say, if they would snicker behind my back. Other folk's opinions didn't matter to me. Plus, they don't know me, and they certainly aren't privy to what I know about Tony. No matter what, Tony is MY man. I've got a promise from God and a rock hard belief system in His abilities. And now, I wait because my relief is coming soon.

"Very well, put him through," I told Rainey.

"Hello, Tony."

"HI, KoShari. I'd like to meet you for lunch this week. I have something very important to discuss with you."

"Can't it wait till later? My lunches are all booked this week. Or better yet, why don't we discuss it over the phone?"

"No. I have to look at you. You think you can make some time for me?" He insisted.

"Sure, Tony. Let's meet at Churrascos Restaurant tomorrow. The one on Westheimer Street. Does noon work for you?"

"Sure."

"Good. I'll make reservations for a patio table outside."

"Thanks, KoShari. See you then. Bye."

"Goodbye, Tony."

"Rainey, cancel my 12 noon meeting with UNICEF tomorrow, and replace it with reservations for 2 at Churrascos, the one on Westheimer, for the same time," I told her.

"Yes, Ms. Bryant."

I wondered what he wanted. Was he ready to come back home? I got butterflies just thinking about it. 'Oh God, could this be the answer to my prayers?' I thought. Is all this, finally over? I got excited. My thoughts began to get the best of me…What if he wasn't ready to come home? What if he just wants to discuss the baby? Oh well, I decided not to stress over it, and that I'd be ok, no matter what he wanted to discuss. Why had he waited so long to contact me? After all, it had been three months…

I arrived at Churrascos on time and parked with the valet. I was on the line with the U.S. Patent Office when driving up to the restaurant. Earlier that day I had placed a call to the patent attorney's office regarding the deadline to present paperwork after filing. I hated filing late court documents. Nothing says incompetence more than late filings and procrastination. The paralegal had given me the information I needed. I hung up just as I walked inside. I saw Tony seated at a table out on the patio. I gestured to the greeter that I'd spotted my party, and proceeded to walk to his table. I tried hard not to smile. I didn't want him to think I was overly-excited to see him. After all, he'd found what he thought was better than me, in Rosie.

"Hi, Shari." He got up to pull out my seat. I was glad to see he still respected me enough to be a chivalrous gentleman.

"Hello, Tony. You look well."

He had no smiles on his face. None at all. He was even more serious than I'd ever noticed before.

"Shari, I won't belabor this. I want a divorce. I think I'm finally ready to move on. As for assets, I don't want anything from you. You can have the house and your jeep, and any money in the liquid bank accounts. You and I always kept separate retirement funds and investments. I'd like to keep what's mine. I don't want any of what you've saved personally, or invested. I only want joint custody of lil Tony. This should make the process easy for the both of us."

I wanted to scream at him about Rosie and how he could be so sure he'd fallen for her. However, I didn't want to hear him whining about my complaints. He placed a briefcase on the table, popped it open, and pulled out the divorce papers. My guess is Rosie had put pressure on him to have them drafted.

"Ok, Tony. Hand me the papers. I'll sign them right now."

"Sooo...You don't want to discuss this, first?"

"No. Let's just get on with it. The sooner I sign the papers, the sooner I can get on with my life. Besides, we haven't spoken in three months. I assume you've had time to carefully think this over. Who am I to stand in your way?"

"KoShari, I…I don't know what to say."

We sat in silence for a moment. He handed me the papers. I signed without fully reading the fine print. I couldn't, anyways. It took all the strength I had to sit there, not cry, and to not appear hurt. We'd both come from wealth. I didn't believe he would try and cheat me out of any money.

'I must remain strong,' I thought to myself.

"Tony, is there anything else?" I was hoping he'd say no. I don't think I could've sat there five more minutes.

His gestures communicated a 'no' reply.

"Well then, Ok. Have a nice day, and a nice life, Tony."

I arose violently while almost knocking over the chair. I walked away. Just as I arrived at the valet podium outside the restaurant, I screamed amid the many others in line to get their vehicles:

"Dear God, HOW IN THE ENTIRE FUCK, has this just happened to me!?"

-End of Part I-

www.ingramcontent.com/pod-product-compliance
Lightning Source LLC
Chambersburg PA
CBHW020929310726
48980CB00007B/689/J

* 9 7 8 0 6 9 2 1 6 0 2 7 5 *